MAX THRUST

Written by James Walker

Edited by Nick Melton

Cover Illustration by Andy Anderson

DEDICATION

Dedicated to Jenny
And to my family
To rocket lovers everywhere
And to the readers: stay curious

CHAPTER ONE

"**A**ttention Soyuz class vessel approaching rendezvous, this is United States Space Force Station *One*. Please identify yourself. Over."

Space Operations Officer Charles Hill lifted his finger from the radio icon on his touchscreen control panel. No response came.

"I repeat: Soyuz vessel, this is U.S.S.F Station *One*. Please identify. Over," he said.

"I could warm him up with a targeting laser," offered Space Weapons Officer John Evans. He floated near his control panel. Their missiles and lasers had only ever been used to blast practice targets into a billion patriotic pieces.

"Not yet, but if he does not reply to my third hail I will authorize an optical ping," Officer Hill responded. Frustrated, he reached toward his panel for a third time.

Before he could touch the screen, the station's speakers crackled to life. A new voice resonated through the crew compartment.

"This is Max. How you boys doing? You ain't grenaded yet?" the voice said.

"He does not sound very professional," Officer Hill said.

Officer Evans shrugged. "Vandenberg did brief us that this guy was a bit of a character."

Officer Hill thumbed his panel and put on his most authoritative voice. "This is Officer Charles Hill of the United

States Space Force. I assume that I am speaking with Maxwell Ardis, proprietor of Thrust Solutions Incorporated. Over."

"Well, you weren't expecting the girl scouts?" Came the chuckling reply. "I don't think the cookie van has orbital capability yet."

Exasperated, Officer Hill pressed his icon again. "Mister Ardis, you are addressing a senior officer of the United States Military. You will observe proper procedure on all communications henceforth. Over."

"Oh, I'm pressing all the right buttons. I checked," came the infuriating reply.

"Mister Ardis, I insist that you use correct radio etiquette. Over," Officer Hill demanded.

"I'm pressing all the right buttons… Sir?"

"Over!" Officer Hill near-shouted into his microphone.

"Uh, the Pacific Ocean, I think."

Officer Hill muted his microphone and took a slow breath.

"Officer Evans. Perhaps you had best take the lead. This gentleman is trying my patience," Officer Hill said.

Officer Evans covered a surreptitious grin. "Yes, sir," he replied.

The United States Space Force Space Station *One* was the inaugural military space station of the nascent US Space Force. It packed enough long-range guided missiles to reduce every single piece of hardware in low Earth orbit to shrapnel. There were more top-secret devices onboard than had ever been deployed on any mobile structure. It represented the pinnacle of United States military technology.

And it was falling.

Officer Evans frowned at his panel. His screen displayed telemetry information about his space station as well as about the approaching spacecraft. The numbers he saw gave him palpitations. He hailed the spacecraft.

"Mister Ardis, this is Weapons Officer John Evans. Your heading looks good, but your closing speed is faster than recommended for proximity operations. Over," he said.

"Yeah, well, I'm in a bit of a hurry today," came the reply.

On his panel Officer Evans flipped to an external camera to watch the approaching Soyuz spacecraft. Cones of propellant gas were jetting from the incoming spacecraft's maneuvering thrusters. Max Ardis appeared to be flying his vessel under manual control.

"Mister Ardis, I appreciate that time is critical, but I recommend that you transfer control of approach operations to your automated docking computer. Over," Officer Evans said.

"Never trust the machines Johnny," Max said over the radio. "That's how they win."

"Mister Ardis. I really must insist that you reduce your speed. My instruments show that your relative closing velocity is two point one five meters per second. The operations manual states that, at this range, closing velocity should never be greater than zero point three zero meters per second. Over," said Evans. He noticed that Officer Hill had tightened the restraining straps of his flight chair.

"Don't trust the manual neither. And don't worry. I am one hundred percent sure that we might not die," Max responded.

There was nothing that either Officers Hill or Evans could do. They could not take evasive action. Their own maneuvering thrusters were dead.

Officer Evans pushed away from his console. Weightless, he floated to the window nearest the approaching spacecraft. Blue ocean filled the view. The Soyuz vehicle was approaching from below. It grew from an indistinct speck of light to a living, window-filling, spacecraft. Hypergolic thrusters flared.

"What an old piece of junk," Officer Hill said. He was strapped tightly into his command chair with his arms crossed.

"But a very functional one," Officer Evans responded.

The Soyuz spacecraft that Maxwell Ardis piloted was one of the oldest spacecraft designs in manned rocketry. Its creation dated back to the 1960s when it was developed by Cold War era Soviets to carry Cosmonauts to the moon. With the failure of the Soviet moon rocket, their moon landing never happened.

However, the Soyuz space vehicle became the most popular and reliable launch vehicle in the world. It was also the cheapest.

Officer Evans admired Max's piloting skill. Retro and maneuvering thrusters pulsed as the pilot bled off his vessel's relative velocity and aligned docking ports.

With an audible thump, the docking ports touched. The clamps connected and sealed, the hatch swung open, and Maxwell Ardis floated into the station.

To Officer Evans' relief the rocket mechanic looked more professional than his conduct over the radio had suggested. Max was a man in his mid-forties, clean shaven, wearing a modern flight suit and carrying a zipped tool bag.

"I hear you boys are having some engine trouble," Max said.

Officer Evans nodded. "Welcome aboard Mister Ardis. We are having trouble with our electric propulsion system. Allow me to show you the readouts," he beckoned Max toward his console. Officer Hill remained resolutely in his seat, pretending to be busy with his view screen.

Max floated to the console. His intelligent brown eyes scanned the data on the screen while Officer Evans described the situation.

"This space station's propulsion system is the largest and most powerful solar-electric unit ever deployed in space. Fifty kilowatts of input power are collected and delivered by our advanced solar panels. The main engine is a Hall-effect ion thruster capable of outputting two newtons of thrust," Officer Evans explained.

"But you're not actually realizing that thrust," Max observed, scanning the readout.

"Not consistently, no," Officer Evans admitted. "We never saw a full two newtons. And seven hours ago, the solar electric system shut down entirely. We attempted a manual override, but that ended up tripping the fuses on the main block. We lost all maneuvering control. Only the control moment gyros are still active for attitude control."

"I can see the tripped fuses along the main block," Max said, pointing at the diagram on the screen.

"We tried to reset the fuses," Officer Evans added, "But the maneuvering system refuses to restart. We ran complete diagnostics twice, but the computer could not solve the problem. We called the ground crew, and they recommended your services."

"You're lucky that I was in the area," Max joked.

He and his rocket had not been "in the area." They had launched five hours ago from the Pacific Spaceport Complex in Alaska in response to the urgent call from the Vandenberg Space Force Base.

"Okay," Max said. "Let's pop the hood. Where is the access panel for the main switches?"

Officer Evans pointed him in the right direction, and Max went to work. He went to the wall of the cabin and unclipped the panel, revealing a spaghetti bowl of wires and cables. Fuse boxes and battery arrays were meatballs in the messy marinara.

"Is that an off-the-shelf commercial multimeter?" Officer Evans asked, watching Max produce his tools.

"Sometimes the simplest tools are the best tools," Max said. He was prodding and poking at connections. He produced a pair of wire strippers and began ripping at insulation, exposing more connections.

"Don't you need to turn off power to this section?" Officer Evans asked, aghast. "The manual says to always turn off the power prior to performing any maintenance near electrical connections."

"Remember what I told you about the manual?" Max said. He pried back another panel and began flipping experimentally at the switches hidden beneath.

"I remember, but isn't that dangerous?" Officer Evans asked. "Those are live wires."

"Officer, you rode to orbit atop a giant missile. We are currently traveling at twenty-seven- thousand kilometers per hour inside of a part of that missile. Our current trajectory will take us back into the atmosphere within five to ten minutes. I think we are past worrying about OSHA regulations," Max said.

Officer Evans watched as Max pushed away from the panels

and floated back to the computer screen at the weapons station. The mechanic flipped through utility screens, lips tightening as he did so.

"You know what? For the next part of this fix, I'm going to need more elbow room. Why don't you two go hang out in my ship for a bit?" Max said.

"Mister Ardis, you certainly cannot expect us to leave you unsupervised," Officer Hill objected, speaking for the first time since Max had arrived.

"I'm going to need to crawl all over this dinghy to find the fault. You don't need to be here to see how the sausage is made," Max said.

Max went back to the electrical panel and began pulling bundles of wiring from the wall. They floated into the small cabin, taking up substantial air space around Officer Hill's seat.

Officer Evans put on a mollifying tone. "Come on sir, we should let the man work. He knows what he is doing. Remember the COMMSAT-19 rescue? That was Max," he said. He floated toward the airlock. An electrical board sailed past Officer Hill's stubborn head to bounce off the wall.

"COMMSAT-19 was a glorified tow job," Officer Hill responded irritably. "If you think that I am going to leave this civilian in control of the world's most advanced military vessel then you are insane."

"With all due respect Officer, nobody is in control of this tub right now," Max said. He unwrapped the insulated ties on another bundle of wires. He was deep in the spaghetti now.

"There may be safety advantages in temporarily relocating to the Soyuz vehicle," Officer Evans insisted. He was thinking of what could happen if there were an electrical arc among the live wires that Max was stripping. He wore a forced smile and beckoned urgently to Officer Hill.

Officer Hill slapped a floating wrench away from his face. It clanged off the bulkhead. Reluctantly, he unstrapped from his seat.

"In response to the counsel of Weapons Officer Evans I will

elect to temporarily relocate to your vessel," Officer Hill said. He pushed away from his chair to float toward the hatch, untangling himself from loops of wire as he did so. When he reached the doorway, he stopped and glared at Max. "But let the record show that I did not abandon my post. Mister Ardis, be aware that all your actions are being closely monitored. I hope that you are as good at your job as your reputation might suggest, and I eagerly anticipate a full military review of proceedings."

Huffily, Officer Hill turned and disappeared through the hatch. Officer Evans followed. Max did not respond. He was busy with another panel. He produced a rubber hammer and began energetically hammering on something. The sound of hammering resonated through the hulls of both vessels and was soon joined by a colorful and creative vocabulary of swearing from Max.

Officer Hill meditated quietly, fantasizing about ways in which he would ensure that Maxwell Ardis would never be allowed near any place of legal employment ever again. Meanwhile, Officer Evans explored Max's spaceship.

Officer Evans had never been inside a Soyuz vehicle before, despite them being just about the only ride to space in the decade after the retirement of NASA's Space Shuttle. The Soyuz consisted of three sections. The first section was the orbital module, which was a spherical, six-cubic-meter space for pressurized cargo, docking hardware, and living accommodations for the crew. This module also included the toilet and acted as an airlock for spacewalks. The next section was the descent module, which held three seats and the main control panels. The descent module was used for flying the craft and for reentry into the Earth's atmosphere. Finally, the third section, the service module, consisted of the main propulsion system and the solar panels. That section was not accessible from inside the ship, but Officer Evans knew that it lay just beyond the next bulkhead.

"It is so simple, but so functional," Officer Evans muttered to himself, admiring the stark machinery and manual flight controls.

"What was that?" Officer Hill asked, irritation evident in his voice.

"I'm just admiring the Soyuz, sir. The Soviets really built them to last," Officer Evans said.

"They are last-century vehicles for last-century problems," Officer Hill answered dismissively. "They still use hypergolic propellants for God's sake."

"The nice thing about hypergolics," Max said as he floated through the hatch, "Unlike your electric engine, when you push the pushy-go button you have a really good chance of getting some go."

"Do not waste our time with idle chatter, Mister Ardis," Officer Hill growled. "Provide a service update. Report."

"Well I've got some bad news and some good news. The bad news is that I figured out the problem and how to fix it. The good news is that you won't have to worry about it too much longer," Max said.

Max braced himself against a stanchion and pulled the space station's hatch closed, which was more awkward from this side than it would have been from the other.

"You see," Max continued, "your engine actually works just fine. Your solar panels and batteries are fine too. They can provide enough power to that fancy electrical thruster gimmick. But the main computer still thinks that it is growing avocados in California. Your space station orbits the Earth every ninety minutes. That means that every forty-five minutes the batteries go from shade to sun and vice versa. The solar panels are fine with this, but the temperature change causes the output voltage from the lithium batteries to rise and fall. They don't much care either. The batteries and engine can handle the voltage changes. But then the main computer sees those weird readings and gets all confuzzled and shuts down the whole shooting match just to be extra special careful-safe."

While Max spoke, he finished sealing the station hatch. He then closed the Soyuz spacecraft's hatch and locked it into place. Once he was satisfied that the hatch was sealed, he turned and pushed off toward the descent module, floating past the two space force officers.

"Why did you close the hatch?" said Officer Hill. "I demand that you open it at once!"

"Oh, you don't want me to do that, you'll get sucked right out into the black and your helmet isn't on," Max said. He pulled himself into the commander's seat and began pressing buttons on the Soyuz's control panel. There was a loud noise which Officer Evans recognized as the sound of the docking ring uncoupling. The Soyuz had undocked from the station. They were floating free.

"You boys might want to hold on to something," Max said. His fingers touched the thruster controls.

The Space Force Officers clung to handholds as a gentle acceleration pushed the Soyuz away from the empty space station.

Officer Hill was livid. "Mister Ardis, you are abandoning your mission! This is treason!" he sputtered. He clung awkwardly as a lateral thruster fired, jerking his body to the side while Max deftly maneuvered his craft.

"Sir, look," Officer Evans said. He pointed out the small window, and Officer Hill followed his gaze.

The USSF *One* was tumbling out of control. Wisps of bright plasma from ionized atmosphere shone around the falling space station. As it spun faster, a solar panel was ripped away. Seconds later the doomed station's hull began to glow with the heat of atmospheric reentry.

"You boys had maybe better come on up here and strap in," Max said. "This ride is going to get a little bumpy."

Minutes later, the scattered debris of USSF *One* smashed to Earth across two thousand kilometers of Australian desert. Meanwhile, the descent capsule of Max's reliable old Soyuz descended under parachutes over the Australian coast.

"You boys like opera?" Max asked. "I was really hoping to get us to Newcastle for the beaches, but I think it might be quicker to take a cab to Sydney."

Officer Hill brooded darkly, but Officer Evans grinned. "Why do you have a label on your control panel that says 'Do Not Eat?'" he asked.

Max laughed. The capsule's retrorockets fired, and they landed safely in a grassy field near the A9 Sydney Bypass.

CHAPTER TWO

Two days later, Max sat in a bar in Anchorage, Alaska. An open bottle of soda sat before him, as did a heavy scientific tome.

"Drinking a soda pop? That is not like you," Georgy said, clapping Max on the back. He sat on the next stool and waved down the bartender. "Two bourbons, please and thank you," he ordered.

"State-dependent memory," Max explained, not looking up. "That's a goof that lots of wrench-turners make. They do their studying while drunk, so when they're working, they gots to be just as drunked to remember what they forgot."

Georgy read the page heading aloud, "Concerning external discharge of high intensity ions from annular containment."

"Turns out ions show up in more than just fancy air filters," Max said.

The two glasses of bourbon arrived. Georgy took one of the glasses and set it on the open book. A splash of amber liquid ran down the side of the glass, making a brown half-moon stain on the page.

Max sighed. He carefully lifted the glass and dabbed at the stain with the sleeve of his flannel shirt.

"Cheers," Georgy exclaimed, touching Max's involuntarily raised glass with his own.

They downed their drinks. Resignedly, Max closed the book and set it aside, whiskey burning fire in his esophagus.

"How was Australia?" Georgy asked. He rapped the bar with his knuckles to get the bartender's attention.

"It was cold," Max answered. "It turns out that when it is summer up here it is winter down there."

"The military is calling your job a failed repair attempt," Georgy said.

"It sort of was," Max said, "technically."

"But their official statement is that nobody was ever in any danger. They say that the space station's deorbit was planned. That the mission was concluded. That your rescue of the two officers was not a rescue at all, but a planned transport back home," Georgy said.

"Do people believe that?" Max asked.

"Nobody intelligent does, but that's how the media published it," Georgy said.

Max shrugged. "That's fine with me."

"Two more," Georgy said to the bartender, holding up two fingers.

"Add some water to mine," Max added. "Just a few drops."

"They say a piece of the space station crushed a kangaroo," Georgy said.

"Did it?" Max asked.

"Yes. And that is a good thing. Kangaroos are awful," Georgy said.

Max gave Georgy a raised eyebrow.

"No, really," Georgy insisted. "I had a friend who knew a guy who got kicked by a kangaroo one time."

"Was this guy of a friend drunk at the time?" Max asked.

Georgy shrugged. "Seems self-evident to me."

Georgy Kaverin was a retired cosmonaut. He was a stoutly built Russian man with dark hair, perpetual five o'clock shadow, and a ready grin. He was also a retired fighter pilot, middleweight boxer, and amateur poet. He was the chief operating officer of Thrust Solutions Inc., and he was Max's best friend.

"You know," Max said. "I think those military boys would have ridden that station right down to the ground."

"Following orders?" Georgy asked.

Max shook his head. "No, that's not it. I think they truly did not understand how much danger they were in. When I arrived they were acting like they had all the time in the world."

"Space has gotten safer," Georgy said. "Hardly anybody has died on a rocket since the space shuttle."

"But space is not safe," Max said, picking up his fresh drink. "Space is dangerous, and they were complacent. That station should at least have had an escape pod."

"We had an escape pod on the International Space Station," Georgy agreed, quaffing his whiskey. "We used a Soyuz actually. Speaking of Soyuz, our suppliers are shipping us a brand-spanking new one."

"New?" Max asked, noting the emphasis on the word. "Not surplus?"

"New," Georgy confirmed. "A Soyuz two-point-one letter A. They made us a good deal on it."

"How good of a deal?"

"Fifty-three million American dollars," Georgy answered. "On the pad and fueled up."

Max whistled. "That is a good deal. And I'm assuming the check from Vandenberg cleared?"

Georgy nodded. "Say what you will about the military, but they pay their bills on time."

"Why so cheap on the new Soyuz though?" Max asked. "That rocket costs at least that much to manufacture, let alone transport and assemble."

"This one is government subsidized. My people are proud of their rockets. They dislike all these dirty capitalists edging in on their business," Georgy said, exaggerating his Russian accent.

"What you are saying is that they are trying to stay competitive," Max said.

There was lots of new competition in the market. Private companies had started offering rides to space, and the price of a passenger seat on a rocket ship was dropping fast.

Georgy shrugged. "Something like that maybe. Plus, you are good publicity. Some people even say that you're a hero."

Max scoffed. "You've been drinking too much," he said. He waved at the bartender. "Two more please."

He returned his attention to Georgy. "So, tell me about this fancy new rocket I'm going to be flying," Max said.

"Eh, the new Soyuz 2.1A is not really all that different from the old Soyuz-FG. The biggest change is the upgraded guidance system. It's all digital now, which saves some weight. It has uprated engines, and there are no more matchsticks. It uses chemical ignition for the first stage boosters and core," Georgy said.

"I'll need the manual," Max said.

"Of course."

"And the simulator?" Max added.

"Already updated. Ready and waiting at the Pacific Spaceport Complex."

"You want to come along next time?" Max asked.

Georgy laughed. "No, my friend. Flying the rocket is your job."

"My father said to always use the right tools for the job," Max responded. "Of course, he said that right after repairing my Huffy with a hair dryer, a framing hammer, and a belt sander, so I think he was being facetious."

The two fresh lowballs of whiskey appeared. Max picked one up, gazing at the amber liquid.

"You could stop flying, you know," Georgy observed. "You don't have to keep spending all of your earnings on the next rocket. You could cash out after any job and retire as a millionaire."

Max gave Georgy a wry grin. "Come now, Georgy, where's the fun in that?"

CHAPTER THREE

The next job came less than a month later.

"They need us to repair a vintage communications satellite," Georgy said. "It's old, but that's why they need it. They've got lots of legacy systems depending on it and nobody makes replacements."

"Clearly they haven't updated to all new hardware like we have," Max said ironically. They both knew that even a second-generation Soyuz was practically an antique.

They stood in the parking lot of the launch complex. In the distance, the new Soyuz rocket was being erected on the launch pad. Massive hydraulics slowly pushed the fifty-meter-tall rocket toward the vertical.

"The satellite in question stopped responding while in the middle of an orbital maneuver. They were dodging a spy satellite," Georgy said.

"Did they dodge it?" Max asked.

"We wouldn't be talking about it if they hadn't."

"Do we have telemetry on this thing?"

"Sure do. It's in a near-circular orbit at an altitude of 576 kilometers. Inclination 89.7 degrees."

"That's a polar orbit," Max noted. "Even with the uprated engines, interception is going to push us very close to our maximum delta-vee."

"Very close," Georgy nodded. "Very close indeed."

Delta-v was rocket lingo for "change in velocity." Delta-v represented how much velocity by which a rocket was able to alter its trajectory when burning fuel. Calculating delta-v could be something of a moving target, as it changed depending on the mass of the vehicle, the efficiency of the engines, and the amount of fuel in the tanks. The total delta-v of a rocket was represented by the simple formula:

$$Delta\ v = Isp \times g0 \times ln\ (mwet/mdry)$$

Where *Isp* represented the specific impulse (efficiency) of the engine, *g0* was standard Earth acceleration due to gravity (9.806 m/s^2), *mwet* was the mass of the rocket when full of fuel, and *mdry* was the mass of the vehicle when the fuel tanks were empty.

If you thought of it like a trip in the family sedan, delta-v would tell you how far you could drive before you ran out of fuel. Bigger fuel tanks and more efficient engines increased delta-v. Heavier payloads and less efficient designs decreased delta-v, and consequently, decreased how far a rocket ship could go.

Max sighed. Running a mission at close to the maximum delta-v of the vehicle meant that by the time he got to where he was going, his fuel tanks would be nearly empty. It left little margin for error.

"And they can't just send up another satellite?" Max asked, knowing what the answer would be.

"Maybe they figured that calling for a mechanic is cheaper," Georgy answered with a grin.

"All right. Let's do it," Max said.

All astronauts had rituals before launch. In Russia, cosmonauts planted a tree, signed a door, and urinated on a bus tire. In Florida, astronauts played cards, had steak for breakfast, and were given a cake that they did not eat. Max's ritual was bearing Georgy's bad poetry. He laid back in his command chair and listened.

"Not bad," Max answered. "But aren't Russians supposed to like vodka?"

"I have never said that I don't like vodka," Georgy answered. His voice was transmitted through the radio built into Max's helmet.

Max was clothed in his flight suit, strapped into the central command seat in the descent module of the new Soyuz vehicle. He lay on his back, waiting for the countdown. The Soyuz rocket had finally finished fueling, but there was still an interminable list of checks that needed to be done before liftoff.

"Service access structure retraction complete," came another voice over the radio. It was a member of the ground crew.

Max checked his checklist. They were on schedule.

"T-minus thirty-five minutes," Georgy confirmed.

Max could not reach the control panel while fully strapped in for launch. That was why he had a handy, extendable metal rod for pressing buttons. He scanned the console, using the rod to flip through status readouts on the LCD screens. He had already customized the controls to his satisfaction and most buttons were now labeled in English. One button read "GO FASTER." The oxygen valves were labeled "DO NOT EAT."

"Emergency escape system armed," Max said, depressing the proper sequence of buttons.

"Confirmed," Georgy answered. "You know, when we rode the Soyuz from Baikonur, mission control would always play us music over our headsets."

"Yeah, and they would make you watch that godawful movie too. What's it called again?" Max said.

"*White Sun of the Desert*, and it's a great movie, and you know it," Georgy said.

"I really don't know that," Max answered.

"Oh no, no, no, it is really good. When you get back, we will sit down together and watch it. You will see," Georgy said.

"I have *seen*, Georgy. I've seen the movie before," Max said.

"Sure, okay, but you have never watched it with me. We will crack open a bottle of bourbon. You will laugh, you will cry. You will have a great time. You will see."

"There's no arguing with you," Max said.

"It's a date then. It will be a good time," Georgy concluded. "Do you want some music over your headset? I have some great Russian love albums here."

"No, thank you, Georgy," Max said.

Max had tried listening to music on prior launches, but it only seemed to make the time go even slower. Each song felt like an egg timer, serving only to remind Max of how much more time there was still to wait. He hated the waiting. It was like being pulled up the first hill of a very tall roller coaster at a theme park, ticking steadily upward, strapped in, with no escape. He closed his eyes and focused on his breathing to calm his nerves.

"Did I ever tell you about the time that I fell through the ice while ice fishing?" Georgy asked.

"Yes, you did," Max muttered.

"The ice cracked under me and I went right in the water. It was so cold that I didn't even feel cold. I felt hot. Like I was burning, but I knew that I was freezing. I was a young man at the time, but every time I tried to pull myself out, the ice would crack and I would slip and fall right back in. I was sure that I was going to die. Do you know what happened then?"

"A wolf came out of the woods and saved you," Max answered.

"You will never believe this, but a wolf came out of the woods and saved me. He was a big gray wolf, bigger than a Dacia, and he saw me struggling. He took my sleeve in his teeth and pulled me right out of the water," Georgy said.

"Have I told you that you've told me this story before?" Max asked, knowing that Georgy would ignore him.

"And what do you think happened next? Did the wolf trot

away and leave me there? No, he did not. He sat down, crossed his front paws, one over the other, and watched me. I was miles from home, soaked to the bone and freezing to death, and the wolf sat and watched while I made a fire, stripped bare, and dried off my clothes. Only then. Only then, once I was warm and dry did the wolf stand, nod with approval, and return to his pack."

"How do you know that he had a pack?" Max asked.

"A wolf like that, a healthy wolf like that, always has a pack. Lone wolves are all skin and bones and hunger and have no wolf humanity at all."

"I didn't believe this story the first time you told it to me and I don't believe it now," Max said.

Georgy scoffed. "Believe? What is believing? The pope believes that good people go to heaven. A pet dog believes that if he is a good boy, he will get a treat. And I believe that, according to Newton's third law of motion, when that rocket engine thrusts downward, the rocket ship will go upward!" Georgy concluded dramatically.

"Pre-launch operations completed," came the voice of a member of the ground crew over the radio.

"T-minus six minutes and fifty seconds," Georgy responded.

Max felt his heart rate rise. He breathed in through his nose, out slowly through his mouth. He felt an overwhelming urge to cancel the mission. He felt trapped in his suit, felt trapped in the small cabin. He wanted to call it off. He wanted to leave and have a beer and forget all about space and rockets and spaceships forever.

Instead, he reached up, closed and latched his helmet.

"Commander's controls active," he forced himself to say.

"Combustion chamber nitrogen purge," came another voice from ground control.

"So, no more matchsticks?" Max asked. The first stage engines on the old Soyuz vehicles had been lit with big wooden matchsticks. It was a primitive system, but it had worked for seventy years.

"No more matchsticks," Georgy confirmed. "Chemical ignition

now. With hypergolics."

"Can we keep some matches on standby, just in case?" Max asked.

Georgy laughed. "Sure, I'll order some for you. Good Russian birch wood. And if we don't need them, we'll use them for a bonfire at the company picnic." Georgy's easy chuckle could be heard clearly over the radio. "T-minus three minutes," he added.

Max ran through abort modes in his head. If the rocket experienced a catastrophic failure on the pad, the launch escape tower would ignite and pull him and the capsule away. If it did not automatically engage, then ground crew could engage it, or he could activate it himself. Should the engines or guidance system fail within the first two minutes of flight, the launch escape system would activate or he could engage it himself. After two minutes the first stage boosters would drop away and the launch escape tower would be jettisoned. If there was a failure during the second or third stages, then he could abort using the engines on the spacecraft itself. He would return to Earth in the capsule, hanging from its parachutes.

Georgy's voice came singsong over the radio:

> *"The only thing Prometheus,*
> *saw after bringing humans fire*
> *was eagles tearing at his flesh.*
> *I hope he knows he thrust us higher."*

"Vehicle is now on internal power," a member of the ground crew announced.

"T-minus sixty seconds," Georgy said in response.

Max thought of all the men and women who had come before him. He wondered what they felt, what they saw, what they heard. He thought of the Atlas. The Titan. The Saturn V. The Space Shuttle. And of all the Soyuz rocket ships that had launched before. He thought of all the pioneers that had launched on rockets much like this one. He thought of them and drew strength from their courage. If they could do it, then so could he.

"Thirty seconds," Georgy said.

"Twenty seconds."

The acoustic suppression system activated. Giant sprinklers blasted thousands of gallons of water at the base of the tower. Without the water, the vibrations of the massive engines could tear the vehicle, and the tower, apart.

"Engine start," Georgy said.

Max felt the rocket come to life. With a rumble, five turbopumps, one for the core engine and one for each of the four booster engines, began to spin. The turbopumps forced refined kerosene and liquid oxygen into four combustion chambers for each engine. They, along with twelve verniers gimbaled for steering, ignited. Altogether, twenty pillars of fire burst from the base of the rocket.

"Ten."

The water of the acoustic suppression system was boiled instantly to steam by the tremendous heat of the rocket exhaust. It billowed about the base of the tower in giant white clouds.

"Nine."

"Eight."

A flock of seabirds a kilometer from the launch pad rose into the air, startled by the sudden roar of sound filling the once-tranquil sky.

"Seven."

"Six."

The turbines howled, increasing in pitch as the energy of the combusting fuel drove their alloy blades faster and faster.

"Five."

"Four."

Thrust reached one hundred percent.

"Three."

The rocket vibrated with energy.

"Two."

Spinning turbopumps screamed, whirling at tens of thousands of revolutions per minute. Kerosene combusted fiercely, exploding with heat and light and sound.

"One."

The rocket strained against its launch clamps.

"Liftoff."

The launch clamps released.

The rocket leapt from the launch pad.

Max was thrust back in his seat.

"Roll to align azimuth."

Max watched his navball rotate as the rocket oriented itself. His fear was gone. It had disappeared when the engines had started. He watched his altitude climb and his velocity increase. The rocket smashed through the speed of sound. It passed through *max Q*, the point of maximum aerodynamic pressure. Quickly, the atmosphere outside began to thin. The jostling and vibration decreased.

"T-plus sixty seconds," Georgy said over the radio. "How are you doing Max?"

"Just another day at the office," Max answered. A force of acceleration more than twice Earth's gravity crushed his body, but he hardly felt it. He was glad that nobody could see him grinning like an idiot.

"All systems nominal," said another voice from ground control.

As the kerosene and liquid oxygen burned off, the rocket became lighter. But since the thrust remained the same, the acceleration steadily increased, forcing Max deeper into his chair. The G-force mounted, passing three times Earth gravity, 3G, and approaching four. Breathing became a chore. Max felt his eyeballs pressed into his skull.

"Launch escape system jettison," Georgy announced.

With a loud bang, audible even over the roar of the engines, the launch escape tower detached. It flew clear of the Soyuz under the impulse of its own solid-fuel rocket motors.

"Booster engine shutdown," Georgy said.

Max was thrown forward against his straps as four out of the five first-stage engines cut off. The spent boosters detached and fell away. They spun in the classic "Korolev cross," named after the original designer, venting their final wisps of propellant as they fell back toward the Earth.

"Booster separation confirmed. We are at t-plus two minutes," Georgy said.

The acceleration began to increase once again as the core stage continued to burn, lightening the load of propellant.

"Shroud jettison," Georgy said.

The aerodynamic fairing fell away, and bright sunlight streamed through the cabin windows.

"T-plus three minutes," Georgy said.

Max checked his readouts. He was already over a hundred kilometers in altitude. The ship was outside of the Earth's atmosphere. His velocity was increasing, already at speeds represented in kilometers per second. If he were closer to the window, he could see the blue Pacific below.

"T-plus four minutes," Georgy said.

"Hey Georgy," Max said. "Do you think you could book me a window seat for the next flight? I hate flying in the aisle." The command chair was the center of the three passenger seats.

Georgy's chuckle came over the radio. "Maybe we could add a couple of extra windows? I have a friend who is pretty good with a power drill."

"Is that friend me?" Max asked.

"Acquaintance, then," Georgy said. "Nearing second stage separation," he added.

Like the booster cutoff, when the core stage shut down Max was thrust forward in his chair. He was shoved backward again as the upper stage engine ignited.

"Stage separation successful," Georgy confirmed. "Upper stage engine performance is nominal. All four chamber pressures of the RD-0110 engine are within expected limits."

The thrust of the smaller, more efficient upper stage engine was much less than each of the engines of the prior stages. But, by shedding those prior stages, the rocket had become much lighter and therefore the smaller engine was more than sufficient to accelerate the spacecraft. The force of acceleration began to build on Max once again.

For four more minutes the G-force increased and Max's velocity rose. Going to space was about more than just going up, but also about going sideways. If you wanted to get to space you just had to leave the atmosphere, but to stay in space, you had to reach orbit. To reach orbit you had to go around the Earth so fast that, by the time you would have fallen back down to the ground, your trajectory carried you all the way around the planet instead. The velocity required was incredible. Just to reach low Earth orbit (LEO), baby's first space-travel, a spacecraft had to travel at 7.8km/s, aka. 28,000 km/h, or 17,400 mph. It took expending all of the massive 312-metric-ton Soyuz carrier rocket, with three separate stages and six powerful liquid-fuel engines, just to push Max and his little 7-ton Soyuz spacecraft into orbit.

After peaking at just under 4G of acceleration, the upper stage engine finally burned out. The upper stage, empty now, detached and fell away, off gassing and curving on its own trajectory. Max was weightless. He ran a system check. All spacecraft systems were nominal. Cabin pressure was stable. Fuel lines were pressurized and ready. Orbital insertion looked good.

Max removed his thick gloves, opened his helmet, and unstrapped from his chair. He floated to the window.

The Earth turned beneath him. Below were white clouds, blue seas, and the translucent mist of atmosphere, hazing the edges of the brilliant globe. Ahead was the terminator. His spacecraft, hurtling faster than the fastest bullet, coasted into darkness. The sun set in a flash of glorious red, and the blackness of space, blacker than ever seen on Earth, was filled with a million-billion untwinkling stars.

Max was in orbit.

CHAPTER FOUR

ax had some free time before orbital maneuvers began. He took in the view while his inner ear adjusted to weightlessness.

"Seasick yet?" Georgy asked over the radio.

"Only when you're driving the boat," Max answered.

"That was only one time, and a tide was running, and the swells were bigger than usual," Georgy said defensively.

"And you spilled chum all over the deck," Max said.

"Okay, let's not point fingers here. Somebody made a mistake that time. But yes, it was me," Georgy said.

Max smiled. He returned to his console and input the command to deploy the solar panels. The electric motors hummed as the panels extended. Sound might not travel through the vacuum of space, but vibrations still resonated through the spacecraft's hull and the atmosphere within it.

"In order to rendezvous with the client's satellite, we can commence orbital maneuvers in one hour and seven minutes," Georgy said. "Uploading calculations to your computer now."

Rendezvous in orbit was never as simple as flying directly toward your target. The Gemini astronauts learned this the hard way. Lower orbits had higher velocities and higher orbits had lower velocities, but when you accelerated prograde (in the direction of your orbit) you ended up increasing your altitude. Accelerating retrograde (backward) meant that your altitude decreased. Accelerating toward something that looked like it was in front of you made you go upward and miss your target. If you turned your ship around and tried again, you would end up slowing your orbital velocity, making your orbit eccentric, and making the whole situation worse. The human brain and eyeball struggled with the concepts of orbital mechanics. You had to trust the math, but Max was old hat at this by now, and the math was fairly straightforward.

Max looked at his computer readout. "A bi-elliptic transfer, huh?"

A bi-elliptic transfer was more complicated than a simple Hohmann transfer. It required an extra engine burn, and it took longer to reach your rendezvous. Max unpacked his pen, paper, and pocket calculator and began checking the calculations shown on the computer.

"Georgy must be trying to save me some fuel," he said. He sketched alternate maneuvers, comparing a bi-elliptic to a Hohmann transfer.

"Georgy knows his stuff. It is a good maneuver," he concluded. He checked the minimum delta-v requirements and shook his head. As he had feared, the mission cut it close on fuel. If he ran out of fuel in space, he would be trapped in orbit, circling the Earth forever, unable to drop his perigee enough get back home. The thought gave him chills. He imagined seeing Earth out his windows, close but unreachable. He would float in orbit until his life support gave out.

Max pushed the thought away. He stowed his pen, pad, and calculator. He still had some time until the first maneuver, so he opened the hatch to the orbital module and floated into the spherical compartment. As dependable as Soyuz spacecraft were, they were cramped in the descent module. The orbital module was spartan, but at least he could stretch out.

In this module was another window, facing forward. Through it, Max could see a half moon rising. He touched the glass. Earthshine brightened the dark regions of the moon's cratered surface. He gazed at it for a long time.

"You will be entering a communications blackout soon," Georgy said over the radio, interrupting Max's thoughts.

"For how long?" Max asked.

"Just nineteen minutes," Georgy answered.

As his spacecraft zoomed above the Earth, there were inevitably times during the orbit, especially over the poles or over the emptier parts of the ocean, when Max was out of range of ground-based communications and relay stations.

"I'll try and not get too lonely," Max said.

Max began the process of shrugging out of his pressure suit. He had an urgent need to use the bathroom.

Once he had relieved himself in the orbital module's vacuum-operated space toilet, he was in shirtsleeves, but did not put his flight suit back on. He stowed it in a locker in the orbital module and floated back into the descent module.

The computer showed that all spacecraft systems were nominal. His trajectory had taken him over Antarctica. In twenty minutes, he would be over the African continent. It was nighttime down below and the spacecraft was in the Earth's shadow. He had twenty-seven minutes until his first orbital maneuver.

"Communications test. You have cleared the blackout zone. Can you hear me, Max?" Georgy said, his voice crackling over the cabin speakers.

"Unfortunately," Max answered, hearing Georgy's reliable chuckle in response.

Max unzipped the cargo bag above his head. In the nearest pocket was a plastic container of beef jerky, and he helped himself to a piece.

"I can hear you chewing, Max. I threw in a packet of borscht for you if you want a snack," Georgy said.

Max felt around until he found a plastic bulb. It was filled with dubious-looking red liquid.

"Oh yeah, I see it here. Yum. Looks delicious," Max said before packing it safely away, pushing it much deeper in the bag.

The sun rose, bright rays slanting through the side window. Max strapped himself in to prepare for orbital maneuvering.

The propulsion system for the Soyuz spacecraft was a work of genius. The brilliance of the system came down to its utter simplicity. To recognize just how simple the Soyuz spacecraft's engines were, one must understand the overwhelming complexity of other rocket engine designs. For example, each of the RD-107A first stage engines of the Soyuz carrier rocket weighed more than a metric ton and contained hundreds of moving parts. A gas-generator turbine, driven by the catalytic decomposition of hydrogen peroxide, drove a turbopump which forced liquid oxygen and highly refined kerosene (called RP-1, or Rocket Propellant-1) into four separate combustion chambers and two verniers (small gimballed nozzles for steering). To make things even more complicated, kerosene and oxygen were different densities, meaning that they had to be pumped at different rates with different plumbing so that they would reach the combustion chamber at the proper ratio. Kerosene and oxygen would not ignite spontaneously, so the booster engines needed to be lit by an independent ignition system, which was a separate hypergolic chemical in the case of the Soyuz 2.1. Finally, the liquid oxygen in the tanks needed to be kept chilled at less than -182 degrees Celsius to keep from boiling off.

In comparison, the Soyuz's KTDU-80 had few moving parts and only weighed three-hundred kilograms. It was a pressure-fed system, which meant that there were no turbopumps; the propellant and oxidizer were forced into the combustion chambers by the pressure in the tanks and fuel lines. It integrated a S5.80 main engine with sixteen high-thrust and low-thrust attitude control thrusters. The system ran on a derivative of hydrazine (N_2H_4) called unsymmetrical dimethylhydrazine (UDMH) and used dinitrogen tetroxide (N_2O_4) as its oxidizer. These two propellants, while highly toxic, had the advantage of being "hypergolic," which meant that they spontaneously ignited when they came in contact with each other. Thus, no ignition system was needed. They were also temperature-stable propellants, which did not boil away like liquid oxygen did.

So, as long as the valves turned and the system remained

pressurized, the spacecraft's engines would work. It was simple. There was lots of redundancy. Max liked that.

The computer monitor told Max his altitude, velocity, and orientation. It told him when the maneuver should begin and for how long the thrusters would fire. A gyroscopically stabilized mechanical globe called a "navball" showed Max his vessel's orientation. He recovered his pen and paper and, once again, checked the computer's figures against his own.

"Everything looks good for maneuvers Georgy," Max said.

"You sure? You want to borrow my slide rule?" Georgy asked.

"That's okay Georgy, I have a pocket calculator," Max answered.

"True cosmonauts use slide rules," Georgy said.

"Even on the Space Shuttle?" Max asked.

"Of course. I had a large one and a little small one as a backup. I taught many Americans how math is done," Georgy answered.

"I know how to do math, Georgy," Max said. "First maneuver in two minutes." He grasped the controls.

At his command, the attitude control thrusters gave a brief pulse. The spacecraft rotated. The thrusters deactivated, and the ship coasted. The only sound was the cycling of the cabin ventilation system. Then, the small thrusters activated again, stopping the spacecraft's rotation.

Max checked his navball. The ship was pointing in the correct direction.

"Go for maneuver," Max said.

"Roger," Georgy said.

The ship's computer was programmed to perform the maneuver autonomously, but Max kept his fingers hovering over the thruster controls anyway. Exactly on time, the fuel valves opened, and the rocket ignited with a throaty rumble. This was no gravity-defying, atmosphere-smashing booster. It was a small, efficient engine. A gentle acceleration held Max comfortably in his seat. He timed the burn with his stopwatch. When the burn was done, the engine cut off automatically.

"Your vector looks good," Georgy said.

Max reviewed his instruments, checked his navball, and redid his calculations by hand before replying.

"Yep," he said.

Max unstrapped from his seat. He floated into the orbital module to gaze out the window. The Pacific Ocean was below. A circular storm system worked its way northward across the limitless blue. He gazed down at the Earth, allowing his mind to turn with the clouds.

The elliptical trajectory of the spaceship meant that Max was gaining altitude. Over the next half hour, he watched the familiar landforms shrink beneath him. As the terminator between day and night passed, the sun flashed red and disappeared in flaming brilliance. In less than ten minutes it was nighttime. City lights glowed with artificial fire.

Many space travelers entertained themselves with hobbies. Some played musical instruments. Some wrote in journals or played games. But Max was content with the silence. He was content with the magnificence outside his window and the time alone with his thoughts.

The elliptical trajectory continued to take him higher, and the Earth's curvature contracted. This would be one of his highest altitude journeys, and he savored the experience. The land below remained in shadow when his spacecraft burst into sunlight. The sun was rising over the Indian subcontinent, and he watched the terminator creep slowly westward, highlighting the peaks of the Himalayas as it came.

Humanity was a swarm. It was a hive, like ants or bees. No individual human really mattered. No individual human could do very much alone. Just as this spacecraft had been designed and built by thousands of people, everything that people made was influenced by the thousands or even millions of others who came before. Maybe "hive" was not even the right term. Humanity was like a colony of bacteria, or the body of a slime mold. It was composed of billions of individuals, but each was entirely interconnected, entirely interdependent on the others and thereby interdependent on the whole. No national borders or political boundaries could be seen from space. The entire idea of separate nations seemed ludicrous from up here.

"Your next maneuver won't be for some hours now," Georgy's voice came over the radio. "Why don't you get some rest?"

"That's a good idea Georgy," Max agreed.

Max checked the time, set an alarm on his watch, and closed his eyes.

CHAPTER FIVE

The gentle buzzing of his watch alarm woke Max up. He felt refreshed. He had been dreaming of falling, but he was not afraid of hitting the ground. He checked the time to find there were ten minutes until the next maneuver. He yawned, stretched, then floated into the descent module and to his command chair.

"You have a good nap?" Georgy asked over the radio.

"Always," Max answered. "I always get the best sleep in space. It's so peaceful up here."

"I could never sleep well in space. I was always too excited," Georgy said.

"You're still too excited, Georgy," Max answered.

When it was time, the attitude control system activated and pushed the nose of the spacecraft into the correct orientation.

"Maybe there are just lots of things to be excited about," Georgy answered.

Max watched the countdown, fingers hovering over the controls. The engine rumbled to life, burned for exactly the predetermined amount of time, and then shut off. Max checked his new trajectory.

"New trajectory looks good," Georgy said.

"Yep," Max confirmed.

"Rendezvous in seven hours and twenty-two minutes," Georgy said.

"That's another nap for me," Max responded.

It ended up being more than a nap. Max had lunch. He ate from pouches of yogurt and peanut butter, washing them down with a pouch of lemonade. He gazed at the Earth's horizon, which, as his altitude had increased, had developed a pronounced curve. He went to the bathroom and then had a long, restful nap.

Seven hours and twenty-two minutes later he was at the controls again. The third and final computer-controlled burn began, and it ended with Max sharing an orbit with a new speck on his radar.

"Distance to target, twenty-three hundred meters," Max said. "Relative velocity positive five point zero one nine meters per second."

By convention, a positive relative velocity meant that an object was getting closer. A negative relative velocity meant that the target object was drifting farther away.

"A good rendezvous," Georgy said.

"I'm going to take it in from here," Max said, assuming manual control.

He oriented the spacecraft, centering the radar blip in his scope, then extended his visual periscope. The target satellite was a gleaming speck against the blackness of space. He watched the distance decrease as he coasted closer, making micro adjustments to minimize translational velocity. Once within one hundred meters he decelerated, matching the satellite's orbital velocity. Once finished, his spacecraft and the communications satellite were less than ten meters apart and motionless relative to one another.

"Thank goodness it's not spinning," Max muttered.

There were numerous reasons for an object in space to begin spinning. Its attitude control system could be faulty, or its gyroscopes could be out of whack. Gas venting could make a spacecraft tumble, or even photon pressure from the sun could start an unstabilized spacecraft spinning out of control. If the satellite had been spinning, then Max would have had to scrap the mission. There was no way for him to work on a spinning satellite, not without a robotic arm or some other fancy equipment.

"Its gyroscopes must still be functional," Georgy said.

"Could you ring up the client and let him know that the doctor is in? I might have some questions for him," Max said.

"Can do," Georgy responded. "Calling the client now."

Max pushed off from his command chair and floated into the orbital module. Strapped against the wall was a special spacesuit. Much larger than the flight suit that Max had worn during launch, the "Orlan" was an Extra-Vehicular Activity, or EVA suit. Its self-contained life support system could keep Max alive for seven hours in space, although he hoped that he would not need that much time.

Max closed the hatch leading back to the command/descent module and sealed it. Then, after donning a special tight-fitting pair of jammies and a padded helmet, Max unhinged the rear of the EVA suit and climbed inside. He slid his arms into the protruding armholes. He used the attached gloves to fasten the suit closed behind him. The cooling undergarment was chilly on his legs, but that would be important in space. Contrary to popular belief, space was not just cold: it was cold *and* hot, depending on if you were in shade or in sunlight. It could be negative one hundred degrees Celsius on the shaded side of your body, and hotter than boiling water in the sunlight. The suit had to compensate for that, adjust for the production of body heat, and provide Max with the air pressure and oxygen he needed to survive.

"We have the client on the phone now," Georgy said.

"Great," Max responded, his voice resonant in the helmet. "Don't patch him through yet, but keep him on the line for me."

Max floated to a control panel on the wall by the exit hatch. The buttons were extra-large because they were designed to be used with spacesuit gloves, and he input the command to depressurize the orbital module. Max's tools were in a special bag lashed to his suit. He checked them while he waited for the pressure to drop to zero. The lights on the control panel flashed. Max opened the hatch and looked out into space.

The dysfunctional satellite floated less than ten meters away.

"Alright, Georgy, give me the client," Max said.

A new voice came over the radio.

"Hello. This is Lucas Danielson with International Telecom Incorporated. How can I help you today?" the voice said.

"You can start by walking me through this satellite failure," Max said.

Max ensured that his space-line was attached to his ship. He checked the line for kinks, then clipped the other end to his suit. That rope would be his lifeline to keep him from floating off into space if something bad happened.

"Certainly, sir. Four days ago, we received a warning that our satellite was on a collision course with a military surveillance satellite controlled by an undisclosed foreign nation. We were advised to take evasive action. The command was sent to initiate a two-point-one-one-seven meters-per-second delta-v retrograde maneuver utilizing the onboard station-keeping monopropellant hydrazine thruster system. Zero-point-two seconds after initiating the burn we lost communications with the satellite." It sounded like the young man was reading from a script.

"Can you tell me anything about the nature of the fault? Is it just the communications system that went out? Is the onboard computer offline? Was there an electrical surge? What about the engines?" Max asked.

The young man on the radio gave a nervous cough. "We were hoping that you could tell us what went wrong."

Max sighed. NASA would have theories about what the error might be. They would have run simulations. But simulations cost money, and this was a corporate job. Max gazed at the broken satellite.

The satellite was shaped like a rectangle four meters tall and one meter wide. On that rectangle were two large solar panels spread like wings. Three large, flat antennae pointed toward the Earth below. Max could tell that the satellite was old by the number of shallow scratches and dents that marred its surface, evidence of hundreds of micrometeorite impacts over the years.

"It is maintaining proper orientation," Max commented.

That meant that the gyroscopes were functional. It also meant that the electrical system for the solar panels was working. At least some parts of the computer system were still operational.

"Can you get any response back from this thing?" Max asked. "Even a ping?"

"Nothing, Sir," Lucas answered.

"No dice from us either," Georgy added. "We tried too."

"Alright," Max breathed. He pushed off into space.

Flying in space was not like swimming. You could not change course. Either you hit what you were aiming at, or you did not. NASA astronauts had fancy jetpacks that could help, but Max did not have such luxuries. He had to rely on his legs, arms, and Mk. 1 eyeball.

Max was drifting slowly. He did not wish to disturb the satellite's orientation when he landed on it. It weighed seven hundred kilograms, but any momentum he imparted would be maintained in frictionless space.

"Hey Georgy, did I want to go for an elastic or an inelastic collision with this one?" Max said.

"It's been a while since I took physics but I think inelastic," Georgy said.

The satellite did not have anything in the way of purpose-built handholds to grab on to, but there were sturdy-looking struts holding up the flat antennae, and Max reached for one of those. His hands closed on it, arresting his momentum. He was riding the satellite.

"And here is a fuse box," Max said. "That was easy."

In front of Max was a metal cover, helpfully labelled with a lightning bolt. Protected by the heavy antennae, the panel was smooth and unblemished by the micrometeorite pocks that covered the more exposed portions of the satellite. It was held on by four screws.

Turning a screw in space was no simple task. For every action there was an equal and opposite reaction. Rotational force was as likely to rotate the astronaut as it was to rotate the screw.

Max produced his pistol-grip electric screwdriver, checked that he had the correct screwdriver bit installed, and centered the tool on the first offending screw. He set the torque low, braced himself against the strut, and pulled the trigger.

Nothing happened.

The tool was working, Max was sure of that. He could feel the pressure of the electric screwdriver's handle in his palm, but the screw was stuck. Max turned up the torque setting of the screwdriver, braced his body, and tried again.

Nothing.

There were at least three reasons that a screw on a satellite could be stuck. Firstly, when the satellite was assembled, a careless engineer could have over-torqued it. Secondly, a small electrical current in the satellite could have begun to weld two dissimilar metals together. Finally, the frequent dramatic temperature variations involved in being in space could have deformed the metal panel, increasing the friction on the screw threads.

"You will be crossing the terminator in ten minutes," Georgy said.

Max was not surprised by this. He only had forty-five minutes of daylight in each orbit, and he had never expected to fix the satellite that quickly. He switched on the headlamp of his suit in anticipation of entering Earth's shadow.

"I do some of my best work at night, Georgy," Max said.

Max left the first screw alone. Maximum torque was likely to strip the head of the screw, and then he would really be sunk. Then, the only way to remove the panel would be to drill through the screw or to cut the screw head off, and Max really did not want to have to do either of those things. He shifted the screwdriver to the second screw.

That screw came off easily. It tried to float away into space, but Max trapped it in a small cage around the head of the screwdriver.

The third screw came off easily as well, but the fourth seemed as stuck as the first.

"Gotta have the right tool for the job," Max muttered, putting the electric screwdriver away. He reached into his bag and removed a simple T-handle screwdriver, modified with an extra-large handle for use with spacesuit gloves. It was difficult to feel anything through the thick gloves, but Max was an old hand with this kind of work. He could look at the creases in his glove material and know exactly how much force he was applying.

Working in space was exhausting. Added to the awkwardness of working in zero G with a restricted range of motion and restricted range of vision, the spacesuit itself inflated like a balloon. It fought his every movement. Early spacewalkers wore themselves out simply moving around. An astronaut had to move slowly and deliberately. It took patience, but Max was good at that. He worked doggedly to unjam the stuck screws. He was so focused that he did not even notice when he, as Georgy has predicted, orbited into darkness.

Finally, Max had the panel off. He felt a surge of triumph when the panel came free in his hand. Carefully, he stowed the loose screws, then he took a piece of gray tape and affixed the panel to the hull of the satellite bus. He did not want it floating away.

"Thank goodness this is the correct panel," Max said to himself.

In front of Max were the primary fuses for the satellite. They were labeled, and Max could see that the circuit labeled "Communications" was tripped into the off position.

"How is it going?" Georgy asked.

"Pretty swell, I think I can see my house from here," Max answered, not looking up from his work. "Luke, are you still there?" he asked.

"Yes, Mister Ardis, sir," Lucas answered.

"I think I see the problem. The fuse for the communications circuit has been tripped. Either you had a power surge or the satellite is generating too much voltage," Max said.

"How do we fix that?" Lucas asked.

"Since the onboard computer did not restore the connection, the best thing to do would be to replace the fuse. You didn't happen to pack me any extra fuses, did you?" Max asked.

"Uhh… no sir. We did not," Lucas answered.

"Sorry Max, no fuses," Georgy confirmed.

Max sighed. Experimentally he flipped the circuit back on.

"We have a signal!" came Lucas's excited voice. "You fixed it, Sir!"

"I wouldn't get too excited yet," Max said. The spring-loaded fuse was trying to switch back under his hand. He considered taping it open, then a sudden puff of white smoke emitted from the fuse.

"We lost it," Lucas said.

Max took his hand away, but the smoke lingered, particles floating weightless in vacuum. "You had all this smoke in your wires. I let it out for you," Max joked.

"What?" Lucas asked, confused. Georgy chuckled.

"The communications circuit is dead," Max said.

"Does that mean that the mission is over?" Lucas asked.

Max grinned in his helmet. "Not by a long shot, Luke."

"Do you have a plan?" Lucas asked.

The sun rose and Max lifted his head to watch the Earth's blue horizon sweep open beneath him.

"I do," Max said. "Normally what I am about to do would be totally unacceptable, but today we are doing it anyway."

CHAPTER SIX

ax decided to bypass the fuse and hardwire the connection directly. He might short out the system and fry the main computer, but the satellite was as good as dead in its current state, basically a useless piece of space junk. Since the circuit briefly closed before the fuse blew, Max thought the old machine might still have some life left in it.

"She can probably handle a little bit of surge every now and then," he said to himself.

Max took out his wire cutters and went to work. The sun rose, washing out the puny suit headlamp, and he switched it off.

"How's it going Max?" Georgy asked.

He checked his watch to find he had been working for over an hour.

"Not too bad Georgy," Max answered. He was nearly done. He drifted away, stabilizing himself against the antenna, and examined his work. "It's not a good solution but it's dishonest so at least it's got that going for it," he added.

Max had fashioned a rudimentary switch from the hardware serving the broken fuse. Each of the new connections on either side of the switch were twisted together. All he had to do was flip the switch to close the circuit.

"I'm going to turn the thing back on. Let me know if baby's vital signs stabilize," Max said.

"Yes, Mister Ardis, sir. I am at my console, awaiting the

satellite's signal," Lucas said.

Max turned to gaze at the Earth. White clouds rippled. Antarctica was a gleaming crystal on the horizon. Tiny islands dotted an endless blue sea.

Max's Soyuz had drifted away, but Max had anticipated that, and there was plenty of space line. It hung slack between him and his spaceship, a tiny lifeline in a vast ocean of black. Max turned back to his work.

"Here goes nothing," he muttered. He pulled himself to the panel and flipped his makeshift switch.

Instantly, Lucas's excited voice came over the radio. "You've done it, sir! We have a good signal from the satellite. All systems are online."

"That's great, let me just put the cover panel back on..." Max reached for the metal panel.

He stopped.

Something was wrong.

The antenna strut was pulling on his hand. No... it was not the antenna. The whole universe was moving. Stars wheeled overhead. The satellite was turning; reorienting itself. He could feel the vibrations as the satellite's gyroscopes rotated. Then the satellite shuddered. Hydrazine fuel was flowing through pressurized lines.

"Luke! Shut off the thrusters!" Max shouted.

But it was too late. A rocket nozzle less than a meter above Max's head blasted into life.

Hydrazine, chemical formula $N2H4$, when used as monopropellant, is a simple but highly effective rocket fuel. When forced over a hot catalyst at high pressure, the $N2H4$ quickly decomposes into ammonia ($NH3$), nitrogen gas ($N2$), and hydrogen gas ($H2$). This is a highly exothermic reaction, achieving nearly instantaneous temperatures of greater than 1,000C and blasting out a cone of exhaust gas at 1,500 m/s.

The fringe of the rocket exhaust scorched Max's helmet. He could feel the heat on the back of his head. The satellite spun, throwing Max against the antenna.

"Shut it down. Shut it off!" Max cried.

"I don't know why it's firing," came Lucas's panicked reply.

"Get out of there, Max!" Georgy shouted.

The Soyuz was nowhere in sight. Max's lifeline quivered and stretched, then whipped tight against the bulkhead of the satellite. With a sudden jerk, Max was yanked into space.

Blue Earth and black sky traded places in his vision. Max's inner ear protested and he felt sick. With a hard jolt he reached the end of the lifeline.

"Max! Max!" Georgy was shouting.

"I'm okay Georgy, I'm alive," Max said.

He was spinning fast. He fought a wave of nausea and attempted to reorient himself. He could see his Soyuz briefly once each spin. The space line appeared to be intact, limply hanging between himself and his spaceship. He could not locate the satellite at first. He spun and spun.

Then, he saw it. The satellite filled his spinning vision. He twisted, trying to track it, then lost it again. On the next turn he saw that it was picking up speed. Its engines were firing. The satellite was headed directly toward the Soyuz. They were going to collide. Such a collision would easily destroy his fragile spacecraft.

"Georgy, take remote control of the Soyuz. Fire the retro thrusters," Max commanded.

"But you are still outside!" Georgy objected.

"Do it now, Georgy! The satellite is on a collision course!" Max insisted.

His spin faced him away from the Soyuz, so he did not see the rocket motors fire. The Soyuz dashed away from the rushing satellite. Max felt another jerk on the space line. His vision squeezed. The universe spun around him. He lost all sense of orientation as Earth and space traded places at a maddening rate.

"Satellite evaded successfully," Georgy said with a relieved sigh.

Max took a deep, even breath. His life support was still functional. He could hear the cooling fan in the suit. His suit integrity was intact, but the nausea was worsening. He needed to stop this mad spin. He needed to get back to his ship.

His vision was useless. The blue-green globe flashed by several times per second. He closed his eyes tight. Blind, he fished for the connection for his lifeline. His hand closed on the rope. He ignored a rotating universe and pulled. The line gave him some resistance, then went slack.

"Max?" Georgy's worried voice came over the radio.

"I'm okay, Georgy," Max said. "I'm okay."

"Are you back in your ship?" Georgy asked.

"No, but I will be soon," Max answered.

Max timed his pulls on the rope so that they would slow his rotation each time. After some trial and error, it began to work. He began to slow his spin. He opened his eyes. The Soyuz flashed by. It was closer than before. He breathed a sigh of relief, then felt acid rise in the back of his throat.

"No, no, no, don't throw up," he muttered. Vomit in the spacesuit would cloud the visor and leave him blind. The vomit would float around and could even choke him when he tried to breathe. He grit his teeth. On his next rotation he saw that the Soyuz had also developed a slow rotation.

"Georgy, my ship is spinning a bit, do you think that you could stop it for me?" Max asked.

"Certainly, just a moment," Georgy answered.

"Actually, leave it," Max changed his mind.

Georgy could stop the ship's rotation from the ground, but Max was still at the end of a long rope, stopping the ship's rotation would increase his relative angular velocity. He needed to minimize the angular momentum of the whole system.

"You're the boss," Georgy said.

Max pulled himself toward his ship. It was awkward, with no way to maneuver except through pulling on the rope. Thankfully, there was no appreciable angular acceleration. The real challenge was fighting the waves of nausea.

Finally, Max reached hatch. He grasped a handhold, oriented himself, and entered feet-first. Before he closed the hatch he scanned for the satellite. There it was, small in the distance and dwindling quickly.

"I figured out what happened," Lucas's voice came over the radio. "You see, sir, there had been a partial maneuver program carried out before the satellite lost communications. After communication was restored, the satellite's programming caused it to complete the initial maneuver that had been started before it lost the connection."

"Thank you, Lucas, but I don't particularly care right now. Georgy, can you kill my ship's spin?" Max said. The horizon wheeled sickeningly below.

"Roger," Georgy said.

The thrusters hissed and Max felt the gentle acceleration. Then the horizon was finally stationary in the sky.

"I can't be sick," Max groaned. He was salivating. He swallowed hard.

Max closed and sealed the external hatch. He pressed the buttons for the cabin atmosphere to cycle. The vents opened and slowly the air pressure in the cabin increased. Max closed his eyes, fighting nausea with tooth and claw.

"Georgy, maybe some music would be nice right now," Max said.

"Coming right up," Georgy answered. His voice was subdued. He seemed to sense what Max was going through. Classical music began to play softly over the suit's speakers.

"Lucas has signed off. It's just us now," Georgy said. "It looks like the satellite is doing just fine."

Max did not answer. It was an interminable wait for atmospheric pressure in the cabin to climb. Finally, a light informed him that the pressure had normalized. He unlatched the rear door of his spacesuit and climbed out. He went to the cache of pharmaceuticals stored in the descent module and found an antiemetic. He removed the soft, white tablet from its wrapper and placed it in his mouth. It dissolved, leaving behind a grainy texture and a sweet-sour taste of artificial strawberry. It began to seem possible that he might not puke.

"Max," Georgy's voice came over the radio again. "We might have a problem."

CHAPTER SEVEN

The problem was the fuel level. The fuel needed to dodge the satellite had been relatively small, but the margin for error for this mission had been impossibly tight. Max floated above his control panel.

"Do I have enough fuel to get home, Georgy?" Max asked.

"It is close," Georgy answered. "Very close. All maneuvers will have to be done with high-thrust and high-thrust alone, main engine if at all possible."

Since the Soyuz's maneuvering system ran off a single shared fuel supply, all the thrusters, small and large, drew from the same tank. It was a truism of chemical rockets that high-thrust was always more efficient than low, as the efficiency of a rocket engine was directly tied to exhaust velocity.

Specific impulse equals thrust divided by propellant mass flow rate:

$$Isp = Thrust\ (N)\ /\ mass\ flow\ rate\ (kg/s)$$

"You should be able to achieve aerocapture," Georgy continued, "but there is less than a ten meter-per-second delta-v margin of error."

"Does this limit my landing options?" Max asked.

"Severely," Georgy answered. "You will not be able to adjust your inclination, and your burns can be only at apogee, where they will be the most efficient in lowering your perigee. Your next twelve orbits will place perigee over the Pacific Ocean, which is a no-go. We are looking into alternate landing options now."

Max exhaled slowly and reached for his notepad. The figures swam before his eyes, but he forced himself to concentrate.

"Delta-v equals specific impulse times gee zero times the natural log of wet mass over dry mass," he muttered to himself.

The Tsiolkovsky rocket equation stared back at him from the paper:

$$Delta\ v = Isp \times g0 \times ln\ (mwet/mdry)$$

"How many kilos of fuel do I have left Georgy?" Max asked. He already knew the Soyuz's dry mass: 6,350kg. The standard acceleration due to gravity was the constant 9.806 m/s^2, and the specific impulse (Isp) of his rocket's engine on high-thrust mode was 302 seconds.

"One hundred and sixty-three kilograms of propellant," Georgy answered.

$$Delta\ v = 302s \times 9.806\ m/s^2 \times ln\ (6{,}513kg\ /\ 6{,}350kg)$$

Max did the math.

$$Delta\ v = 75.05\ m/s$$

"Seventy-five point zero five meters per second," Max muttered to himself.

Max gazed at the notepad, willing the numbers to change. He could not create more fuel. He could not change the efficiency of his engines. But he could, perhaps, make his spacecraft lighter. The orbital module weighed about 1,300 kilograms. If he could ditch it, he could make his remaining fuel go farther. He ran the equation again with different numbers:

$$Delta\ v = 302s \times 9.806\ m/s^2 \times ln\ (5{,}213kg\ /\ 5{,}050kg)$$

Which came out to:

$$Delta\ v = 94.07\ m/s$$

"Ninety-four point zero seven meters per second," he concluded, triumphantly.

"What was that?" Georgy asked.

"Ninety-four meters per second, Georgy, what could we do with that?" Max asked.

"We could get you dead-center at White Sands," Georgy said, naming their original intended landing site in New Mexico. "That would be superb, but how are you going to get ninety-four meters per second of delta-v?"

"By ditching the orbital module," Max answered.

The sound of Georgy sucking air through his teeth came over the radio.

"I see," Georgy said finally. There was a silence, broken only by the muffled noise of Georgy conferring with one of the ground crew.

"We have a landing solution that does not require you to detach the orbital module prior to maneuvers. After fourteen revolutions there are three potential landing sites in northern Canada, between 60- and 70-degrees north latitude," Georgy said finally.

"In the trees, Georgy? I don't like that. And how long until recovery?" Max asked.

There was muffled conferring again before Georgy responded. "We can scramble a rescue crew in not more than twenty-four hours," Georgy said.

"I'd rather land in White Sands and be home by breakfast," Max said.

"Standard procedure is for retention of the orbital module until after successful completion of the deorbit burn," Georgy said.

"Yeah, I know. But what do I always say about following the manual?" Max said.

"It is your choice, Max. We will support you either way,"

Georgy said.

Max closed his eyes and tried to think. He was dizzy. His throat was sour and he had a headache. Detaching the orbital module early could strand him in the capsule if there was any issue with the descent burn. But landing in the taiga of northern Canada was dangerous too. He knew that the region was all tall pine trees, steep slopes, and a long distance from recovery.

Max trusted his gut, and his gut told him that detaching the orbital module and going for a landing in New Mexico was the right thing to do. He opened his eyes.

"Sometimes bad solutions are the best solutions," Max said. "I'm ditching weight and going for White Sands."

"Okay, Max. Calculating new reentry vectors now," Georgy said.

It did not take long for Georgy to get back to him. "First maneuver in forty-two minutes," he said.

Max looked at the readout. He checked the math. The trajectories looked good. He would adjust inclination near apogee, swing around the planet one more time, then burn retrograde when he was half an orbit from the landing site.

"Looks good. I'm going to use the space toilet before it gets blown into space," Max said.

He did that, then shrugged into his pressure suit. He went through the capsule and threw everything he would not need into the orbital module. That included his toolkit, which he consigned to space with a wistful sadness. He needed all the weight savings he could get. He closed the hatch to the orbital module and strapped himself into his command chair. He depressed a sequence of buttons. The orbital module was depressurized, and all connections were separated. Then, there was shudder and a bang as the explosive bolts fired and the orbital module separated. He watched it float away on his periscope. The entire module and EVA suit would float in the infinite vacuum until the slight drag of attenuated atmosphere deorbited it in a thousand years. Max's slimmed down spaceship was free to return home.

Max performed the first maneuver without incident. Two

hours later, the second maneuver was completed, and the ship was on a free-return trajectory back to Earth. He had burned ninety-nine-point-eight percent of his fuel. He detached the service module and the main engine. Unshielded, they would burn up on reentry. The descent capsule oriented heat-shield down with its final puffs of hydrazine. Max was on his back in the command chair as the deceleration force began to build. He could see wisps of plasma through the window as molecules of atmosphere, ionized by the ship's screaming passage, glowed brilliant magenta.

The radio went dead, but Max was not alarmed. Loss of contact during reentry was expected due to atmospheric ionization. Max watched his velocity decrease as the atmosphere slowed the ship. The heat shield would be glowing white-hot as it ablated away, burned by the tremendous heat of atmospheric compression. The G-forces grew. For five minutes Max was crushed into his seat by 4G of deceleration.

"Still there, friend?" Georgy said when radio contact was reestablished.

"I'm strapped in. I can't go walking off," Max answered, catching his breath.

"Your trajectory looks good. Parachute deployment in three minutes," Georgy said.

Max was falling free. Finally, the parachutes deployed: first, the drogue, and then the main parachute, each with a bump and jolt. There was a gentle swaying motion as the capsule descended. The heat shield was jettisoned, and the air valves opened, allowing the pressure inside and outside the ship to equilibrate. Max opened his helmet to breathe the fresh desert air that wafted into the cabin. The retrorockets fired at touchdown, softening Max's landing.

He was home.

CHAPTER EIGHT

The recovery team opened the hatch and helped Max climb out of the capsule. It was a cool morning as the sun rose over the New Mexico desert.

Max was led to a black SUV, then driven to the military base for the usual debriefing and medical exam. He smiled, responded to questions, and felt strangely numb after his near brush with death. It was well past lunchtime by the time they were finished.

"Is there a good place to get a hamburger around here?" Max asked finally.

Airman First Class Samantha Priestly, Max's guide and escort, wrinkled her nose.

"You could try the base cafeteria if you are starving, but I would not recommend it. There are decent restaurants in Las Cruces though. I can drive you," she said.

"Great, let's go," Max answered.

"Don`t you have anything to retrieve from your ship?"

"Nope."

"Okay, but it is about an hour drive. If you're really hungry you could just eat here."

Max's stomach growled. "I'll take quality over convenience any day. Lead on, Airman," he said.

The car ran down the empty four-lane highway, distant mountains on the right, scrubby desert on the left. Samantha was blissfully quiet. Max felt exhausted but sleep evaded him. Every time he closed his eyes, he saw spinning blackness. He opened his eyes and gazed, unseeing, out the window.

The grand scenery transitioned to the gravel drives and homes of small-town America as they eventually left the highway. Airman First Class Priestly drove the car through a quiet downtown and pulled into the parking lot of a restaurant.

"We are here, sir," she prompted him.

Max gazed at the gaudy storefront.

"Don't you know anything a bit more… divey?" Max asked.

"Ahh, you aren't big on chain restaurants. I should have guessed. Well, I might know just the place." She returned the car to the street.

"And, I just wanted to say that I think that you astronauts are so brave," she added, now that the spell of silence was broken.

"I am not an astronaut, I am a civilian contractor," Max corrected her.

"Well whatever. You go up into space and all that. That must take some serious courage. Why do you do it?" she asked.

"Why did you go into the Air Force?" Max asked.

She shrugged. "ROTC paid for my college," she answered.

"Exactly, I do it for the money," he said.

She frowned. "I don't believe you."

"Well, I don't do it for free," Max said.

"I wouldn't expect that, but it is too dangerous of a job for money to be the only motivation," she said.

"Glory, then," Max said.

"I believe that even less," she snorted.

She parallel-parked the big vehicle on the main street. Outside of Max's window was a dive bar, replete with neon signs for brands of beer. A large motorcycle was rudely parked on the sidewalk. The two-wheeled chrome abomination would have blocked pedestrian traffic had there been any.

"This looks like my kind of place," Max said. He reached for the door handle, then stopped when he noticed that Airman First Class Priestly was frowning at him.

Max sighed. "Has anybody ever told you that you remind me

of my ex-wife?" he said.

"I am much too young to be your ex-wife," she said.

"True, but she always saw through my bull. That is why we worked. And that's also why we didn't," Max said.

Airman Priestly cocked an eyebrow at him.

"When was the first time you saw a rocket launch?" Max asked.

"I saw the last launch of the Space Shuttle *Atlantis* back in 2011," she answered.

"And how old were you then?"

"I would have had to have been…" the young woman counted on her fingers. "Eight or nine."

"And did you tell your parents that you wanted to be an astronaut?" he asked.

She looked surprised. "Yes, I did," she said.

"And what did they say?"

"They said that being an astronaut was too dangerous," she answered.

Max nodded. "Rockets are like cigarettes: they are an addiction that begins in childhood. Little boys and girls see a rocket, they hear the whoosh and boom and see the bright flame and they get hooked. The allure of rockets is like a forbidden drag on a ciggie behind the schoolyard dumpster. Your parents tell you that rockets are too dangerous because they do know better. They steer you away from them. But once you are addicted it takes an act of God to quit. And just like cigarettes, those addicted to rockets are bound to be killed by them someday."

Max opened the car door and stepped out.

"Do you need a ride back to base later? Do you need a car or a hotel or anything?" Airman Priestly yelled after him.

Max waved dismissively. "I'm a big boy. I can take care of myself. Thanks for the lift," he said. He walked to the grimy bar and opened the door.

The establishment had few patrons. Max took a seat at the bar and ordered a cheeseburger from the disinterested-looking bartender. When the burger came, it was moist and greasy, perfectly medium-rare and dripping with mayonnaise and the juice of several thick slices of ripe, red tomato. It looked wonderful.

But it was like ash in his mouth. He ate mechanically. He felt no satiety from it. When he was half done, he pushed the plate away and hailed the bartender.

"I will have a beer, please," Max said.

"What kind of beer?" the bartender asked. She was a white woman in her fifties, with dyed-blonde hair and a loose-fitting t-shirt and jeans. When she was not glancing at him, she was playing a game on her smartphone.

"Whatever is cheap," he answered.

She poured a sloppy pint and slid it across the bar. He started on it at once.

"That didn't take you long," she said soon after, looking at the empty glass. "Want another?"

"If you insist," Max answered, sliding the glass back to her. She returned it with a foamy pour.

"You know, physics doesn't want us to leave this planet," he told her.

"Mmm," she grunted, tapping on the screen of her cell phone.

"If the Earth were just a little bit bigger, or if the atmosphere were just a little bit denser, rockets wouldn't work at all," he added.

The bartender looked up. "You must be one of those rocket men from the base," she commented. "Don't recognize you though. You want another?" she asked, indicating his empty glass.

"A whiskey please," he said.

"What kind?"

"Surprise me. And with just a drop of water," he added.

The drink appeared. It burned going down.

"So, rockets have to be designed at the absolute edge of their material tolerances. Bulkheads are as thin as paper. Tanks are full to bursting. Engines run at redline."

"Another?" she asked.

"Please," he answered.

"When a rocket launches, everything, every single little thing has to be absolutely perfect. Every single time. If anything is not perfect, the rocket goes boom, and in a bad way," he continued.

"Uh huh," she grunted. Her phone screen flashed and beeped under her tapping fingers.

"So rockets must be perfect, but rockets are built by humans," he said.

"Another?" she asked.

"Yes, please," he answered.

"And humans are not perfect," he concluded.

Max's phone buzzed. He dug it out of his pants pocket and saw that it was Georgy calling. He muted the phone and returned it to his pocket.

"How many was that?" he asked.

"Six," the bartender answered.

"Make it seven," he declared. "Have you ever nearly died?" he asked.

"I crashed my motorcycle once," she answered, brightening. "Woke up in the hospital with a concussion and two cracked vertebrae."

"Have you ever felt so filled with panic that you could not think? That you could not move? That time raced but you were frozen in place?" he asked.

"I really don't remember much from the accident," she said.

"Have you ever wondered what our purpose is? As thinking beings, so small, on a tiny round planet, spinning in blackness?"

"I was reading on the internet that the Earth is actually flat. Makes a lot more sense if you think about it," she said.

"Is there a good motel around here?" he asked.

"Motel? Yes. Good? No. Take a right out the door. Go a block. You can't miss it," she said.

"Put it all on my card," he said, managing to sit up straight and fumble out his wallet before stumbling out the door.

It was bright outside and he covered his eyes against the red sunset.

CHAPTER NINE

Max woke up in a motel room with a splitting headache. His mouth tasted foul. He was lying in bed fully dressed, alone. Two empty beer bottles were on the nightstand. He checked to make sure he still had his wallet and cell phone and noticed four missed calls from Georgy.

He sighed and went to the bathroom. Luckily, this was one of those motels that correctly assumed that its occupants forgot their toiletries. The bathroom counter was stocked with cheap toothbrushes, soap, toothpaste, mouthwash, and etcetera. Max used the amenities, scrubbing the sour taste from his mouth. He took a shower. When he was done, he had only his clothes from the day before, but they were clean enough. After dressing, he checked out of the hotel and went outside. His phone rang.

"Georgy?" Max said, answering the call.

"Good morning my elusive friend. Out celebrating last night, were we?" Georgy asked.

"Yeah big party. College kids. We tore up the town," Max lied.

"Is there even a college in Las Cruces?" Georgy retorted.

"Who knows. And are you tracking my phone again?" Max asked.

"I wish. That nice Airman lady told me where she dropped you off. You really should let me implant a tracker in your skin. It would be so much easier to keep an eye on you," Georgy said.

"We've talked about this Georgy. No chips. Skin, mind control, or otherwise," Max answered.

Max's hung-over brain was only slowly taking in his surroundings. It was early morning and he stood at a crossroads near the center of a small New Mexico town. Cars drove lazily by as a gentle wind rustled the evergreen trees that lined the sidewalk. It was already warm and the sky was clear. It was promising to be a hot, dry desert day.

"You didn't call Heather, did you?" Georgy asked. Heather was the name of Max's ex-wife.

"Hold on," Max said. He took his phone from his ear and checked his call history. "Nope," he told Georgy.

"You know my sister has some very nice single Russian friends who would love to date you. Strong Russian women, with strong Russian values. Much better than weak American women," Georgy said.

"Georgy, your wife is American. I am going to tell her that you said that," Max said.

"Please do," Georgy said. "She likes strong Russian women too."

Max laughed, regretting the instant headache that came with it. "What's news Georgy? Do we have a new job?" he asked.

"No new job. Not right now. I was thinking that you deserved some vacation. Somewhere warm. I booked you a flight," Georgy said.

"I am already somewhere warm," Max said, which was true. He unbuttoned the first two buttons of his shirt as the desert sun peeked above the opposite buildings.

"Somewhere warm and near rockets," Georgy appended.

"I'm already warm and near rockets, Georgy, the White Sands Missile range is only an hour away," Max said.

"Somewhere warm and near rockets and in Florida," Georgy said.

"What's going on in Florida?" Max asked.

"NASA is testing its new moon rocket. Certainly, you haven't forgotten about that. They invited me and you to view the first flight from the Kennedy Space Center. I e-mailed you your plane tickets," Georgy said.

Max felt an involuntary flutter. Georgy was referring to the inaugural launch of the Space Launch System, the SLS. It would be the first rocket powerful enough to take people to the moon since the Saturn V.

"Is this trip really a vacation or is this work related?" Max asked.

"No?" Georgy said evasively.

"Okay, Georgy. I'll meet you in Florida," Max said. He hung up the phone and found that he was grinning.

Two hours later Max was at El Paso International Airport, boarding an Orlando-bound Airbus. After finding his seat he scanned his phone screen, refreshing his memory on the specifications of the rocket he would soon be viewing. The SLS was 111 meters tall. The first stage had four RS-25 main engines and two massive solid rocket boosters with a combined total thrust of 40,000 kilonewtons. The Orion capsule massed 10,400 kilograms, carried a crew of four, and had 9 cubic meters of habitable volume.

Max eventually dozed off, lulled to sleep by the gentle turbulence of the airplane.

After the plane landed, Georgy met Max in the terminal. Georgy was wearing a t-shirt, cargo shorts, and open-toed sandals with calf-high white socks. He carried two duffel bags, one of which he handed to Max.

"Am I your porter now?" Max asked.

"That is your luggage. I know that the only clothes you have are the ones on your back, so I packed a bag for you," Georgy said.

"Thank you," Max said. He unzipped the bag and looked inside. It was neatly packed with a selection of his own clothes from his home in Alaska, including a set of swim trunks and a neatly folded blue business suit.

"Am I going to be interviewing or swimming?" Max asked.

"Who knows. Maybe both?" Georgy answered with a smile. "Come on."

They walked through the busy airport. At the exit was a black limousine, waiting, apparently for them. Georgy led the way without a word, and soon the two of them were alone in the spacious interior of the limo.

"Take us here," Georgy said, showing the driver his cell phone screen. The limo moved off.

"This isn't the first time I've been kidnapped by Russians; I'll have you know," Max said.

"Your birthday doesn't count," Georgy retorted. He leaned forward and opened the glass door of the small refrigerator across from his seat. "Soda?" he asked.

"Yes, please," Max asked, accepting the cold beverage.

The limo left the airport and ran eastward on State Road 528. The wooded lowlands of the Florida coastal plain slid by. Max sipped his soda.

"Excited to see some of your old NASA buddies?" Max asked.

"Of course," Georgy answered. "But I have a secret to tell you."

"Okay," Max said.

"Something I didn't mention before," Georgy continued.

"Obviously, that is implied," Max said.

"They secret is that you are not my plus one for this NASA invitation," Georgy said.

"What do you mean?" Max asked.

"I am *your* plus one! They invited you first, but they said that it would be fine if I were to tag along too," Georgy said, beaming.

"So what? What does it matter?" Max asked.

"It means that somebody at NASA wants to talk to you. They might have a job for you," Georgy said.

"You mean like a contract job or like a *job* job?" Max asked.

"I don't know. They would not say," Georgy said.

Max chewed on that news while he sipped his soda.

"I like my job, Georgy," Max said finally.

"Jobs are like women," Georgy said airily. "You should hold on to a good one but always keep an eye out for a better one to come along."

"I am telling your wife that you said that too," Max said.

Georgy only chuckled. He gulped down his soda, tossed the empty bottle into the waste bin built into the limo's bar, and laid down across the seat. He sighed and closed his eyes, and the two of them lapsed into companionable silence.

They arrived at an oceanfront hotel in Cocoa Beach in the early evening. Georgy checked them in, then they hauled their luggage to a second-floor suite overlooking the pool.

"The launch isn't until tomorrow afternoon, so we have plenty of time to relax. I, for one, would like a large meal and then a float in the pool," Georgy said.

"Sure," Max assented. "Lead on."

"Do you want a shower or anything? Your hair is very greasy," Georgy said.

"I don't need to clean myself. You already said that we are getting in the pool," Max said.

"Fair enough," Georgy answered.

They changed into swimsuits, ate at the hotel restaurant, then made their way to the hotel pool. The sun was low in the sky, but the evening was still Florida summer hot when Max cannonballed into the cool water.

When Max came back up, he found Georgy sitting on the edge of the pool chatting with a middle-aged man who stood in sandals, khaki shorts, and a collared shirt. Max paddled over to the side. The stranger kicked off his sandals and sat beside Georgy, soaking his bare feet.

"Max, I want you to meet my friend, Adams Leverrier," Georgy said.

The water was shallow enough for Max to stand. The stranger grinned and extended his dry hand, Max shook it with his dripping one. The man's grip was strong.

"I know who you are. You were a Space Shuttle pilot," Max said.

The man nodded. "Three times," he said. "Twice with Georgy here as my copilot," Adams said.

"Are you sure that you were not the copilot and I was the pilot?" Georgy asked with a smile.

"Quite sure," Adams said.

"Well, I remember it differently," Georgy said. "Would you like a drink?" he added.

"I wouldn't say no to a cold lemonade. This muggy Florida heat doesn't let up even when the sun goes down," Adams said.

Georgy waved to a passing server. Max snagged an abandoned pool float and lounged on it. Children splashed nearby. The poolside bar was rowdy with patrons.

"You do good work Max, I have read about your missions," Adams said.

"We are not fancy enough to have missions. We just call them jobs," Max said.

"Your rescue of those two men from the USSF *One* was heroic. My own calculations of the orbital trajectories would have placed your ship in the upper atmosphere within seconds of decoupling," Adams continued.

The official statement from the US Space Force implied that the station's deorbit was planned, but Max was not surprised that Adams knew the truth. Rocket men generally knew how to read between the lines.

"Max is a hero," Georgy beamed. "A true American hero. And those stiff-necked military men would never admit that they made a mistake."

"Don't call me a hero, Georgy. 'Hero' is a title given to somebody dead or soon to be dead," Max said.

"They could have given you more credit for what you did. You saved those men," Adams said.

"It wouldn't do to embarrass an employer by calling them out. Their official report is safe enough. The press was more interested in the kangaroo that was squished by falling debris than anything that happened in space," Max said.

"Kangaroos are nasty," Georgy offered. "A friend of mine knew a guy who was kicked by a kangaroo."

The drinks arrived. Georgy paid the server with a handful of damp bills and passed Adams a lemonade. He handed Max a twelve-ounce beer, then opened his own and took a sip. Max took a gulp. There was a cup holder built into the flexible plastic of the pool float where the can took a break from dispensing its cool beverage across his lips.

"I am glad to see you here, Max. I had been hoping to speak to you," Adams said.

"Oh?" Max asked.

"About the Space Launch System. I have been training for the Orion capsule as crew for Artemis 2," Adams said.

Georgy snorted, spraying beer. "Congratulations, my friend! I did not know that. Old Adams is going back to space? Who would have thought?" Georgy guffawed and slapped his friend on the back.

"I am fifty-two years old Georgy. I am not that much older than you are," Adams said mildly.

"You wanted to talk about the SLS?" Max prompted.

"I want to hear your opinion on the rocket," Adams said.

"Well, it is the most expensive rocket ever made. That means that it has to be the best. That is just science," Max said.

Adams gave a wry smile. "Setting aside the program's cost for a moment, fertile topic for discussion that may be, what do you think of the rocket's design?"

"The SLS has four reused Space Shuttle RS-25 hydrolox engines on the first stage, with two stretched Space Shuttle solid rocket boosters strapped on the sides. Second stage is basically the same as a Delta rocket: a cryogenic hydrolox upper using RL-10 engines. Slapped on top is the Orion capsule with an Airbus ATV for mobility," Max said. "It should be able to lift about 100,000 kilos into low-earth orbit and take about 25,000 kilos to the moon."

"So, do you think that it will fly?" Adams asked.

Max shrugged. "I don't see why not. Those are all time-tested components and a pretty straightforward design."

"Unlike the Space Shuttle," Georgy interjected. "God, I hated that thing."

"I thought you liked the Space Shuttle, Georgy," Adams said.

"I did like it. I loved it. And I hated it too. The Space Shuttle was like a dangerous woman. It was intoxicating and exciting. It was the greatest thrill of my life, but you never knew when something was going to go wrong. There were so many things to go wrong," Georgy said.

"You could say that about any rocket," Adams pointed out.

"Yes, but the Space Shuttle is the only rocket that killed fourteen astronauts," Max interjected.

They were all quiet for a moment. Max took a drink of his beer and laid back on the pool float, closing his eyes. The poolside noise washed over him. Glasses tinked at the bar. A woman laughed. Children shouted and splashed.

"I am worried about the SLS," Adams said.

Max opened his eyes. "What are you worried about exactly," Max asked.

"Let us just say that I have a professional concern for its success," he said.

"We will see tomorrow," Georgy said. "Nobody will be onboard for this flight, so if it explodes, we enjoy the fireworks."

CHAPTER TEN

M ax sat with Georgy in the crowded bleachers on the north lawn of the Kennedy Space Center. He finished a concession-stand hot dog and wiped his hands on his khaki pants. Two large video screens showed the rocket, an enormous orange and white missile, sitting on the launch pad. Clouds of white gas, which Max knew was the condensation of atmospheric water vapor triggered by the venting of excess cryogenic oxygen, could be seen from the first stage tank. From where they sat, Max and Georgy could not see the rocket with their own eyes; the launch pad was seven miles away and hidden by a line of trees. Their first direct view of it would be after liftoff when it rose above the tree line.

"I expected VIP treatment," Georgy grumbled.

"Where did you want to be? In the Launch Control Center?" Max asked.

"Sure. Or at least in a nice office with some windows and air conditioning," Georgy said.

"Well I think it's nice to be out of the office," Max said.

"You don't have an office," Georgy pointed out.

"T-minus five minutes," the announcer announced.

"So, what do you think of the Space Launch System?" Georgy asked.

"Well, I don't want to get too technical, but I understand that when the flame shoots down, the rocket goes up," Max said.

"Be serious with me, friend," Georgy said.

Max sighed. "Well, the fact that the SLS is built from reused leftovers of the Space Shuttle is disappointing. That means that we are not doing anything new. Artemis is made from old technology. The SLS isn't any more capable than the Saturn V, and the Saturn V launched nearly sixty years ago."

"The Soyuz design is even older still," Georgy pointed out.

"Sure, but the Soyuz is a relatively simple vehicle. The flagship of the next generation of human spaceflight should be capable of so much more."

"If you don't like the SLS, then why did you agree to come to see the launch?" Georgy asked.

"Because the SLS is the first rocket capable of taking people back to the moon. Maybe once we start doing that, we can try and make the next jump to Mars and then, who knows?" Max said.

"That's sounds surprisingly optimistic, coming from you," Georgy countered.

"It's not optimistic, Georgy. It's desperate. Humanity needs progress in order to survive," Max said.

"T-minus three minutes," the announcer announced.

Georgy waved his hand at the screen. "So, if the SLS is not as great as you would have liked, what should it look like instead? How would you have designed the rocket?"

"I don't know Georgy. I'm a mechanic, not an engineer," Max said.

"Don't you have a PhD in Aerospace Engineering?" Georgy asked.

"I don't see how that's relevant," Max said, then he sighed, "I would think that looking into reusability of the first stage might be worthwhile."

Georgy nodded. "It does seem like a shame to drop so much hardware into the ocean," he said.

"Private corporations have started landing first stage boosters, so we know that it is possible. And the RS-25 engine is one of the very best engines ever made. They could be flown again. They were designed to be reusable for the Space Shuttle. Recovering those would be good. Speaking of the Space Shuttle, those solid rocket boosters strapped on the side are really familiar," Max said.

"They fixed the O-ring problem," Georgy pointed out.

Max nodded. "True, but SRBs are still dangerous. They limit your launch abort options. Detonation of a solid rocket motor releases a cloud of superheated debris that melts any parachutes attached to any capsules with any potentially reusable people inside them."

"The Space Shuttle avoided that problem by never having any launch abort options," Georgy chuckled.

"One less thing to go wrong," Max said dryly.

"T-minus sixty seconds," the announcer said.

"Why is it orange?" Georgy asked.

"Orange is the color of the foam insulation they spray on the first stage fuel tank to keep the cryogenic hydrogen and oxygen cool," Max answered.

"It is a really ugly color," Georgy said.

"Hideous," Max agreed.

The final countdown began, and at t-minus zero there was brilliant flash of light as the two solid rocket boosters ignited. The rocket heaved itself off the pad, tremendous power and acceleration were matched by the skyscraper-height of the vehicle. Soon, it cleared the tree line and Max could see the rocket with his own eyes: an orange and white spear, climbing steadily, riding on a pillar of flame and smoke. Thirty seconds later the roar of rocket sound reached them, filling the world with its energy. The SLS was twice as tall and had ten times the thrust of Max's Soyuz, and even at this distance Max could feel the heat from its mighty engines.

The audience erupted in cheering, and the rocket began its gravity turn, nosing over to fly eastward. It climbed higher and higher, shrinking to a pinpoint of light tracing an arc of solid white smoke. Just before it was outside the limit of vision, Max saw the solid rocket boosters cut off and fall away, spinning toward the blue Atlantic sea.

Max shifted his attention to the large television screen. The core stage burned on and on, continuing to accelerate. Finally, the fuel and oxidizer tanks ran dry. The first stage decoupled and fell away. Then the second stage RL-10 engine lit and accelerated the Orion capsule, striving for orbital speed.

Max stood.

"I'm going to go for a little walk. Let me know if anything exciting happens," he said to Georgy. He climbed out of the stands, and with his hands in his pockets, strolled toward the museum complex.

Georgy found Max two hours later. Max and Adams Leverrier were standing, silent, under the giant engine bells of the Saturn V Museum display, gazing at the titanic machine.

"Max, I want to introduce you to Doctor Ohemaa Thompson," Georgy said.

Max turned to see that Georgy was standing beside a well-dressed black woman with long dark hair and a broad smile. A badge on a lanyard was around her neck, identifying her as a "NASA Administrator."

"It is wonderful to finally meet you Doctor Ardis," the woman said, extending her hand.

"Just 'Max' is fine," Max responded, returning her firm, confident handshake.

"I have read quite a bit about you, Max. You are a genius in your field," she said.

"I don't know about that. I mostly just turn wrenches," Max said.

"And yet nearly everything that you touch seems to get fixed," Doctor Thompson said.

"Not USSF *One*," Max admitted

"Given more time, I suspect that you could have fixed that too," she said.

"It's the funniest thing. Whenever I'm trying to figure out what's broken, it always ends up being the last thing I try," Max responded.

Doctor Thompson gave him a knowing smile. "I will be straight with you, Max. The success of Artemis is my priority. I want you on the project. Your skills are invaluable, possibly unique. I have no doubt that you will find ways to improve the vehicle and mission design."

Max shrugged. "Maybe I can. Maybe not. But I can look at it and see what I find," he said.

"Georgy guessed that would be your response. Can you start tomorrow?" Doctor Thompson asked.

"I can start tonight if you want," Max said. He was not sure yet how he could contribute, but this rocket was important. He would help if he could.

"Tomorrow will be fine. Come to the headquarters building at six o'clock in the morning and we can provide you with a badge and computer access and give you a tour. Do you have any questions?" Doctor Thompson said.

Max shook his head. "No questions. Get a badge and do other boring stuff in the morning. Then I fix your rocket. Got it," Max said.

"It is good to have you on board. I will see you tomorrow," Doctor Thompson said. She nodded to Adams and walked away.

"I am very glad to hear that that you are joining the project," Adams said, his expression grave. "Artemis must succeed. The very future of humanity is at stake."

Max nodded in mock gravity. "Sure, yeah, of course. And I'll come over and hit it with my hammer and see if I can make it better," he said.

Adams gave a wry smile. "You may hide behind your sarcasm, but everyone at NASA understands the gravity of what we do. The world is watching, Max."

Adams walked away. Georgy suppressed a chuckle.

"What a character he is," Georgy prompted, watching Adams walk away. But Max did not respond. He was looking at the Saturn V, his mind turning.

Georgy stepped close to Max and touched his arm. "You do know that the future of humanity is not actually at stake with this, right?" he asked seriously.

"It is for him. He is going to be the one riding the rocket," Max said.

Max strolled around the Saturn V, examining where the five massive engines met the bottom of the fuselage.

"Do you think these F1s have had their powerheads removed?" he asked.

"Did you know that we can't build any F1 engines anymore?" Georgy said. "They were hand-fitted and hand-welded and we have lost the necessary know-how."

"I could take a crack at one. I'm pretty good with a torch," Max said.

"You are," Georgy agreed.

They shared a moment of silence together, then Georgy spoke again.

"You know that you working here puts me out of a job," he said.

"Just temporarily, Georgy. I'll have their rocket straightened out in a week or two, then we'll be back to old tricks," Max said.

Georgy chuckled. "I am happy that you took the job. This is a great opportunity for you to work on something really special," he said.

"I can ask around if they have any odd jobs you could do. I am sure that there are some floors that need mopping or telephones that need answering. Maybe you could be a guide in the museum," Max offered.

"See if they need anybody to mow the lawn. I have always wanted to drive one of those riding lawnmowers," Georgy said.

"I'll ask tomorrow," Max said.

CHAPTER ELEVEN

The next day Max did not ask about riding lawnmowers. He was too busy. After a brief security check, Max was provided with a badge and security access and shown to his desk, which was a nondescript cubicle. Max was not entranced by the cubicle, but happy to see that they had provided him with a brand-new high-performance computer with two large, high-definition LED screens. It booted with Max's new login.

The security officer who led him to his desk, a middle-aged man with a tan uniform and easy manner, turned to go.

"Oh, and Doctor Thompson said she would be by later to give you more of a tour," he said. Max nodded, but his attention was already focused on his screen as the security officer left.

The computer gave him access to a shared mainframe with thousands upon thousands of files. There were hundreds of executable programs and applications.

"Where to even start?" Max mumbled. He experimentally opened a computer-aided design program that he recognized from his school days.

"Hello, and welcome to the office," a voice said. Max looked up to see a genial young man leaning on his cubicle. His hair was up in a purple mohawk and was drinking coffee from a mug with the logo for the "Kerbal Space Program" videogame emblazoned across it.

"I'm Max," Max said, extending his hand.

"Javid Gilani," the young man said, shaking it. He frowned suddenly, staring at Max's ID badge. "Maxwell Ardis? I know you. You're an astronaut. What are you doing here?" he said.

"I'm not an astronaut," Max corrected him. "I dropped out of the astronaut program. I got bored of waiting for my turn to go to space."

"Yeah, but then you've been to space like a dozen times now," Javid said. "I know your missions. I've recreated most of them in the simulator."

"My chosen profession takes me to certain near-Earth, near-death objects from time to time," Max admitted.

"What brings you to our humble workplace?" Javid asked.

Max glanced down at his ID badge. "It says 'Consultant'" he read. "So, I guess I am here to 'Consult?'"

"Neat," Javid said. He took a sip from his mug.

"What do you do, Javid?" Max asked.

"I am a systems engineer, but mostly I design computer simulations," Javid answered.

"Can you show me?"

"Sure. Step into my office," Javid said.

Max followed Javid to his cubicle, which was liberally plastered with sci-fi posters and memorabilia. Javid had to move a model spaceship so that Max could see the screens.

"These are the programs that I use," Javid said, showing him. "We can simulate any aeronautical system that you can imagine and adjust these physical parameters. You are limited only by your imagination."

Max leaned over Javid's shoulder. "Show me the Artemis program," he said.

"Sure," Javid said. His fingers raced over the keyboard and the mission unfolded before them.

They had just reached the first separation event when Doctor Ohemaa Thompson found them.

"I'm glad to see that you found the place, Max," Doctor Thompson said.

"If I weren't here, I would be somewhere else," Max

responded.

"I have come by to give you a tour of the facilities. Shall we?" she asked.

"Yes, please," Max said to her, then turned quickly back to Javid. "And I have access to all of this from my computer as well?"

"Yep. There are template files that provide starting conditions and launch plans. They can be modified at will. Would you like me to show you?" Javid asked.

"Yes. Later," Max answered. "Thank you, Javid."

Doctor Thompson took Max to the Launch Control Center, then to the Multi-Payload Processing Facility, the Tracking Station, and finally to the Vehicle Assembly Building. A giant orange first-stage hydrogen tank was there. Vertical, quiescent, and awaiting integration into the world's largest rocket.

"So, what exactly is my job supposed to be here, Doctor Thompson?" Max asked finally.

Doctor Thompson gave Max a half smile. Her arms were crossed against the lapels of her perfectly fitted blue suit.

"I could give you precise directions, Max. There are many specific tasks that would aid the project, but I also know that some minds are best left untethered. Right now, I want you to take a look at the project as a whole. I want you to see the rocket. I want you to understand the mission. Artemis, Orion, and the Space Launch System have been in development for more than two decades. Many ways of thinking have become restricted. Perhaps you will see things that we cannot. Take your time, look around, and then come and tell me what you think. If you fail to have any brilliant flashes of inspiration, then I can provide more specific guidance," she said.

Max turned away from her and considered the orange fuel tank. The Vehicle Assembly Building in which it stood was the largest single-story building in the world. His eyes tracked upward; up and up and up to a distant gray metal ceiling, imagining the perfect blue sky that lay beyond, and the blackness that lay beyond that.

"Okay," Max said.

Max stayed at his desk all that day and all that night. By the next morning he had a question.

"What is this?" he asked, pointing at his computer screen.

Doctor Thompson looked at the schematics that were pulled up on Max's display. She noticed that Max's previously spotless new desk was now liberally distributed with crumpled paper coffee cups.

"That is an adapter. It links the 8.4-meter diameter first stage to the 5.0-meter diameter interim cryogenic propulsion second stage," she said.

"I want to see it," Max said.

"We do not have that component here. It is manufactured by one of our commercial partners and then shipped to the Michoud assembly plant in Louisiana for testing and integration," she said.

Max stood. "Let's go, then," he said, suppressing a yawn.

They landed in New Orleans that afternoon and took a private car to the assembly facility. Max had slept on the flight but still gulped down a black coffee as they left the airport. He carried a messy three-ring binder of newly printed schematics and freshly scribbled notes. He continued to take notes in the margins as the car cruised along the highway. He had hardly spoken to Doctor Thompson in two hours, but she only smiled. She knew that Max was hooked.

The Michoud facility was a broad series of hangars and manufacturing bays. First and second stage components were in various stages of assembly. Orion vehicles were being prepped for Artemis 2 and Artemis 3. Max and Doctor Thompson were met by two assembly engineers and guided to the component Max was interested in.

The adapter in question was a conical piece of aluminum alloy, 8.4 meters in diameter on one end, tapering down to 5 meters on the other. It was suspended on an upright stand, its lower end lifted about a meter and a half off of the ground. Without ceremony, Max stooped underneath it. The two assembly engineers stood nearby, watching him closely.

"Yep. Just like I thought. See this here?" Max tapped with his ballpoint pen at one of the supporting members that ran along the interior of the structure.

"The struts?" Doctor Thompson asked, joining him.

"This adapter component is over-engineered. You can remove one in three of these supporting members without compromising vertical load-bearing capacity," he said.

Doctor Thompson glanced at the two nearby engineers.

"What about shear forces? Torsional stress in max-Q?" one of the engineers asked.

Max nodded confidently. "It can handle it. Remove this one, this one, this one, this one, and this one. It will save at least fifty kilograms," he said, tapping the indicated structural members.

Doctor Thompson glanced back at the watching engineers.

"We can run simulations," the first one said helpfully.

"Do it. Then make the changes and run practical testing," Doctor Thompson ordered. "Is that all, Max?" she asked, turning back to him.

Max looked at her, looked at the metal structure, checked his notes, and then looked back at her.

"Yes," he said simply.

"Alright. Thank you, Max. And you two, make this your priority. I want updates by this evening," she said.

The engineers nodded and turned away. Max yawned.

"I'm going to rest my eyes for a bit if you don't mind. Is there a break room around here?" Max asked.

Max was led to a break room with two tables, eight chairs, and a large couch. Groggy and exhausted, he laid down and promptly fell asleep.

Doctor Thompson woke him four hours later.

"You were right," she said. "The preliminary results from simulations indicate that the stage adapter was over-engineered."

"Yeah, I know," he answered, rubbing his eyes. "I had a hunch when I saw the schematics, but I had to lay my mark one eyeball on it to be sure. That piece of metal was designed by somebody that was not a veteran of the Delta rocket or the first stage of the

SLS. That designer was focused only on that one piece, and thus was too cautious."

"Lightening that component is a significant weight savings. Every kilogram we shave so high in the stack dramatically increases the payload that we can put into orbit," she said.

"And increases delta-v for stage two and delta-v for the spacecraft. And as somebody that flies spaceships every now and then, I know that you want every meter-per-second of delta-v that you can possibly get," Max said. He yawned hugely. "Got any coffee?" he asked.

Doctor Thompson pointed at the machine in the corner and Max heaved himself to his feet. He lumbered over, poured himself a cup, and then sat in a chair at the nearby table. Doctor Thompson poured herself one too and joined him.

"You are a valuable asset to the Artemis mission," Doctor Thompson said.

"Even a blind squirrel finds a nut every now and then," Max said.

Doctor Thompson shook her head. "You are not blind, Max. You have a gift, and I am determined to use it."

Max shrugged, silently fighting his body's sudden craving for a drink. A couple shots of whiskey in this coffee would be heavenly. Had he not earned it? He had a gift. He was a genius. He should celebrate. Max took a gulp of his coffee and pushed the cravings away.

"Well, you have seen more of our facilities now, any other flashes of insight for us?" she asked.

"There are hundreds of different components being checked out in those hangers right now. How many contractors are working on the SLS?" he asked.

"Components for the SLS are manufactured in forty-nine US states and in over one hundred separate congressional districts," she said.

"You're saying that you have over one hundred different suppliers? Quality control must be a nightmare," he said.

Doctor Thompson nodded. "It is. We have had to develop the

capability to test and verify each and every component that we receive. Our materials scientists are the best in the world. Even nuts and bolts are x-rayed for stress fractures and material imperfections. Sending parts back for remanufacture is not uncommon," she said.

"But wouldn't it be better to vertically integrate the supply chain? There have to be some common processes that would streamline this whole thing."

"Better? Sure. Several of the commercial rocket companies are doing exactly that with great success. But this is where politics comes into my job. Artemis is funded by the taxpayer and has to be approved by congress. Those politicians are more concerned with protecting jobs in their districts than they are with improving our manufacturing efficiency," she said.

"So, the rocket has to suffer?" Max asked.

Doctor Thompson shrugged. "Is the process perfect? No. But I am willing to make compromises because we must. Because we have no choice. If we did not play the game of politics, the rocket would not exist," she said.

Max looked troubled, but he let the topic slide and finished his coffee with a convulsive gulp.

"I do have other ideas," he said, standing decisively. "But I cannot explore them here. I need to go back to KSC and talk to that operations engineer with the mohawk."

"Doctor Gilani?" Doctor Thompson asked.

"That's the one," Max confirmed.

Doctor Thompson stood. "I will book us seats on the next flight back to Orlando," she said.

CHAPTER TWELVE

"So where are you sleeping now?" Georgy asked on the telephone.

"At my desk for the past two nights," Max admitted.

"I can arrange for you to have a nice apartment set up nearby," Georgy said.

"Just keep a room for me at the hotel," Max said.

"That hotel does have pretty great room service. I got lobster last night," Georgy said.

"Keeping yourself busy, Georgy?" Max asked.

"Not at all. I've been at the beach. And I changed my mind, don't ask about that gardening job. I don't want to drive a lawnmower anymore. I'm going to work on my tan instead," Georgy said.

"All right Georgy. It is good hearing from you. I must get back to work now. Bye bye," Max said before hanging up the phone.

"Shall we run the simulation again?" Doctor Gilani asked.

"Yes Javid. Please do. And with the new parameters I specified," Max said.

They were the only two people in the expansive Launch Control room at Kennedy Space Center. Above them were the projector screens on which the simulation was shown, lighting the otherwise darkened room.

"And here are when the problems start," Javid said.

On the screens something was going wrong. The simulated rocket was still ascending, but it was not accelerating. The projected trajectory showed it failing to reach orbit, instead destined to eventually fall back through the atmosphere and crash into the ocean.

"And what are the potential failure modes that could cause this?" Max asked.

"There are several. Early first stage engine shutdown, delayed stage separation, delayed second stage ignition, or insufficient second stage thrust," Javid said. "This particular scenario is a failure of the second stage RL-10 engine to ignite."

The big orange fuel tank, with its four main engines, separated itself from the rest of the rocket and fell away. The rest of the rocket was centered in the screen. That included the upper stage, with its single vacuum optimized engine, as well as the Orion spacecraft, with its attached service module, fuel tank, and small engines.

The single RL-10 engine of the second stage stayed cold. Error messages showed in bright red. Other screens showed the evolving trajectory for the vehicle.

"How likely is it that the RL-10 engine would fail?" Max asked.

"Just the engine alone? Very unlikely. The RL-10 is a reliable engine. But this high return trajectory would be shared by a number of failures causing abort in mid-ascent," Javid said.

"What's our projected apogee?" Max asked.

"Two hundred and seventy-three kilometers," Javid answered.

"Initiate abort procedure," Max said.

On the screen the simulated Orion vehicle, with its service module, separated from the dead second stage. Its small engines lit briefly as it pushed itself safely away from the failed stage, which had become a dangerous, explosive hunk of debris traveling at over three kilometers-per-second.

"Could the engines on the Orion service module shallow out the descent?" Max asked.

Javid shook his head. "No. Not even if the module had enough time to burn all of its fuel, which it does not," he said.

The simulated Orion capsule, with its simulated crew, was in freefall. The capsule jettisoned the useless service module and oriented itself to reenter the atmosphere heat-shield first.

"Time to reentry?" Max asked.

"Thirty seconds," Javid said.

They watched silently as the simulation played out on the screens. The Orion capsule accelerated in the gravity well as it fell silently toward the blue ocean below.

The vehicle struck the atmosphere. Too quickly, the heat shield glowed hot and bright. Warning lights flashed and continued flashing.

"How many G-forces are we seeing on the crew?" Max asked.

"Too many," Javid said. "Twenty G's maybe. Lethal levels."

"And what is the status of the heat shield?" Max asked.

"Bad. The reentry temperature is too high. The shield cannot handle it," Javid said.

On the screen the capsule flashed and then disappeared.

"Capsule disintegration. Mission failure," Javid said solemnly.

Max sighed and sat back in his chair. "Good thing it was just a simulation," he said.

Javid frowned. "Well how do we keep this failure from happening? Could we flatten the first stage trajectory? A shallower ascent would mean a shallower descent and a safer reentry," he said.

"We can't flatten the first stage ascent. The rocket wouldn't be able to make orbit. The second stage has plenty of delta-v, but it doesn't have the thrust. The RL-10 engine is incredibly efficient but lacks oomph. The first stage needs to have a steep ascent trajectory to give the second stage enough hang-time to push the Orion into orbit," Max said.

Javid was quiet for a while. His fingers ran across his keyboard while he checked Max's assertions. "You're right," he said finally.

"We need to add more thrust to the second stage," Max said.

"How?" Javid asked.

"More RL-10s would do it. That's what they did with the Centaur," Max said.

"How many?" Javid asked.

Max shrugged. "At least two. Four would be better," he said.

"That's extra weight. That will decrease the payload capacity of the upper stage," Javid said.

"Yep," Max said.

"And it will decrease the delta-v available," Javid said.

"Yep," Max said.

"Want me to reset the simulation with those parameters?" Javid asked.

"Yep," Max said.

They sat and watched the simulation play out. This time with a new trajectory made possible by building the second stage with more RL-10 engines. They simulated three different failure states. In each one the capsule survived abort.

"It works," Javid said. "More thrust on the second stage allows a shallower ascent profile which expands safe abort windows throughout the launch."

"What does it do to our payload capacity at trans-lunar injection?" Max asked.

"Extra engines mean extra weight, so payload capacity is decreased. However, it should still be sufficient to carry the Orion, and that's all that will be flying on the early Artemis missions," Javid answered.

"Good job, Javid. Go home. We can go to Doctor Thompson with our findings in the morning," Max said.

"You upgraded our room," Max commented, stepping through the door with his new hotel keycard.

Georgy spread his arms expansively. "If we are going to be here for a while, we might as well do it in style," he said.

When Max's car service had dropped him off, the hotel concierge had waylaid him in the lobby and directed him to a new penthouse room on the top floor. It was a deluxe suite, with an expansive living room and a kitchenette, in which Georgy was currently standing. He was wearing an apron and assiduously stirring a steaming pot with a wooden spatula.

"That smells good," Max said. The cooking pot filled the room with a smell symphony of rich spices.

"Creole is my most favorite American cuisine. It is the blend of disparate cultural influences that gives it its totally unique character," Georgy said. "Have a seat. It is done and ready to be served."

Max sat at the small table and Georgy produced two bowls and spoons. He half-filled the bowls with rice and then ladled the seafood gumbo on top.

"I don't think you've ever cooked for me before," Max said. He lifted his spoon and found that he was ravenously hungry. He scooped into the gumbo then blew on the steaming spoonful, suspecting that it was too hot yet to eat.

"I have cooked for you. You have eaten at my home many times," Georgy protested.

"I assumed that your wife did the cooking," Max said.

"We take turns, although she is the better chef," Georgy said.

Max blew again then put the spoon in his mouth. Spicy cayenne and allspice competed with the temporizing okra and bell pepper and glutinous rice. Max found himself shoveling another spoonful into his mouth before the first one was swallowed.

"So, how was work?" Georgy asked.

"Busy. There are a lot of things about the rocket that could be improved," Max said.

"I was myself wondering if the TLI payload capacity does seem a bit low for how powerful the first stage is," Georgy said.

Max nodded. "The second stage is essentially a placeholder, copied from the Delta rocket. It was not built from the ground up for the SLS," Max agreed.

Georgy went to the small refrigerator. He opened the door and took out two beers in glass bottles.

"Want one?" he asked.

Max gazed longingly at the frosted glass, then he shook his head. "No, thank you," he said. He knew that when he had one, he would want a second. And if he had a second, he would want a third. He did not want to start tomorrow morning with a headache and a dull mind.

Georgy put one of the bottles back and opened the other for himself, taking a long drink as he sat back at his half-finished bowl.

"So, what are you going to do?" Georgy asked.

"I'm going to keep giving advice until they stop listening to me," Max said.

"The Artemis project is twenty years old. There must be substantial sunk costs. I am sure that there will be things that they are unwilling to change," Georgy pointed out.

"When they stop listening to me, that is when I will know that my time on the project is done," he said.

Georgy elected to change the subject. "Have you seen what some of the private companies are testing?" he asked.

"First stage reuse?" Max asked.

"And in-orbit refueling," Georgy said.

"It's never been done to any significant scale," Max said.

"But it would open up a lot of possibilities if they could do it," Georgy said. "There are blueprints for truly massive spaceships, even bigger than the SLS, but to get anywhere beyond low-earth orbit, they will have to refuel."

Max chewed on that for a moment. "Do we have any more?" he asked, lifting his bowl.

"Yes," Georgy said, taking the bowl from his hands. He refilled it from the pot and then set it back down in front of Max.

"The Saturn V was more capable than the SLS," Max said. "Each Apollo mission was capable of sending an entire mission to the surface of the moon and back. Trans-lunar injection was performed with the third stage. The command and service module placed into lunar orbit, moon lander and lunar ascent vehicle all on a single launch. They even put moon rovers on the last three launches just to show off."

"I wish I could have seen it fly," Georgy said wistfully. "I was born just a few years too late."

"But the SLS cannot do that. A moon lander cannot launch on the same rocket as the Orion crew capsule. The payload capacity is too weak. A moon lander would have to be launched separately and the lander and Orion would have to rendezvous in space," Max said.

"Maybe that's a good thing. Maybe instead of cramming a tiny capsule and a tiny lander together on the same rocket, we can specialize and get bigger, better versions of each on separate launches," Georgy offered.

"Perhaps. But it galls me that we are not so much better than this by now. We have supercomputers that can fit in your pocket and automated manufacturing techniques better than the greatest machinists of the twentieth century, but it has been sixty years and we still haven't been back to the moon," Max said.

Georgy shrugged. "Priorities have changed. Going to the moon was a Cold War game. That catalyst does not exist anymore."

"We're putting our resources into all the wrong things. We could have a moon base by now and be working our way toward colonizing Mars, but instead we build more nuclear missiles and fighter jets and aircraft carriers," Max groused.

"Aircraft carriers are pretty cool too," Georgy said.

"Sure, but rockets are cooler," Max said. "And I'd rather build missiles to send us to the stars than missiles to blow each other up."

"Cheers to that," Georgy said, raising his beer. Max raised his water glass in return. Georgy drained his drink with a long pull, then put the empty bottle on the table. Max slurped the last of the gumbo from his bowl, his mouth tingling from the spices.

"I'd better get to bed, Georgy. Tomorrow I've got a rocket to save," Max said.

CHAPTER THIRTEEN

Max and Javid showed Adams and Doctor Thompson their findings in the morning. Javid ran the results of their simulations on a projector screen that took up most of one conference-room wall.

"I am impressed. The change you propose does increase the safety margin for crewed missions," Doctor Thompson said.

Adams wore a freshly pressed suit and tie and a frown on his face. His arms were crossed on his chest.

"I cannot dispute Doctor Gilani's and Doctor Ardis's findings; however, I must express my concern that any significant changes in the design can only set back our timetable. Am I not mistaken, Doctor Thompson, in saying that Artemis is already over budget and behind schedule?" Adams asked.

Doctor Thompson nodded. "That is true as well. It is too late to implement these changes on the next launch of Artemis without significantly disrupting workflow. Artemis 3 would be the first time that we could increase the number of engines on the second stage," she said.

"As long as we are suggesting changes," Max interjected, "then I would like to add that everything on the SLS from the second stage and up is underpowered. The first stage is capable of boosting more than just a modified version of the Delta Cryogenic Second Stage. The Orion's service module could be upgraded with larger fuel tanks and more powerful engines. We can wring a lot more performance out of this vehicle than we are seeing with the current design. The Saturn V massed three million kilos and could carry one hundred and forty thousand kilograms to low earth orbit. In comparison the SLS masses three point six eight million kilos, and in its current configuration can only launch ninety-five thousand kilos to low earth orbit, despite having more efficient engines. It is an inefficient design."

"The SLS was designed the way that it is because it is using existing, verified components from smaller systems. The Delta Cryogenic Second Stage is a tried and tested design. Artemis 1 was a success, you saw the launch with your own eyes," Adams said.

"I know that, but I am saying that with a redesign we could dramatically increase payload capacity, both to low earth orbit and to trans-lunar injection," Max argued.

Doctor Thompson spoke up, "You are right, Max, but Adams is right too. Increasing the baseline capability of the rocket will have to wait. We have to move forward with our current architecture if we are to launch on schedule."

"But we can add the extra engines to the second stage going forward?" Javid asked hopefully.

"Based on what I have seen here, yes. That is a change that we can afford to make. Not on Artemis 2, but on Artemis 3," Doctor Thompson said.

Javid grinned, but Max was troubled. The deeper he got into this project, the more changes he wanted to make. He found himself dreaming of orange and white rockets at night, and in each dream the rockets got bigger and better.

"Thank you for the presentation, gentlemen. If that is all, then we will conclude this meeting," Doctor Thompson said, standing.

"Thanks for listening," Javid said.

Max and Javid sat for lunch together in the employee cafeteria.

"So, what's your story, Javid? What brought you to NASA?" Max asked over a tuna salad sandwich and bag of potato chips.

"My parents were super disappointed when I went into engineering. They wanted me to be a doctor or a lawyer. They said that there were no jobs in engineering. But I always wanted to work on rockets. I loved science fiction, and I dreamed of going into space and meeting aliens," Javid said.

"Not much chance of that," Max said.

Javid sighed. "It's a shame we haven't met any aliens yet. Statistically they must be out there. There are four hundred billion stars in the Milky Way alone. Alien civilizations are probably just too far away for us to contact them," he said.

"Far in distance or far in time. The universe is almost fourteen billion years old. We might have just missed them by a couple million years," Max said.

Javid looked glum. "That's a depressing thought," he said.

"I comfort myself by remembering that aliens are probably just as cruel as humans are," Max said.

"Humans aren't all bad. There's as much good in humanity as there is evil. Maybe more," Javid said.

"So, any aliens we find will be half evil?" Max said.

Javid chuckled. "There is only one way to find out. But rockets aren't going to get us far enough into space to find aliens. We need some new breakthrough in technology," Javid said.

"Like what?" Max asked.

"Like nuclear engines. Or a warp drive," Javid said.

"So, science fiction stuff," Max said.

"Nuclear thermal engines have already been tested. They're twice as efficient as chemical rockets, you just have to make an investment in nuclear reactors and find a way to manage the radiation they produce. Clean fusion power is definitely possible, we just haven't figured it out yet. Pair a small fusion generator with a big ion drive and you'll have a great deep space drive. It still wouldn't be enough to get you to another star in your lifetime, but it would make getting around in this solar system much easier. For long distance travel, it is warp drives that I am most hopeful for," Javid said.

"I didn't think that they were possible," Max said.

"Space is bendy. The math is good. We just need to figure out how to bend it. Anything is possible, Max, if we are smart enough," Javid said.

"And if we don't blow ourselves up in the process," Max said.

"That too," Javid said.

Over the next three weeks Max found himself and Javid continuing to work closely together. The young engineer was brilliant at designing simulations that stressed the rocket in every conceivable manner. They modeled failures in all of the rocket's stages and all of the rocket's systems, building contingency plans for any number of incidents. Max felt confident that they were helping make the rocket safer. He wanted to make the rocket better, but there was little that he could do to increase the rocket's performance without a redesign.

The agency was building up toward the second launch of Artemis. Artemis 2 would be the first crewed launch of the Space Launch System. Adams Leverrier would be the pilot and co-piloting would be a veteran astronaut named Iris Wimberly. Lee Cheng, an electronics and navigation expert, was in the third seat, and Jonquil Daniel, an experienced Navy pilot, would be in the fourth. They would ride the Orion capsule for a moon flyby. It would be the first time that humans had been so close to the moon, and so far from the Earth, since the flight of Apollo 17.

As the launch date approached, the energy was palpable. Components came in from Michoud and from Stennis. In the Vehicle Assembly Building the rocket neared completion.

"I love the RL-10," Javid said one day, gazing at the diagram displayed on their screen.

"It's not that exciting of a rocket engine. It's a really old design. It's efficient but it doesn't have a lot of thrust," Max said.

"That's what gets me about it. It dates back to the 1950's. But it's still one of the most efficient engines that we have. It manages to get more delta-v out of a tank of hydrolox than just about anything anybody's been able to make since," Javid said.

"That's just the nature of expander cycle. The turbopumps are driven by expanding hydrogen as it warms. You don't need a pre-burner so you don't waste any fuel. It's a very simple trick of chemistry," Max said.

"Exactly. A simple trick. Nothing fancy. It was just some designer with a brilliant idea," Javid said.

"That's what you want to do, isn't it? Have the brilliant idea that changes everything?" Max asked.

"The idea that changes the world is going to be something simple. Something that we will slap ourselves for not thinking of first," Javid said.

Javid was an easy coworker to have, as likely as Max to work late and spend long hours diving into one rabbit hole after another. They updated the emergency manual. They would be prepared when launch day came.

When he sat down one morning, Max found the telephone on his desk ringing.

"Hello?" Max answered.

"Good morning Doctor Ardis. It's Adams," Adams said.

"Hi, Spaceman. What can I do for you today?" Max said, leaning back in his chair.

"I have been re-reading the mission manual. The book has gotten heavier, and I understand that I have you to thank for that," Adams said.

"It's only heavy if you print it out Adams. When you're in the capsule you'll have it all on your electronic tablet," Max said.

"You can't make a plan for every possible contingency, Max. I know for a fact that you are practiced in improvisation," Adams said.

"I'm more comfortable taking chances when it's just me that could get hurt," Max said.

"Nothing great was ever achieved without taking chances, Max. Risk is a part of this business. We are the pioneers. We pave the way for future generations. You have to trust us. You have to trust that we can do this," Adams said.

"I do trust you," Max said. "I don't trust chaos. The universe is trying to kill us. Eventually it is going to succeed."

"We cannot change our fate. We can only decide how we live. But I did not call to criticize; I called to thank you. You have done a great job on this manual, Max. I want you to know that I appreciate your work," Adams said.

"You're welcome," Max said.

Adams hung up the phone. Max replaced the handset and stood. He went to the window and gazed toward the distant launch pad. Artemis 2 would launch tomorrow.

CHAPTER FOURTEEN

Launch day opened on a cool autumn dawn. Max stood on the grassy field and gazed eastward. A sun pillar heralded a sunrise that began deep crimson. He watched the sky climb the spectrum of color through ochre, amber, and finally to a brilliant, joyous gold.

"I wonder what a sunrise looks like on Mars," said a voice.

Max turned to find that Adams had joined him. He, too, was gazing at the cloud-flecked sky. His hands were in the pockets of his pressed khaki pants and a distant smile was on his face. The usually uptight astronaut looked more relaxed than Max had ever seen him.

"Mars has blue sunrises against orange skies. Iron oxide dust in the atmosphere scatters the longer wavelengths. Aren't you supposed to be suiting up?" Max asked.

"Not for another two hours. Then I'll be in my flight suit and climbing aboard for preflight checks. Just like the Soyuz, they make us board before fueling. They say it is safer that way," Adams said.

"The time before the launch is always the worst part. The waiting kills me," Max said.

Adams shook his head. "I don't mind it. When I am on the spacecraft there is nowhere else that I need to be. There is nothing else that I need to do. I can be fully present in the moment, at peace," he said.

On the launch pad the rocket awaited, a thirty-story white and orange missile. It was impatient to perform: to defy gravity, and atmosphere, and all common sense to blast its way to space. Max watched it with trepidation. Eventually, he left Adams and walked back inside.

Max's terminal in launch control was next to Javid's. Javid was already there. They put on their headsets and checked their computer programs. Doctor Ohemaa Thompson's assigned terminal was nearby, but the administrator rarely sat down. She paced the room, checking on the engineers.

Four astronauts boarded the Orion capsule, then the fueling procedures began. In Houston, Texas Mission Control would take over Artemis following the launch. The flight director's station was there, and his voice could be heard over their headsets. He began the calls for "go" or "no go."

Weather was "go."

Range was "go."

Crew was "go."

He continued through the various teams and spacecraft systems.

Max and Javid were ready. They waited for their cue. Automatic abort systems would activate the escape tower and pull the crew to safety if there was a catastrophe during the fueling process. Recovery crews waited downrange, the furthest was all the way in Hawaii. When it was their turn, Javid gave a "go" for the abort team.

"I got you a present," Javid said to Max. He produced a small cardboard box and placed it on Max's terminal.

Max opened the box and took out a ceramic mug. It bore the Artemis program logo: a stylized capital letter "A" with a spacecraft's trajectory curving redly through it. A blue arc of Earthly globe filled the foreground, with the distant gray circle of the moon beyond.

"Thanks, but I didn't get you anything," Max said.

"It's okay, I got one for myself too," Javid said, reaching into his backpack and producing an identical mug. "I got them from the gift shop. It's my little tradition before launches." He produced a large silver thermos. "Want some coffee?" he asked, unscrewing the cap.

"I've already had two cups, but okay," Max said, holding out his mug. Javid poured the steaming black elixir and Max sipped gingerly. He set the mug down to cool.

Vehicle fueling finished and the final countdown began. Service umbilicals detached. The service tower walkway swung away at T-minus six minutes.

One of the big screens in the launch control room showed the faces of the astronauts. They were in two rows, one "above" the other, lying on their backs in preparation for the launch. Adams, in the command seat, spoke.

"I would like to thank every man and woman who made today possible." His voice came through clear and confident. "Not just the employees at NASA or our commercial partners. Not just the engineers and scientists and technicians who are a part of the project. I also want to thank the husbands and wives and partners and children. Thank you for supporting all those who work on Artemis. Only four of us get to go to space today, but returning to the moon will be an achievement shared by all humanity."

Doctor Thompson was walking by. "Not bad," Max overheard her murmur. "Not a bad little speech, Mister Leverrier."

At two minutes to launch, the rocket switched to internal power.

"Initiate startup sequence," the flight director said.

"Flight termination system is armed," Javid said into his headset.

"First stage is 'go' for launch," said the first stage team.

"Second stage is 'go' for launch," said the second stage team.

"Orion is 'go' for launch," said the Orion team.

"SLS is 'go' for launch. Let's light this candle," the flight director said finally.

At T-minus five seconds the four RS-25 liquid fuel main engines ignited and began to throttle up. At T-minus zero seconds they were at max thrust and the two solid rocket boosters ignited.

The launch clamps released and Artemis 2 rose on a pillar of flame.

"We have liftoff," the flight director said.

The Launch Control Center exploded in cheering. The rocket accelerated, gaining altitude as it rolled to align to flight azimuth and then began its gravity turn.

Max watched the rocket ascend. If anything were to go wrong now, it would happen faster than any human could react. They had to depend on the automatic abort systems that he and Javid had so painstakingly revised. Soon the solid rocket boosters would run out of fuel and then detach. At that time the rocket would go from abort program 1A to abort program 1B.

"What was that?" Max asked suddenly. His microphone was not active, so only Javid had heard him.

"What was what?" Javid responded.

But Max did not answer. He squinted at the screen that showed the live feed of the rocket engines.

"What was what, Max?" Javid asked again.

"I thought I saw something. There was a flash in engine three," Max said.

"I didn't see anything," Javid said. He flipped through his status screens. "All four RS-25 engines are reading nominal," he said.

"Nothing at all? No difference between the engines?" Max asked.

"They are all in the green," Javid said.

Max pulled up the engine sensors on his own screen.

"Chamber pressure is low on engine three," Max said.

"Only by a few hundred pascals. It is well within the normal range," Javid said.

Max tapped his screen. "But there is a change in the mixture. Look, the pressure downstream of the hydrogen turbopump dropped at T-plus zero point two seconds. The engine computer is increasing oxidizer delivery to maintain thrust. With the increase in oxygen in the combustion chamber, heat is up. There is a hydrogen leak somewhere," Max said.

"It must be a small one to not trigger any warnings. Do we need to abort?" Javid asked.

Max's thoughts raced. The liquid oxygen consumption rate of engine three was high, but still within allowed tolerances. Thrust was nominal. Engine temperatures were slightly high, but not at dangerous levels. All other systems remained nominal.

"No," Max answered. "Don't abort, but I want to figure out what caused that flash. Take over monitoring the abort modes while I dig into it."

The SLS was two minutes into flight. On schedule, the solid rocket boosters ran out of fuel.

"Booster separation," the flight director said.

The twin boosters detached and fell away, spinning as they fell toward the Atlantic Ocean.

Max tore his eyes away from the overhead screens and focused on his terminal. He pulled up the engineering videos of the engines and rewound to launch. He watched the playback carefully.

"All systems still green up here," Adams could be heard saying meanwhile. He looked comfortable in his flight chair. "And acceleration is very gentle. Without the boosters, Artemis is a smooth ride, Houston."

"Acceleration is low because it's still early in the stage and they are still full of fuel. Stage one is a very long stage. Acceleration will build as they burn off fuel. They will feel plenty of G's before stage separation," Javid muttered, microphone muted.

Max played the video back again. He was sure that he saw something.

"There it is," Max said to Javid. Javid leaned closer to Max's screen, and Max went through the first moments of launch frame by frame.

As Max suspected, something had happened inside the engine bell of engine number three. Just after engine ignition, there was a tiny flash of yellow flame against the brazed tubes of the bell nozzle. It was hard to see, only a few pixels of yellow and only for an instant, but there was a yellow flash in the near invisible blue-flame of the hydrolox exhaust.

"Something struck the inside of the engine three bell nozzle zero point two seconds after engine ignition," Max concluded.

To keep the RS-25 engine nozzle from melting in the 3500K (thirty-five-hundred degrees Kelvin) exhaust, the nozzle was regeneratively cooled by cryogenic liquid hydrogen. The liquid hydrogen, at a temperature of just 20K, flowed through over a thousand tiny metal tubes that made up the nozzle's surface. Something had struck those tubes and broken them, causing liquid hydrogen to leak out of the system and directly into the exhaust.

"What could have caused it?" Javid asked.

"I'm not sure," Max said, frowning at his screen.

"Could it have been some debris from the pad?" Javid asked.

"Possibly," Max said. "But the way that it impacted the inside of the engine bell, it really looks like it was flying down from the combustion chamber."

"But all the sensor readings look too good for parts to be falling out of the engine. Temperature and oxygen consumption are only a tiny bit up, and thrust is within one percent of its expected value," Javid said.

"You're right. The hydrogen leak is small. The SLS will be able to reach orbit just fine. But I want to find out what happened. Whatever caused that flash has the potential of doing a lot more than just nicking the engine bell. That was a small, hard object travelling at very high speed. Lots of bad things could happen. I don't like bad things," Max said.

Javid nodded at those sage words and returned his attention to his terminal.

Meanwhile, fairing separation occurred. The fairing was an aerodynamic shell that protected the Orion capsule during the supersonic transit through the denser parts of the atmosphere. When it detached, the Orion was finally open to space. Bright sunlight streamed in through the spacecraft's windows, drenching the astronauts in light.

"Escape tower jettison," Javid said into his microphone.

"Copy that," the flight director answered from Houston.

No longer needed, the escape tower lit its solid rocket motors, detached from the capsule, and flew off into space. The first stage of the rocket kept burning, pushing its occupants faster and faster, closer and closer to the 7.8 kilometers per second needed to keep from falling back to Earth.

"Acceleration building, Houston," Adams grunted. A force of three times Earth's gravity pushed him and his fellow astronauts back in their chairs. "All systems green," Adams added, although the acceleration was such that he could no longer hold his head up.

"Stage one is a long stage," Javid said again. And it was. For the next five minutes fuel burned and the rocket got lighter, increasing the acceleration, closing in on 4G's.

Finally, the first stage ran out of fuel. The rocket's trajectory was a steep parabola, extending hundreds of kilometers out of the atmosphere. Only a short second-stage burn at apogee would be necessary for orbital insertion.

"Stage separation," the flight director said over the radio.

The first stage detached but did not fall away. It coasted, apparently motionless relative to Artemis, but travelling at over twenty thousand kilometers per hour relative to the ground.

"Second stage ignition," Adams said.

The engine bell of the single RL-10 rocket engine was visible on the feed from the upper stage engineering camera. Its ignition was invisible. There was no exhaust flame in the vacuum of space. The only evidence of its action was the sudden dwindling and disappearance of the floating, now-inert, first stage fuel tank.

"Orbital insertion burn complete," the flight director said.

Cheering erupted. Artemis was on its way.

CHAPTER FIFTEEN

In the Launch Control Center, engineers stood at their terminals. They stretched tight muscles and they smiled away the recent creases of anxious frowns. Involuntary laughs were the catharsis of bound nerves.

But Max did not stand. He did not stretch. His tension was held in his bowed shoulders and furrowed brow.

"Something happened to that first stage engine, and I am going to figure out what that was," Max said to Javid.

Thus Max was insensible when, two hours later, the upper stage engine restarted for translunar injection – the maneuver that would place the Orion capsule and its crew on a free-return trajectory around the moon. Max was deep in the schematics for the RS-25 engine, searching for the component that could have caused the damage he had spotted on the high-speed cameras.

Sometime later Max felt a hand on his shoulder.

"Come on, Max. There's nothing more for us to do here. Houston took over flight operations. It will be three days before the Orion reaches lunar orbit," Javid said.

Max looked around, blinking. He and Javid were alone in the control center. The overhead screens were turned off. The terminals were dark.

Reluctantly, Max shut off his terminal. He had been several hundred pages deep into the maintenance records of the refurbished RS-25 engines.

"Yeah, okay," Max said.

Meanwhile, one hundred and fifty thousand kilometers away, the Orion capsule and its human crew raced toward the moon. They covered ten kilometers every second, flashing through the empty space between worlds.

Max slept the sound sleep of exhaustion that night, but even his unconscious brain continued to chew on the problem. He woke to the smell of brewing coffee in the morning.

"I cannot imagine what would cause that flash that you are describing," Georgy responded while eating a room-service blueberry scone. "I am well acquainted with the RS-25 engine, but there are no moving parts downstream of the injectors. Maybe a mechanic left a loose nut or bolt after its most recent refurbishment?"

"That is possible," Max admitted, "but I have a feeling that there is something big that I am missing. I wish I could inspect the engine, but it is resting at the bottom of the Atlantic Ocean."

"There is no sense in looking backward. We can only look forward," Georgy said.

"You're right Georgy. Whatever happened to that engine could happen to others. I need to take a close look at the engines for the next Artemis rocket," Max said.

Max spent the next day pouring through the maintenance records of the RS-25 engines. Each engine had a long and storied past. Each one had flown to space and back and had been refurbished many times. By the end of the day, he looked away from his computer to find that the office held an atmosphere of restrained anxiety. Milling engineers spoke in strained, hushed voices.

"What's up Javid?" Max asked. "People seem tense."

Javid stood at his desk, glancing uncertainly between his two monitors, both overflowing with figures.

"It is the solar forecast. It looks like we are due for some bad space weather," Javid said.

"Sunspots?" Max asked.

Javid nodded. "And solar flares, and a very high risk of coronal mass ejection," he said.

"But the Orion spacecraft is hardened against solar radiation," Max said.

Javid shrugged. "Against ordinary solar radiation that is true, but a coronal mass ejection is another matter. Solar energetic particles traveling at five hundred kilometers per second, hot plasma filling a quarter of the empty space between the Earth and the Sun, a cloud of particles that carries its own magnetic field – everything depends on how big the CME is and exactly where it is traveling. A close brush from a big one could cause an electromagnetic pulse in Orion, overloading the spacecraft's systems. Or there could be a lethal dose of radiation. There is no guarantee that the crew would survive a direct hit from a CME."

Max chewed on that for a moment. "When will we know for sure that the CME may be dangerous to Orion?" he asked finally.

"I don't know," Javid answered.

"We have approximately thirty-six hours," Doctor Thompson announced to the waiting engineers the next morning. They stood crowded in the gaps between cubicles. "That is our best estimate of the time before the CME reaches the vicinity of Earth's orbit. It is traveling faster than the solar wind, and the shockwave of its passage will fill all of space between Earth and the Moon. Damage to satellites and ground stations is reckoned to be significant, but our most pressing concern is Artemis. The ionizing radiation from this solar event could be very dangerous to anybody beyond the Earth's protective magnetosphere. We must protect the crew at all costs."

"What about bringing them home?" one of the engineers spoke up. "The Orion spacecraft is still as close to the Earth as it is to the moon. Is there a trajectory that could bring the crew home safely before the radiation storm hits?"

Doctor Thompson shook her head. "Translunar injection has placed the Orion on a free return trajectory. It would take over three thousand meters per second of delta-v to reverse their course. With their remaining fuel, they have less than one thousand."

"Could they fashion a radiation shield?" Javid asked. "Using their onboard water, food, and computer equipment could they rearrange the cabin to block out the worst of the radiation?"

Doctor Thompson nodded. "Yes. We have already informed the Orion crew of the situation and that was their first response. Engineer Harding has set up a replica of the Orion capsule in the testing facility. Javid you should join them. Your expertise with radiation modeling would be invaluable to their efforts."

"I will go now," Javid said. He went to his cubicle and snatched up his laptop before heading for the door. Doctor Thompson sent four members of the engineering team along with him. Max raised his hand.

"Yes, Max?" Doctor Thompson said.

"Exactly how much delta-v does the spacecraft have to play with?" he asked.

"Eight hundred and forty three meters per second," Doctor Thompson said.

Max went back to his desk. Doctor Thompson watched him go. She finished assigning tasks to the rest of the engineers, then glanced at him again. He was hunched intently at his keyboard. The spacecraft's trajectory was displayed on the screen before him. She let him be and returned to her office.

Thirty minutes later her telephone rang.

"Max?" she answered.

"I think I have a solution," Max said.

She went to his desk. He turned his monitor so that she could see.

"Javid was right," he said. "Shielding is the answer, but using makeshift shielding onboard the spacecraft will not be enough. Even putting the engines and fuel tanks between the crew and the sun will not work, there is just too much radiation to block out. But there is a bigger shield out there in space. A radiation shield that is thirty-five-hundred kilometers across."

"You mean the moon?" Doctor Thompson asked.

"Yes. If the crew adjusts their trajectory, they can close their perilune to less than fifty kilometers, skimming the lunar surface. Once at that closest point, they must burn retrograde and enter low lunar orbit. That will give them approximately a one-hour window where the moon will be between them and the sun, blocking most of the fast-moving energetic particles from the coronal mass ejection," he said.

"A one-hour time window is not much. Our estimates of the arrival time of the CME are just approximate. We cannot say for sure exactly when the shockwave will arrive. Is there any way to increase the sheltered window?" she said.

"We can lengthen the window by increasing altitude. The farther they orbit from the moon's surface, the slower the spacecraft will travel in its orbit. However, as we increase altitude, we may lose the moon's shielding effect. I cannot say exactly how far into space the moon's protective shadow might extend," he said.

Doctor Thompson looked at Max's proposed trajectory, possible pros and cons already turning in her head. "What are some potential disadvantages of this plan?" she asked.

"There are a number of risks, but the biggest is the risk of an electromagnetic pulse. On the Orion's current free-return trajectory, even if EMP from the storm knocks out the spacecraft's guidance and propulsion, they will still swing around the moon and come safely back to Earth to splashdown in the Pacific Ocean. Their propulsion system can be knocked totally offline, and they would be fine. No adjustments need to be made to bring the spacecraft back home on its current trajectory. However, if we change their orbit, and then an EMP knocks out their propulsion systems, they will be stranded in lunar orbit," Max said.

"If that happens, it looks like they would smash into the moon within a few days," Doctor Thompson observed.

"Yes, this would not be a stable orbit. Gravitational perturbations from the moon's mascons will make the orbit increasingly unstable until perilune intersects regolith," Max said.

"That is one risk, what are the others?" she asked.

"If we make the maneuver too early, they could exit the moon's shadow while the CME radiation is still too high. If we make the maneuver too late, the ship will be struck by the shockwave, which is where electromagnetic radiation is greatest and the chance of an EMP knocking out their systems is highest. Burning retrograde also moves the engines and fuel tanks orthogonal to the crew module with respect to the sun, negating any shielding effect they could provide for the duration of the maneuver. Further retrograde burns during the CME event could keep the ship in the moon's shadow for longer, but at the risk of running too low on fuel to fly home," he said.

"If it were you on that spacecraft, what would you do?" Doctor Thompson asked.

"I'd go for it," Max said.

"Let`s put it to the crew. We will let them decide," she said.

They went to the control center. Adams's face was centered on the screen. His crewmembers joined him, floating weightless in the crew compartment of the Orion.

"Max, explain your proposal," Doctor Thompson said.

Max detailed his plan and Adams, being familiar with orbital mechanics, needed no visuals to understand what Max was suggesting.

"Deviating from the free return trajectory will doom the capsule and my crew if our propulsion system is rendered inoperable by an electromagnetic pulse," Adams interpreted.

"Yes," Max answered.

Adams turned to look at his crew. Iris, the mission's navigator, could be seen plotting the proposed trajectory on her screen. Lee's face held a serious, considering expression. Jonquil grinned and shrugged, her dark hair floating loose in the cabin.

"We will have to discuss and get back to you," Adams said.

"Understood. You have thirty hours to make your decision. Time to CME arrival is approximately thirty-four hours. In the meantime, our engineering team will be in contact with suggestions for restowing ship cargo for optimal radiation shielding," Doctor Thompson said.

The screen cut off. Max fiddled with his pen.

"Anything else, Max?" Doctor Thompson asked.

"Yes. I need to see the remaining RS-25 engines. All of them," Max said.

CHAPTER SIXTEEN

Javid found Max in the assembly building late that night. A team of mechanics was helping him disassemble one of the RS-25 engines as it lay sideways in a metal cradle. They had nearly finished detaching the rocket nozzle, and Max was working busily to separate the powerhead. He set his torque wrench down when he saw Javid approach.

"You're really getting into that engine," Javid commented. "Reading the inspection reports didn't solve the mystery?"

"On the contrary, I think that the reports already gave me my answer. I just need to see it with my own eyes to be sure," Max said.

"What's wrong with the engines?" Javid asked.

"I'll tell you all about it once I am done. How are things in the testing facility?" Max said.

Javid shrugged. "Not great. I have been modeling radiation scenarios all day, but there are too many unknowns. We cannot tell how close the ship will be to the center of the CME or its exact velocity, which affects the CME's arrival time and the power of the shockwave of the solar wind. The error bars on all the estimates are too wide. In a best-case scenario, the crew will only receive a mild dose of radiation. In a worst case, there could be lethal doses for all four of them and a concomitant electromagnetic pulse that shuts down not just propulsion, but also the spacecraft's life support."

"How wide are the error bars on the CME's arrival time?" Max asked.

"Twenty-seven minutes plus or minus," Javid answered. "Though our precision gets more accurate the closer the CME comes."

Max whistled and looked away. He still believed in his suggestion that the spacecraft and crew hide in the shadow of the moon, but their orbit would only allow a one-hour window of safety.

"They will need to be very lucky," Max said.

"I don't think that luck is on their side. A solar flare this large is a once-in-a-lifetime event, and it comes at the worst possible time," Javid said.

"We will just have to hope that luck works both ways," Max said with a wan smile.

Eventually Max dismissed the engine team and went back to the hotel. But the freshly cleaned linen of the hotel bed was no comfort to him. He slept fitfully.

"The news is saying there is going to be a big solar flare," Georgy said in the morning. "Planes are being grounded. Server farms could lose their data. Power grids have issued surge warnings."

"Could I have another cup of coffee, Georgy?" Max asked.

Georgy complied, filling his cup. "A solar flare means a coronal mass ejection. What does that mean for Artemis?" he asked.

"The Orion capsule is more hardened against radiation than any spacecraft has ever been before, but it might not be enough," Max answered.

Georgy sat heavily. "That's not good," he said.

Max said nothing. He drank his coffee.

"What can they do?" Georgy asked.

"Rearrange the cargo to absorb some of the radiation, but it won't be enough. I advised Adams to drop his lunar orbit and hide in the shadow of the moon," Max said.

"The timing for that would have to be perfect," Georgy said.

"What did Adams say?"

"He said that he and his crew would think about it," Max answered.

Georgy nodded.

"And there is another thing," Max said. "There is something wrong with the engines for the SLS."

"Which engines? The stack has eight different rocket motors."

"The first stage RS-25s. The reused Space Shuttle Main Engines," Max answered.

"What could be wrong with them? They've all flown before. If they haven't blown up yet, they shouldn't blow up now," Georgy said.

"I'm not so sure about that," Max said.

A massive cloud of charged particles and radiation barreled toward the Earth, and the rocket engineers watched it come. It came so fast that it made a shockwave in the solar wind. As estimates of its arrival time and power became more and more precise, estimates of its effect on the spacecraft and its crew became more and more unfavorable.

Max avoided his nervous coworkers. He went to the assembly facility and dove into the teardown of the RS-25 engine.

"Max, the crew of Artemis would like to speak with you. We have them onscreen in the control center," Doctor Thompson said.

The injector plate of an RS-25 engine sat on a large table before him. Max was holding an ultrasound report in his hand. He put the papers down and followed her to the control center.

"We have decided to take your advice," Adams said on the video feed.

"I am elated to hear it," Max said.

"You have given us several trajectories to choose from, and each seems to carry different advantages and disadvantages. We would appreciate your input," Adams said.

Max sat at a terminal and pulled up the four alternate trajectory plots that he had provided to Doctor Thompson.

"Trajectory number one brings you as close to the surface as possible and minimizes transit time. Trajectories two and three are variations on the first, but slightly advance or retard arrival time at the moon. Trajectory four raises apolune to increase loiter time in the moon's shadow," Max said aloud.

"Which would you recommend?" Doctor Thompson asked.

"How long until the CME arrives?" Max asked.

"Three hours and forty two minutes," Doctor Thompson answered. "With an estimate margin of error of twenty minutes."

"I recommend trajectory number two. It is the most aggressive maneuver. Dive down toward the moon right now, brake hard at perilune, and be safely in the moon's shadow before the CME hits," Max said.

Adams turned toward his crewmates. One by one they nodded.

"Okay," Adams said.

The video feed cut out and Max stared into the blackness left by its absence.

"We have confirmation of prograde burn. They are diving toward the moon," one of the flight engineers said. On a separate screen the Orion's flight trajectory could be seen. Max watched as the spacecraft accelerated. By shortening their transit time, the moon would be effectively "earlier" in its orbit by the time the spacecraft arrived, allowing the spacecraft to skim close to the moon's sunward surface before swinging low around the moon's nighttime hemisphere.

"We will lose contact when they swing around the far side of the moon," Doctor Thompson said. "But they will not be shielded from the CME until they are a further ninety degrees beyond that."

Max nodded to Doctor Thompson. Wordlessly he stood and left to return to his work on the engine.

But three hours later he was back. The control center was crowded with every mission officer and engineer who could claim a chair or standing space. Javid was already at his console and Max joined him.

"The CME just swept past the Deep Space Climate Observatory," Javid said.

The Deep Space Climate Observatory, or DSCOVR, was a NASA satellite that sat at the L1 Lagrange Point, a stable gravitational eddy between the Earth and the Sun. It hovered, 1.5 million kilometers away, monitoring the sun and the solar wind that blew toward the Earth.

"The CME is just as big and as fast as we feared," Javid continued. "It will hit the Earth, the Moon, and the spacecraft all at roughly the same time."

"And when exactly will that be?" Max asked.

"In thirty-nine minutes," Javid answered.

The Orion was skimming the sunlit side of the moon's surface at less than 20 kilometers in altitude and at a screaming velocity of over 2,000 meters per second. A live feed from the spacecraft showed the cratered surface of the moon scrolling by, shockingly close.

"Initiating retrograde burn," came Adam's voice. The numbers on the screen updated as the capsule slowed. The trajectory changed. It went from a figure-8 that collided with the Earth in three days, to a tight circle, hugging the moon.

"We have achieved lunar orbit," he said.

There was subdued clapping in the Control Center, but none of the energetic cheering heard earlier in the mission.

"In thirty seconds you will orbit to the far side of the moon and radio contact will be lost," Doctor Thompson said.

"Copy that. See you again soon," Adams said.

The radio gave a brief crackle, then a red light came on the screen. CONNECTION LOST.

"Cape to Artemis. Do you copy?" Doctor Thompson asked experimentally.

But there was no reply. The moon's bulk stood between the Earth and the capsule.

"They are not safe yet," Javid observed. "They are on the other side of the moon from us, but they are still in full view of the sun. They will not rotate into the moon's umbra for another fifteen minutes."

"And the CME will be here any moment," Max muttered.

There was nothing more anybody could do. The staff waited, tense at their consoles. Doctor Thompson stood, arms crossed, and watched the capsule's tiny dot creep across the trajectory screen.

Suddenly the control center lights flickered. It was a tiny thing, the briefest diminution of luminosity, only noticeable when contrasted against the nighttime sky outside the broad glass windows. But Max knew the magnitude of what that flicker represented. An electromagnetic pulse of tremendous magnitude had impacted the Earth. Most of its energy had been absorbed by the Earth's massive magnetic field, but a tiny percentage of that power had gotten through. It had passed through the atmosphere and touched the electric fields that ran along the power conduits through the complex.

The Kennedy Space Center was resistant to such pulses, but many power grids were not. Blackouts and power surges swept across the Earth, tripping breakers and overloading transistors. New York City went dark. A transformer station exploded in Hyderabad, starting an electrical fire. Water pumps in the Hong Kong sewers sputtered and died, flooding the downtown area with a mix of rainwater and sewage. Israel's largest desalination plant shorted out, needing to be restarted with diesel generators.

"That was a big one," Javid said quietly.

"The capsule made it into the shadow of the moon before the EMP. It is ionizing radiation that I'm worried about now," Max said.

On the heels of the shockwave, a cloud of highly charged particles surrounded the Earth and Moon, filling space with crackling energy. The Earth's ionosphere absorbed the energy, precious atmosphere shielding the delicate life from dangerous ionizing radiation. But vessels in deep space had no such protection.

"Thirty more minutes until communication is restored," Javid said.

The minutes crawled by.

"Artemis this is Cape Canaveral, do you copy?" Doctor Thompson said finally.

There was no response.

"Artemis," she said again. "Are you there?"

"They should be back in contact by now," Javid murmured.

But no voice came back from space.

"Artemis," Doctor Thompson said a third time, "do you co-"

"Artemis here," Adams voice was suddenly audible through a burst of static. "All spacecraft systems green."

A tremendous cheer arose from the gathered engineers. The video feed on the main screen showed Adams's smiling face floating upside down in the small cabin.

"We took only a small dose of radiation," Adams continued. "Nothing that we can't handle."

"I am glad to hear that Adams. Let`s run complete system diagnostics starting with-"

"Just a moment," Adams interrupted. "I think that you guys are going to want to see this."

Adams detached the small camera. He swung the lens around the cabin, revealing the rest of the crew clustered around one of the windows. He floated closer, and the crew moved away. He put the camera against the glass, pointing it out into space.

The moon was dark shadow on one side of the image. The stars twinkled across the arc of the cosmos on the other. Centered in the view was the Earth, and it was an Earth the likes of which no one had ever seen.

From pole to pole of that blue-white globe shone a dazzling green aurora. The shifting light obscured continents and oceans with its radiance. It was a light made by the ionization of the earthly atmosphere by a gale from the sun. Earth was wreathed in fusion fire, glowing emerald bright with the power of the sun's breath.

"What a view," Adams breathed. "What an incredible view."

CHAPTER SEVENTEEN

For three days the crew of Artemis 2 travelled back to Earth. They reentered the atmosphere, deployed parachutes, and splashed down in the Pacific Ocean. They were fished out of the water by the US Navy and ferried back to Florida. Therefore, Adams was standing, dry and healthy, in Dr. Thompson's office when Max opened the door. They broke off their own discussion to watch him as he walked across the room. On Dr. Thompson's desk Max placed a small golden object.

"What is this?" Doctor Thompson asked, picking the object up. It was a tapered cylinder about two and a half centimeters long and only a fraction of a centimeter in diameter.

"It is a golden pin. They are used to deactivate liquid oxygen injectors in the RS-25 engines when X-Ray scanning indicates a risk of structural failure," Max said.

"I am familiar with those. They are a safety measure against metal fatigue in the injector plates," Adams said.

"One of those came dislodged during liftoff of Artemis 2. It blew down through the injector tube then out of the combustion chamber, striking the engine bell and damaging two of the hydrogen cooling tubes in the nozzle extension," Max said.

"Yes. I am aware of this. Three flight engineers have already reported the incident," Doctor Thompson said.

"If it had damaged any more of the cooling tubes the hydrogen leak could have been catastrophic. The mission would have failed.

The entire rocket could have been destroyed," Max said.

"I am sorry that you were not present at the meetings about this, but we have reviewed this issue extensively. There is a very low chance of mission failure from this fault," Doctor Thompson said. Setting the gold pin back down on her desk.

Max leaned forward and retrieved the object. "There are over two hundred pins like this in the remaining engines. Any one of them could fail," Max said.

"This is not the first time this has happened, Max. Space Shuttle mission STS-93 had the same failure. Three hydrogen tubes were lost then and the mission was still a success," Adams said.

"That only makes it worse! If this has happened twice now, it could happen again. It could happen on Artemis 3!" Max exclaimed.

"Control yourself, Doctor Ardis. I do not condone shouting in this office," Doctor Thompson said mildly.

Max took two deep breaths. "It is not just the risk of damage from the golden pin bouncing around the engine. The purpose of the golden pins is to deactivate weakened oxygen injectors. Without the pin, the damaged injector could collapse, taking a chunk of the injector plate out with it. No engine could survive that."

"I have been assured that there is a less than one percent chance of that happening," Doctor Thompson said.

"One percent for what? For each engine? For each injector pin? How is this okay?" Max said, his voice rising again.

"Accepting risk is an integral part of this job. You should know that better than anybody," Adams replied.

"I do understand calculated risk, but this is the best funded space program in the world. This is the biggest rocket ever made. We can do better than this," Max insisted, brandishing the tiny pin.

"What would you have us do? Throw out all the engines and start over?" Adams said.

"Sure. Maybe. Or replace all of the injector plates," Max said.

"All of these engines have been tested extensively. All of them have flown before on Space Shuttles. There is no reason to think that they will fail now. The RS-25 is the best rocket engine in the world," Adams said. "The SLS is a good system, Max."

"No, the SLS needs a total redesign," Max said.

"The SLS is composed of time-tested components. It is as venerable and stalwart as any rocket design could reasonably be," Adams said.

"That is the problem. It is an old design. Its capability is disappointing. It cannot integrate a moon lander with an Orion launch. It is using an underpowered second stage. We have some of the greatest minds in the world working here. We can design a better rocket than this," Max said.

"We are designing a better rocket. The upper stage is due to be upgraded for Artemis 4, and the boosters are due to be upgraded for Artemis 8," Adams argued.

"It's not enough. Those are just incremental improvements. They do not change the fact that the SLS is cobbled together from pieces of old rockets. Eventually those pieces are going to run out. A fresh design could not help being worlds better than what we have now," Max said.

Doctor Thompson shook her head. "That's impossible, Max. It took the SLS program twenty years to get to where it is today. If we were to attempt a radical redesign it would only result in cancellation of the whole program. There are a lot of politics at play here. We rely on Congress for approval of our budget. We have to keep our suppliers happy. We have to cater to our commercial partners," Doctor Thompson said.

"That's just a sunk-cost fallacy," Max argued.

"No, Max. If we stop now, we lose everything. If we are to return to the moon within our lifetimes we must keep going. We have to do our best with what we have. We have to play the game," Doctor Thompson said.

Max was quiet for a moment. He fingered the golden pin, then he leaned forward and dropped it onto Doctor Thompson's desk.

"I told myself that I would work here until you stopped

listening to me. That day has come," Max said. He removed his ID badge and laid it on Doctor Thompson's desk alongside the shining pin. With his hands in his pockets, he turned and walked away.

Ohemaa Thompson and Adams Leverrier watched Max leave. They looked at each other.

"He's not entirely wrong, you know," Ohemaa said.

"He is wrong," Adams said. "He lacks faith in the project, and he lacks the determination to see it through."

And Max left the building, determined to find a bad bar and get good, and thoroughly, drunk.

CHAPTER EIGHTEEN

"I found you!" Georgy exclaimed.

Max sat hunched in the corner booth of a Florida diner, a steaming cup of black coffee in front of him.

"Congratulations," Max muttered.

"I heard you walked out on NASA," Georgy said, sitting across from Max. Georgy wore a pastel collared shirt over palm-tree print shorts and open-toed sandals with calf-length socks.

"That is correct," Max said. Max wore an unbuttoned button-up, khakis, and a pained expression as the morning sunlight struck his face.

"I also heard that you were spotted drinking at a dive bar in Palm Shores," Georgy said.

"You have spies everywhere," Max accused.

"Yes," Georgy nodded. "I do."

"Can I get you anything?" asked their server, a young man who appeared by the table.

"Yes, please. Two eggs over easy, an order of hash browns, three sausages, and pancakes with syrup. And a coffee. With cream and sugar please," Georgy said.

The server nodded at Georgy, scribbling on a pad, then turned to Max. "And anything besides coffee for you, sir?" he asked.

With an involuntary shudder Max shook his head. The server disappeared.

"It is bad form to walk out on a job, Max," Georgy chided.

"And worse to go out drinking all night without your best friend."

"I am never drinking again," Max groaned.

Georgy reached into his shirt pocket and pulled out two loose pills. "I thought you might say that, so I brought you these," he said.

"Cyanide?" Max asked hopefully.

"Aspirin," Georgy explained, handing them to Max.

Max swallowed them with a convulsive gulp of his coffee then gave Georgy a rueful smile. "You're going to tell me to back to NASA," he said.

"Do you want to go back?" Georgy asked.

"I want to kick some sense into them," Max said.

"But they won't listen?" Georgy asked.

Max frowned. "On the contrary, I think they heard me." He shook his head. "But I am not needed there."

"So, what is next?" Georgy asked.

"You are my Chief Operations Officer. I should be asking you that," Max said.

"The check from International Telecom cleared. We can afford another Soyuz," Georgy offered.

"Or we could finally retire," Max said.

Georgy said nothing. He sat back and folded his arms. Together they looked thoughtfully out the window. Max toyed with his coffee cup.

"I was seven years old when I saw my first rocket launch," Max said. "I remember it so well. It was a cold day in January."

Georgy stiffened.

"My parents promised that we would go to Disney World, but we would stop off and see a rocket launch first. They knew how much I liked watching them on TV. I was holding this little model of the Space Shuttle. It was just plastic, but it felt so alive in my cold hands. I took off my gloves so that I could touch it," Max mimed holding it, lost in his memory.

"So I held my toy, and I waited. The grass on the lawn was dead and yellow. My mother kept asking me if I was cold and if I wanted to go back to the car. I said 'no' because I didn't want to miss anything. What if I never had a chance to see a rocket launch ever again?" Max said.

Max paused his story and stared out the window for a while. He took a sip of his coffee.

"Finally, the rocket launched. I remember the heat and the light. It was warm on my face. I held my hands out and it was warm on my palms. After that came the roar of the engines. The shuttle climbed on a solid pillar of exhaust, like it was being pushed up by this connection to the Earth. As it rose, my heart rose with it, I remember laughing with joy. I was still laughing when it exploded."

The server returned with the platters of Georgy's breakfast. Georgy nodded his thanks.

"I could not believe it at first. I could not understand what had happened. The rocket was climbing and climbing, then there was a big cloud of smoke and flame. The sound of the explosion came a moment later. It was felt more than heard. It was like being hit in the chest. My mother screamed and tried to cover my eyes, but I wanted to see. I had to see. I pulled her hands away and watched. Flaming debris rained over the ocean," there were tears in Max's eyes. "I saw this big piece. Bigger than the others, and I watched it as it fell. I heard later that the crew lived through the explosion. They lived until they hit the water."

Georgy cleared his throat, but no words came out. He picked up his fork and started on his eggs. Max watched him eat. Eventually Max wiped his eyes and finished his coffee. He flagged down their server.

"I would like a stack of pancakes please," Max said. "And some bacon."

Sometime later Max and Georgy stood. Georgy left bills enough for the both of them and Max followed him outside.

"Come with me," Georgy said. "There is somebody that I want you to meet."

They went to the airport, boarded a plane, and flew to Texas. After they landed, Georgy rented a car and drove. Max, exhausted, slept. It was late, nearing dusk when they stopped on a stretch of road near a group of boxy buildings and two large satellite dishes.

"Where are we?" Max asked, blinking. "A radio observatory?"

"Not exactly," Georgy said, passing Max a canned coffee and a granola bar.

Stomach growling, Max started on the granola bar at once. By the time he had cracked open the coffee, there was a man walking toward the car. He was a middle-aged man with a broad smile. He wore a dark blue blazer over a black t-shirt and blue jeans with brown dress shoes. He strode to the passenger side window. Max lowered the window, instantly greeted by the dry Texas heat.

"Georgy!" the strange man exclaimed, beaming at Georgy, "So good to see you again. And you must be Max. Hi. So wonderful to meet you," the man stuck his hand in through the open window. Max shook it awkwardly.

"You're David Steins," Max said, recognizing the man. "Head of SpaceTech."

"Call me David. Come with me. You don't want to miss it," he said.

"Miss what?" Max asked.

"Where should I park?" Georgy asked.

"Just leave your car here," David said.

"In the middle of the road?" Georgy asked.

"People can get around you. There is plenty of space," David said.

"Okay," Georgy said. He turned the car off and opened his door. David began walking, beckoning to the two of them.

"Where are we going?" Max asked, opening his door.

"Just up the road. We could watch it by video from the command center but that's no fun. I prefer to see it with my own eyes," David said.

David set off walking at an energetic pace and Georgy matched him. Max followed behind, taking in the scenery. They were on an empty stretch of asphalt road. Sandy coastal plain stretched away on both sides, greened by short, scrubby grasses. In the distance rose sand dunes and the faint sound of ocean surf. A flight of pelicans flew westward toward the sinking sun.

"Is that it?" Georgy asked, pointing.

"Yes. That's our first prototype. Isn't it beautiful?" David said.

"The grain silo?" Max asked, taking a gulp of his coffee.

David laughed. "That's no grain silo. That's our rocket. We can stop here."

In the distance stood a silver tower. It was tall and shiny. It was standing on three tall legs, and Max finally noticed the engine bells protruding below. He could identify the connected propellant lines and recognized the distinctive clouds generated by the off gassing of cryogenic oxygen. It was surrounded by a small tank farm that provided the fuel to fill the rocket.

"We call it Big Test Rocket One. Not the most creative name, I know, but it has all come together so quickly that we haven't had a chance to come up with a better. It is the prototype for our next generation of really big rockets. They will be fully reusable and capable of on-orbit refueling. It really looks like Tintin's rocket doesn't it? Have you ever read Tintin, Max?" David asked.

"No, I can't say that I have," Max answered.

"They are great. Literary classics. I will have my assistant send you a copy," David said.

"When will it launch?" Georgy asked.

David checked his watch. "In two minutes," he said.

"How big is it?" Max asked. On the empty plain there was nothing to give the vehicle scale.

"Fifty meters tall, give or take. Same height as your Soyuz, but quite a bit bigger around. The final version will have a booster stage underneath. That will make it more than twice as tall," David said. "This version can't quite reach orbit yet, but it should be able to go up a few thousand meters and come back and land. That would be enough to test the engines and guidance system."

"And what is the purpose of the rocket? I don't see a payload fairing," Max observed.

David chuckled. "The rocket is the payload. You don't need something this big to launch satellites. This will be for sending humans to colonize the solar system. Once we have the kinks worked out, we will be booking round trips to the moon and to Mars," he said.

Max looked at him quizzically, but David seemed earnest. He grinned at Max, looked back at the quiescent spaceship, then checked his watch. "Ten seconds!" he exclaimed.

"Nine, eight, seven," he said, providing the countdown in an ever-rising voice. "Six, five, four," he continued. Max took another sip of coffee from his can.

With a flash of light and a mushroom cloud of smoke, the rocket exploded. Max dropped his drink. All three clapped their hands over their ears in anticipation of the noise. Five seconds later the sound of the explosion reached them with an earth-shaking boom. Shiny bits of debris rained down on the grass.

David's phone rang. He fished it out of his jacket pocket and answered. "Yep. Yep. I saw it. I will be there in a second. Thanks," he said. He replaced the phone in his pocket and turned to Georgy and Max with a rueful grin.

"That's okay. We will have another prototype ready to go soon. We will get this cleaned up and try again. 'Try, try again,' that's the SpaceTech motto! I have to go and talk to the team. I will see you guys tomorrow!"

With this, David turned away and began jogging toward the burning wreckage. A fire truck emerged from the orbital tracking station, turned on its siren, and barreled down the road past Georgy and Max.

Georgy looked at Max and shrugged. The two walked back to their rented car. The driver's side windows had been blown out by the concussion. Broken glass was on the ground, but Max's passenger window was intact. He rolled the window up, leaned his seat back, and went to sleep.

CHAPTER NINETEEN

ax awoke in a roadside motel the next morning. He climbed out of bed, brushed his teeth, showered, and dressed. For once, Georgy was still asleep, snoring gently. Max was hungry.

"I'm going to borrow the car," Max said aloud. Georgy kept snoring.

Max fetched the keys from the bedside table, then he went outside. The paved lot was almost empty. The sun had not yet risen, but the predawn light was growing in the east. Max went to the car, started the engine, and drove down the highway. He did not have to go far. Within a few miles he saw a sign reading "Hon's Biscuit and Breakfast." Max drove into the lot and parked. He could see staff busy in the small diner, but the sign on the door indicated that they would not open for another five minutes. Max sighed and took out his cell phone.

He had two missed calls from Heather. He had been avoiding this. Reluctantly, he pressed the button to return his ex-wife's phone call.

She answered. "Max?" she asked.

"Hi, Heather," Max said.

"You called me yesterday," she said. "Very early in the morning."

"Yes. I know. But I don't remember what I said," he said.

"You were drunk," she informed him.

"I know. I'm sorry," he said.

"Thank you for apologizing," she said.

"I hope I didn't say anything too embarrassing," he said.

"Just the usual," she said. She did not elaborate.

"I'm sorry," he said again.

"I know you are, Max. But being sorry and being ready to change are two different things," she said.

"I mean that I am sorry for hurting you. For everything I've done. I never meant to hurt you," he said.

"I know you didn't. You're not intentionally cruel," she said.

Max did not know what to say. Heather saved him by changing the subject.

"How is Georgy?" she asked.

"He is good. He's here with me in Texas. We are meeting the SpaceTech people," he said.

"I've heard of that company. They are growing fast," she said.

"Yep," he said.

There was another long silence.

"I didn't leave you because of your work," Heather said, finally. "When you called yesterday you accused me of leaving you because you were too busy."

"I don't remember what I said last night," Max said.

"I left because I was tired of feeling helpless. I was tired of feeling guilty that I could not help you. You're reckless, Max," she said.

"I have a dangerous job," he said.

"It's not the job. Why do you drink so much?" she asked.

"I don't know," he admitted.

"That's a question that you need to answer," she said, "for yourself."

The restaurant's door sign swung to "OPEN" and Max's stomach rumbled.

Heather sighed. "I still care about you, Max. But I can't spend my life worrying about you. If you want to call and talk sometimes, that's okay, but don't call me when you're drinking," she said.

"Okay," he agreed.

"I have to go now. Take care of yourself," she said.

"Goodbye," Max said. The phone beeped and the line went dead.

Max returned to the hotel with a bag of biscuits and two hot coffees. Georgy was just stepping out of the shower, wet towel wrapped around his waist.

"That smells good," Georgy said, taking the bag and peering inside.

"What's the plan for today?" Max asked.

"David has invited us to come to the SpaceTech offices and look at one of their projects," Georgy said.

"It looks like they can blow stuff up just fine without my help," Max said.

"The Big Test Rocket is just a side project for them. Their primary focus is on space capsules. They want to make crew shuttles for low-earth orbit. They are testing one next week," Georgy said.

Max chewed on a biscuit. Georgy considered his face. "What do you want to do, Max?" he asked.

"Let's check it out," Max said, finally.

The corporate offices of SpaceTech were modern and clean, situated in a quiet Texas suburb. David Steins met Max and Georgy in the lobby. The CEO shook their hands, greeted them warmly, and led them past a receptionist's desk and into the office hallways. The walls were plastered with photographs of rockets through the years.

"First, let me get you acquainted with our new workhorse, the Hawk rocket. It's sixty meters tall, has two stages, and can lift about fifteen thousand kilos into low earth orbit. It's similar to the capability of your Soyuz, Max," David said.

"It's not my Soyuz. It's the company's Soyuz. They get mad if I use it for personal travel," Max said.

David laughed. "Except that our Hawk rocket is partially reusable, and thus much cheaper to operate," he added.

"That must give you guys an advantage," Max said.

"Very much so. That's how we're going to smash the competition," he said. David's phone buzzed. He pulled it out of his pocket, typed a quick message, and put it away. "Lower prices, more stuff in space. Let's go in here." David opened a door and led them into a conference room. There were five people sitting around a long table. At the head of the table a woman was giving a presentation on a large computer screen. They went silent when David strode in.

"Oh, hello, I didn't mean to interrupt. What are we doing in here?" David asked.

The woman who had been giving the presentation spoke. "Mister Steins," she said. "These are the two newest members of the HR department. I was just going through the new employee orientation."

"Human Resources!" David exclaimed, "Our most valuable resource. Hello. Nice to meet you. Call me David," David said, going around the table to shake hands.

"No, no, please sit. Do not get up. I won't take but a minute. These are my friends Georgy and Max. Georgy is a retired astronaut and Max is a mechanical genius with rockets," David said.

"Hi," said Max. He leaned against the wall by the door. Georgy pulled out a chair and sat down at the table.

"They will be consulting with us on the Hawk rocket," David continued. "While we are all here, let's talk about the Hawk. Does anybody have a whiteboard marker?" David asked.

The woman who had been giving the presentation produced a black marker and David turned to the blank white wall.

"Don't worry, we have all our walls painted with special paint so that I can draw on them. So, this is our rocket." With quick strokes David drew a sketch of the Hawk on the conference room wall. It was a simple cylinder, divided into two stages, with engine nozzles at the bottom of each stage and a rounded payload fairing at the top.

"Does anybody notice anything special yet?" he asked,

continuing to sketch.

"Your rocket has landing legs," Max said.

"Exactly. After releasing the second stage for orbital insertion, the first stage re-enters the atmosphere and lands itself on the launch pad where it's ready to be refueled and launched again," David said. He stepped a pace to the side and sketched a rocket trajectory as he talked.

"And that is why your rocket is so much cheaper," Max concluded.

"Yes. We don't throw the hardware away. Going to space will eventually be just as cheap as the cost of fuel," David said.

"And the cost of the second stage," Max observed. "I don't see any landing legs on that part."

"One day we will land that too," David said. "Maybe you can help us figure out how."

"You could try and catch one with a helicopter. With a parachute and a hook," Max said. "Although that might void the warranty on the helicopter."

David blinked at him. He turned back to the wall and began sketching an exploded view of the second stage. "That could work," he mused. "We would need a new heat shield…"

David stared at his work in silence. The room gazed at him, waiting.

"Max," he said suddenly. "I know that your company has a lot of cash sitting in the bank, would you like to invest it all in this project? You would have a very good return on investment if it works."

Max glanced at Georgy, who gave him a grin.

"Not… not right now," Max said.

"That's okay," David said. "But let me know if you change your mind. Private investment is the lifeblood of our venture. Let me show you to my office."

David dropped the pen and left the room. Max and Georgy followed him out.

"I know that you have been working with NASA on Artemis," David said. "But the Hawk is a totally different project. The Hawk cannot take people to the moon. It is just a cheap ride for satellites and for shuttling people to LEO."

"And how can we help you?" Max asked.

"How can we help other than giving you all of our money," Georgy clarified.

"We have already used the Hawk to launch some unmanned payloads and commercial satellites, but now we are testing the Hawk system with a human-rated capsule. As an expert in human spaceflight, I want you to observe the system. Tell us what we are doing wrong," David said.

"You already assume that you are doing things wrong?" Max asked.

"Of course. It would be unreasonable to assume that we got the system perfect on the first try," David said.

David led them through an open office area. Dozens of engineers worked at their computers or collaborated at round tables. None took any notice of them. He went to a glassed corner office, opened the door, and led them inside.

"You can use this office," David said.

"The door says that this is your office," Max observed.

The door indeed read "David Steins, CEO." A terminal sat on a large metal desk. An eclectic collection of books was crammed onto bookshelves that lined every wall. Max noted a few textbooks on physics, and a large number of science fiction novels.

"Yeah, it's my office but I never use it. I just come in here for books from time to time. You're welcome to have it. I made you both new user profiles for our computer system. Let me jot the usernames and passwords for you," David said. He took a pen and sticky note from the desk and scribbled a series of characters and numbers. "And let me give you my cell number too," he wrote his phone number and handed Max the note. Max passed it to Georgy.

David's phone buzzed, and he answered. "Yes, I am on the way, I will be there in a minute," he said into the phone, then turned back to Max.

"I have to run, but I will be back soon. Feel free to call me at any time. Really, I work all the time. Just give me a call. If it goes to voicemail, I will call you right back," he said. He shook Max and Georgy's hands one more time, then left the office.

CHAPTER TWENTY

Max sat in the large office chair and logged in to the workstation. Georgy pulled one of the guest chairs around the desk and booted up a laptop set in a docking station adjacent to the first computer's monitor.

"Overall, the flight profile looks pretty orthodox," Georgy said after studying for some time. He was looking at a screen that showed burn times, thrust to weight ratios, and acceleration rates for each of the Hawk rocket's stages. "The Hawk is similar to the Atlas V rocket, except that the second stage is kerolox instead of hydrolox, and the first stage is oversized to account for the boost-back burn and powered landing."

Max nodded. "And no accommodation has been made for solid rocket boosters," he responded. He inspected a diagram of the interior of the spacecraft's capsule.

"Take a look at this, Georgy," he said. Georgy shifted to look over Max's shoulder. On the screen were images of the interior of the Hawk crew capsule.

"Nice looking cabin. Very modern. Lots of legroom," Georgy said.

"I was looking more at the controls," Max said.

"Where are the controls?" Georgy asked.

"My question exactly," Max said.

"Surely the spacecraft is not fully autonomous?" Georgy said.

"Maybe it is," Max said.

Georgy sat back and looked thoughtful. "We are accustomed to seeing manual controls in our spacecraft, like on the Soyuz and the Space Shuttle, but with the way computers are today, are they really necessary?"

"The computers have gotten better," Max allowed, "but I do like having manual backups."

"Maybe the touchscreens allow some kind of direct override?" Georgy offered.

"Maybe. We need to ask somebody," Max said.

Max stood and went into the hallway. The first person he saw was a woman sitting at a nearby desk. She met his eyes and smiled as Max approached.

"Hi. I'm Max. I'm new here. I was wondering if you could help me," he said.

"I know who you are Doctor Ardis. My name is Victoria Amahale. It is nice to meet you," she extended her hand and Max shook it. "And you must be the famous astronaut Georgy Kaverin. It is an honor." She stood and shook his hand as well. "How can I help you two?"

"We were wondering if somebody could help us understand the pilot interface for the Hawk crew capsule," Max said.

"You have come to the right person. I designed it," she said. "What is your question?"

"We were wondering about the flight controls. How does a pilot adjust the craft's trajectory?" Max asked.

"You are going to be flying the thing after all?" Victoria asked with a smile.

Max blinked. "I never agreed to that. David Steins just asked me to review the system and make recommendations," he said.

Victoria chuckled. "David was telling me that he wanted Max "Thrust" Ardis to be the first person to fly on the Hawk. I had heard that you were working on Artemis, so I told him it would not happen. But here you are," she said.

"I've agreed to nothing of the sort," Max said, shaking his head. "About those flight controls though?"

"Let's go take a look," she said.

Max turned to go back into David's office, but Victoria beckoned them down the hallway.

"Don't you want to see the real thing?" she asked.

Victoria led Max and Georgy to an exit door. They left the building and crossed a stretch of asphalt to a metal hangar. Victoria punched a code into a keypad and a reinforced door swung open. They went inside the workshop.

Divided by tall plastic barriers, engineers worked in brightly-lit bays containing rocket motors, fuel tanks, aerodynamic surfaces, and hydraulic components. Victoria strode to a large central space that housed the crew capsule.

The capsule was a truncated cone five meters tall and four meters in diameter. It was painted in white and blue, and emblazoned with the SpaceTech logo. It was raised from the floor and a set of mobile stairs was pushed against its open door.

"Go on in," Victoria said.

Max climbed the stairs and crawled through the door.

"It's a bit more spacious than the Soyuz descent module," Max commented, crawling inside.

"Almost twice the interior volume," Victoria agreed.

The seats were oriented orthogonal to local gravity. Max climbed into the nearest chair, laying on his back. A large computer screen was immediately in front of him. It was blank.

"How do I turn this thing on?" Max asked, poking at the screen with his finger.

"The circuit is tripped open. Let me close it for you," Victoria said, turning away. Georgy crouched in the doorway.

Seconds later the screen flickered to life. Diagnostics ran across Max's field of vision.

"We could run a docking simulation," Victoria offered from outside the door.

"Please," Max said.

An image of the international space station appeared, centered in the screen. Windowed numbers and figures displayed the spacecraft's simulated orbit, orientation, and relative velocity.

"Our closing velocity with the space station is 0.01 meters per second," Max read aloud. "What if I wanted to take manual control?" he asked.

Victoria edged past Georgy to crawl into the capsule alongside Max.

"Well, you would not take direct manual control. You would request a new vector and then the computer would take care of the maneuvers," Victoria said. She reached past Max to touch the screen. She opened a new virtual window and input a command. There was a brief delay, then there was a simulated puff of gas from the thrusters. The closing velocity to the station now read "0.02 m/s."

"What if I wanted to do something more complicated, like fly a circuit around the station?" Max asked.

Victoria pursed her lips. "Well, something like that would need to be authorized by ground control. We are very careful around the ISS," she said.

"I just want to know how it could be done," Max said.

"We would first bring your relative velocity to zero," she touched the screen and entered another command. Simulated maneuvering thrusters fired and the craft came to a halt, relative to the station. The image of a simulated Earth turned below.

"Then..." Victoria hesitated. She shrugged. "Then you would contact ground control and they could upload a new set of vectors," she said.

Max scanned the screen. "What about an even simpler maneuver. What if I wanted to impart a lateral thrust of 1 m/s of delta-v?"

"You would touch the screen here to open this set of inputs," Victoria said, showing him. "Then you would dial in the vector and magnitude. Then you would confirm. The panel closes and then the computer performs the maneuver." She completed a series of commands and then, after a brief delay, there was another simulated puff of gas. The image of the space station began to drift laterally in the screen.

"That was four commands for a single impulse," Max observed.

"How many should it be?" Victoria asked.

"One," Georgy chuckled.

"This spaceship does not have a control system designed for a pilot. It has a control system designed for a passenger," Max commented.

"In our simulations, human error is responsible for a lion's share of mistakes," said another voice. Max looked up to see David Steins crouched in the doorway. "We have done everything that we can do make the system as simple as possible," David said.

"So, you have idiot proofed your system," Max said. "But sooner or later somebody invents a better idiot."

Max rolled out of the command chair and made his way to the door. Victoria and David shifted to let him pass. He walked down the stairs to inspect the exterior of the capsule.

"I see that you have reaction control thrusters here and here," Max said, indicating nozzles on the outside of the spacecraft. "What about high thrust maneuvering?"

"Gross orbit adjustments are made with the thrusters in the service module," David said, following him.

"I will have to see that too," Max said.

"Certainly," David responded. "But I take it that you are less than satisfied with the control system of the capsule?"

"Piloting a spaceship is hard. Maybe it is best that the computer manages most of the maneuvers most of the time, but a pilot would like the option to take over," Max said.

"Do you want to fly it?" David asked.

"He does," Georgy interjected.

"If the craft is so good at flying on its own, let's see it do that first. I want to know it won't blow up before I put my fragile human body inside of it," Max amended.

"That's fair," David said.

"When is the next launch?" Max asked.

"How about tomorrow?" David said with a grin.

CHAPTER TWENTY-ONE

Max and Georgy met with David and Victoria the next morning.

"We do things a little differently than NASA does," David said.

They stood outside of the small metal buildings of the ad-hoc launch control station. In the distance, the new rocket stood on the launch pad while Max squinted against the brilliant dawn.

"NASA is cautious and intolerant of mistakes. But we don't mind blowing things up if it gets us to space faster," David said.

"Talking about blowing things up isn't selling me on being your test pilot," Max said.

David laughed. "What I mean is that we believe in rapid, iterative testing. Our goal is to achieve a cost effective and reliable rocket as quickly as possible. We don't mind making a few mistakes along the way," he said.

"I assure you that pilot safety is the highest priority for the crewed system. Our Hawk rocket is already validated," Victoria clarified. "It is only the crew capsule that is new to the system."

Max gazed at the distant rocket. It was the same height as the prototype vehicle that had stood on that same pad, but slenderer. It was like Max's Soyuz rocket, but without the four boosters at the base. Atop the rocket was an aerodynamic fairing which sheltered the crew capsule and service module.

"Let's launch this thing," David said, and he led them into the nearest building.

Within the double-wide trailer were twelve laptop computers on various folding tables. The ceiling and opposite side of the building's sheet metal exterior had been cut out and replaced with plexiglass to make a tall, curved window. Engineers already filled most of the folding chairs.

"Are we ready?" David asked.

A chorus of "sure," and "yes," answered him and he sat at the nearest chair. Victoria sat beside him where her own laptop was waiting.

"Where are we on the fueling?" David asked.

"It is done, sir," one of the engineers replied.

"Range safety?" David asked.

"Range is clear."

"Rocket systems?" David asked.

"All green," another engineer answered.

"Capsule?" David asked.

"Crew capsule is a 'go,'" Victoria answered, checking her screen.

"Then let's not waste time. Start the countdown at ten seconds," David said.

After a tapping of commands on her keyboard Victoria began counting.

"Ten, nine, eight, seven..." she began.

"They really are not wasting any time," Max muttered.

"...six, five, four, three, two, one," Victoria continued. She struck a key on her keyboard.

Suddenly, the tall rocket began rising. There was flame, but no smoke as the missile rose into the air.

"Clean burning engines," Georgy grunted. "And a fast acceleration."

"There are five keralox engines on that vehicle, and they are deep-throttle capable. That allows us to keep the acceleration steady between 1.5 and 3.0 G's for the whole ride," David said.

"All systems green," Victoria said. "Passing through max-Q now."

Max watched the rocket turn toward the sun. It climbed silently into a blue, cloudless sky. The sound of the rocket finally reached them with a roar that rattled the metal walls of the trailer. A radar dish outside panned to track the Hawk as it flew eastward. Eventually the rocket grew too small to see and Max shifted his gaze to the laptop screens. Victoria monitored sensor readings. David watched the rocket's trajectory as it gained speed and altitude.

"Approaching main engine cut off," Victoria said. A few seconds later she added, "We have MECO."

The velocity for the rocket had stopped increasing. David touched his keyboard, and his screen showed the live feed from an onboard camera aimed backward. The blue water of the Gulf of Mexico took up most of the image. A distant yellow-green fleck was the coast of Texas.

"Stage separation," David said.

The first stage of the rocket detached. Max watched it rotate, drifting behind the now-freed second stage engine bell.

"Second stage ignition confirmed," Victoria said.

In the vacuum of space there was no flame, but the newly exposed engine glowed red, the first stage receded into the distance, and the velocity numbers on the computer screen began to grow once again.

"This is the coolest part," David said. "Keep looking out that window."

High in the sky outside there was a glint of light. Max squinted through the plexiglass ceiling and the distant speck descended. The first stage of the rocket was falling, tail first. It grew larger and Max could see aerodynamic surfaces rotating on the top of the rocket. The rocket was steering itself toward the launch pad. It fell, faster and faster, growing larger and larger, and Max braced himself, expecting it to crash. At the last second the engine fired, and the rocket caught itself, balanced on a fountain of flame. Landing legs sprang down and the rocket settled softly on the pad.

"That is pretty cool," Georgy said.

Meanwhile, the second stage continued to accelerate. Max watched it on David's screen, glowing engine bell and turning Earth below as the velocity climbed. Suddenly the screen went black.

"We lose the video feed when the rocket goes past the horizon," David explained. "Lack of bandwidth. But we still have telemetry." His screen switched to showing a digital simulation of the upper stage, oriented parallel to Earth's turning surface, engine still burning.

"The orbital insertion is going well," Victoria commented. "Only a few more kilometers per second and we will be in orbit." She sat back in her chair.

"This is a nicely streamlined operation that you have here," Georgy said.

"Thank you, Georgy, that means a lot coming from you. I know how lean you run," David said.

"We get by," Georgy said.

"Any thoughts on the rocket so far?" David asked, looking at Max.

Max shrugged. "You don't need my opinion when things are going well. I am a mechanic. I am waiting for something to break," he said.

David smiled. "Then let's hope something does break. I would not want to have brought you all the way out here for nothing," he said.

On the launch pad the first stage of the rocket was venting its last reserves of cryogenic oxygen. Service crews were moving about in its shadow.

"How many times can you re-fly the first stage?" Georgy asked.

"We are hoping for an infinite number of flights," David said.

"Our limiting factor is turnaround," Victoria added. "The system is still experimental so we don't know how much we need to tear down and rebuild. Currently we overhaul every engine and disassemble the fuselage and fuel tanks for structural assessment. The eventual goal would be to simply refuel and launch again."

"That would save some money," Georgy said.

"Yes," David said, "If we could bring the cost down enough, then cheap, reliable spaceflight is just one of the benefits. We could offer a suborbital passenger service. Orlando to Kyiv in an hour!"

Victoria eyed her computer screen. "Coming up on second stage engine shutdown," she said. After a pause, she continued, "we have achieved orbit."

The small control room gave a brief cheer. Engineers leaned out of their seats to high-five. On David's screen was a simple graphic representation of the spacecraft. Solar panels deployed from the conical vessel.

"Prepare to test orbital maneuvering operations. First..." Victoria trailed off. She frowned at something on her screen. "There is a problem," she said.

"What?" David asked.

"I am seeing unexpected fuel consumption," she said.

"The vessel is not supposed to be making any maneuvers now. What is burning fuel?" David asked.

"The RCS is reading active," Victoria answered, referring to the vessel's Reaction Control System, the small thrusters responsible for minor course adjustments. "The attitude control thrusters are firing."

"But the ship's attitude is constant," David said.

David leaned to look over Victoria's shoulder and Max did the same. On the screen the spacecraft appeared to be unmoving. Its heading was not changing and its velocity was a steady 7.79 km/s. Trajectory showed an elliptical orbit of 25.59 degrees inclination. The fuel reading for the spacecraft was ticking down. As Max watched, it dropped from 97% to 96%, then to 95%.

"Maybe there is a fuel leak?" David offered. Fuel level read 94%.

"It can't be," Max interjected. "A leak like that would release pressurized gas to space. That would necessarily impart an acceleration to the spacecraft. But there is no acceleration on the telemetry."

"Then maybe our telemetry is wrong?" David said.

"Running diagnostics on that now," Victoria said. "So far everything checks out. Our spacecraft appears to be in a stable orbit. It is not rotating or maneuvering but the RCS system is active. The thrusters are firing, and we are losing fuel."

"How could the thrusters be firing but the vehicle not be moving?" David mused.

Nobody answered. The control room had gone quiet. Slowly, the fuel reading was ticking down. 92%. 91%.

Max leaned against the wall. Georgy unfolded a nearby chair and took a seat. Victoria typed on her keyboard. David abandoned his own computer and watched Victoria work as they went through diagnostics again.

"We will be orbiting over our downlink center in French Guiana momentarily. We will have enough bandwidth to view the feed from the ship's onboard engineering cameras," Victoria said.

Soon her screen showed live images from the spacecraft. They could see close ups of the maneuvering thrusters. Two of them were firing white propellant into space.

"That's it!" Victoria exclaimed. "Thruster one and thruster seven are firing at the same time. They are diametrically opposed, so they cancel each other out."

"That explains how we're losing fuel but not changing the spacecraft's trajectory," David nodded. "So how do we turn them off?"

"Like this," Victoria said. She leaned forward and input a series of commands.

"Nothing happened," David said.

"That's odd. I told the RCS system to reboot. The spacecraft received the command, but it's not shutting down. We cannot shut off the engines," Victoria said.

"Could the fuel valves be stuck open?" David asked.

"For two engines? That just happen to be diametrically opposed?" Victoria made a face. "Unlikely. It has to be a software error," she said.

"What now?" David asked.

For a moment Victoria did not respond. She tried inputting several more commands, but to no avail.

"I don't know," she said.

Fuel reading was 88%.

CHAPTER TWENTY-TWO

Max watched the SpaceTech engineers. They were trying to wrangle their misbehaving spaceship as it coasted through space. He uncrossed his arms and went to the window.

Shimmers of heat came off the swampy land as the sun rose in the cloudless sky. Nearby, a heron drifted on outstretched wings. Farther, a flock of birds leapt into the air, flowing in a mass of tawny feathers.

Max put his fingers on the transparent plastic. It was warm and soft. His mind drifted. He thought of the advances in materials science that allowed such a thing as an inexpensive, durable thermoplastic. Humanity had made such advances in the past few hundred years, which was only a blip of cosmic time, just a heartbeat in the life of the Earth. Max felt like he was floating, skimming on the edge of time.

"David," Max said, turning around. "What would be the best outcome for your spacecraft now?"

David looked up from leaning over Victoria's shoulder to blink at him. Victoria answered instead.

"At this point we would be happy to bring the spacecraft home so that we can inspect it and find out what went wrong," she said.

"Where can we bring it down?" Max asked.

"Anywhere in the Gulf of Mexico would be fine. We have recovery boats and spotter planes ready to go," she said.

Max strode to David's abandoned chair. He flipped through screens on David's laptop until he found what he was looking for.

"Rather than use a launch escape tower you guys incorporated the launch abort system into pusher motors in the service module?" Max asked.

"Yes," David said.

"And it runs on the same propellant as the reaction control system?" Max asked.

"That's right," David answered.

"Can we turn 180 degrees and point retrograde?" Max asked.

"The vessel is frozen along the 'X' axis by the firing thrusters, but if we use the reentry thrusters we can pitch along the 'Y' axis," Victoria answered.

"Do it. Flip to point retrograde," Max said.

"Okay," Victoria said.

On his screen Max watched the vessel rotate. The left and right yaw thrusters were still opposing each other, burning through precious fuel, but a small thruster in the nose of the rocket burned. The spacecraft turned, first pointing away from the Earth, and then pointing backward relative to the spacecraft's orbit.

"How much delta-v is left in the tanks?" Max asked.

"Two hundred and sixty-five meters per second and dropping. Two hundred and sixty-four. Two hundred and sixty-three," she read aloud.

"Keep reading that off to me. When I say so, activate the abort motors at full thrust," Max said.

"Wait," David objected. "The craft is opposite to the Pacific Ocean. If we burn retrograde now, it will reenter somewhere east of Australia. We don't have any recovery craft out there."

"I can get the capsule to the Gulf of Mexico. You are just going to have to trust me on this one," Max said. "Where are we on delta-v Victoria?"

"Two forty-nine. Two forty-eight, two forty-seven" she said.

"Nose down three degrees," Max said.

"Roger, pitching down three degrees," Victoria said.

"Cosine losses," Georgy understood, nodding.

Max waited a moment, watching the trajectory.

"Burn now," he said.

Victoria depressed a button on her keyboard. The large rocket nozzles on the back of the service module came to life. The vehicle's acceleration leapt from 0.0G to 4.2G. Max watched the orbit trajectory degrade. The vehicle was on a suborbital path now, and its projected perigee dropped rapidly through the upper atmosphere. After four seconds the acceleration suddenly stopped. The craft had run out of fuel.

"I don't understand," David said. "We are taking it down in the Pacific Ocean?"

Victoria laughed. "It may be entering the atmosphere over the Pacific but look at that inclination. Look at how shallow the angle of attack is."

"Can we get a systems check on the spacecraft?" Max asked.

"Sure," Victoria answered. "The solar panels snapped off during the abort, they were not built to withstand that kind of acceleration while deployed, but we have plenty of onboard battery power left. Comms and navigation are both green. Life support in the crew capsule is intact. We are bingo fuel."

"Good. Go ahead and detach the service module now," Max said.

"Without any fuel, the capsule will not be able to orient when entering the atmosphere. Isn't there a chance of it tumbling?" Georgy asked.

Max nodded. "Yes, but truncated cones tend to stabilize in the proper orientation. Spinning is more likely than tumbling."

"The capsule is on a ballistic course into the Pacific Ocean. We will have to scramble recovery crews," David said. He pulled his phone out of his pocket.

Victoria winked at Max. "No you don't," she told David. "Just keep watching the screen."

David frowned at her but put his phone back in his pocket. He gazed at the video feed. It was not long until the first tenuous wisps of plasma began to cling to the falling capsule. Molecules of gas were smashed by hurtling vehicle. Atmosphere was heated, ionized, and trailed away in incandescent streamers of green, purple, and blue.

Max stared intently at the projected trajectory. The capsule began to lose velocity as it encountered the upper atmosphere. The perigee fell lower and lower, seeming to graze the surface of the blue Pacific Ocean. The heat shield glowed, warming from atmospheric compression.

On the video feed there was a sudden flash of light. The discarded service module, tumbling free half a kilometer away from the capsule, exploded in a shower of shimmering aluminum, burning fragments spreading in a fast-receding cloud.

The video feed died. The projected trajectory froze. All the rapidly changing numbers on the computer screen went still.

"We've lost communications because of reentry plasma," Victoria said.

"We will get it back soon," Max said.

A smidge too little reentry speed, a little too steep of an angle and the capsule would be lost in the Pacific, far from hope of rescue. Max took a breath, closed his eyes, and waited.

"Communications restored!" Victoria exclaimed. "We have a good trajectory. Apogee is climbing."

"It bounced off of the atmosphere!" David exclaimed.

"Like skipping a stone on a pond," Max said.

"Did the capsule actually generate lift or was the trajectory just too shallow to complete aerocapture?" Georgy mused aloud.

Max checked the final trajectory. The capsule would reenter over the Gulf. He glanced at Victoria.

"You have it from here?" Max asked.

"Absolutely. Thanks Max," Victoria said.

Max walked out the door. Georgy followed him. They stood in the dusty parking lot. The sun had climbed halfway up the eastern sky. The door closed behind them. A steady breeze blew from the ocean, bending the marsh grasses. A pelican drifted overhead. If Max held his breath, he could hear the sound of the distant surf.

"SpaceTech is an interesting operation," Georgy said.

"They have a high tolerance for mistakes," Max said. He could see the first stage of the rocket, landed on the distant pad.

"But they are making great strides too," Georgy said.

A cheer came from inside the trailer. The door opened and Victoria and David emerged. Max and Georgy turned to meet them.

"The parachutes deployed," Victoria explained with smile. "Look," she pointed.

Max followed her pointing hand. High in the sky a silver jewel hung beneath three circles of orange.

"Our boats will have it picked up within the hour," David said.

They stood and watched. The descending capsule looked like a flower, drifting toward the unseen waves.

"Max, will you command our first manned flight?" David asked.

"Are you sure that the rocket is not going to blow up?" Max asked.

"Pretty sure," David said.

"How about a compromise?" Max asked. "If you have one unmanned flight where nothing goes wrong, I will fly on the next one after that."

David and Victoria glanced at one another. "That sounds fair," Victoria said.

David grinned and stepped forward to shake Max's hand. "It is great to have you on board, Max. The future is bright," he said.

CHAPTER TWENTY-THREE

Max had dozed off when he got the call from Adams. He was on a towel beneath an umbrella on a Texas beach. The sun was low, and Georgy was floating in the gentle surf, hoping for a wave big enough to skim his surfboard along the desolate beach. Max found his buzzing phone in his hand.

"Yeah?" he answered.

"Hi, Max," said Adams.

"Hello, astronaut. Make it back to the moon yet?" Max said, yawning.

Adams' chuckle could be heard. "Not yet, but soon. I heard that you took a job with SpaceTech."

"Are you nervous that I'm helping the competition?" Max asked.

"SpaceTech is not NASA's competition," Adams said. "NASA does not have competition. We are all in this together."

"Is there something that I can do for you?" Max asked.

"Come and have dinner with my wife and me. We may not be co-workers anymore, but I would like for us to be friends," Adams said.

"I don't know, Adams, I am pretty busy," Max said.

"Who is it?" Georgy called, walking up the beach.

"It's Adams," Max called back, "he wants to have dinner with me but I told him that I'm busy."

"You're not busy," Georgy scoffed.

"Okay," Max sighed. "Let's have dinner."

Max deplaned in Florida, where Adams picked him up from the terminal in a modest four-door sedan.

"You don't have any luggage?" Adams asked.

"I figured you might have an extra toothbrush I could borrow," Max said, settling into the passenger seat as Adams drove them away from the airport.

They soon reached Adams' home in the Orlando suburbs. His wife greeted them at the door. She was a small Asian woman with a broad smile and kind eyes.

"I am Naomi," she said, shaking Max's hand. "Take off your shoes and put them on the rack over here. Welcome to our home." Naomi turned to Adams. "Can you make dinner, honey? Seki needs help with her homework."

"Of course," Adams said. He kissed his wife, then led Max into the kitchen. It was a simple kitchen, with an economical oven and electric cooking range. A window overlooked a small garden. Adams put a pan on the stove and began taking ingredients from the refrigerator.

"Would you like some coffee?" Adams asked.

"Please," Max said. He leaned against the kitchen counter, feeling like a stranger. "Is there anything that I should be doing to help?"

"Sure. Make me a cup of coffee too," Adams said, pointing at the coffee maker. He handed Max a bag of coffee grounds.

Max poured the grounds and checked the water level in the familiar machine. Soon the pot began to fill. The skillet sizzled, and soft music was playing somewhere in the house.

Adams chopped vegetables on a wooden cutting board. He wore khaki slacks and a white button up shirt with the sleeves rolled up past his elbows. He was engrossed in his work. Each knife cut was purposeful and precise. He added diced pepper to the hot pan and began cubing tofu.

"Where do you live when you are not working, Max? I know that you usually launch out of Kodiak Island in Alaska, but is there anywhere that you call home?" Adams asked.

"Georgy rents me a small apartment in Anchorage. I am a low-maintenance spaceman," Max said.

"You don't have anything more permanent? A place to put down roots?" Adams asked.

"Georgy lets me sleep under his desk sometimes, but he is bad about remembering to water me," Max said.

Adams glanced up, searching Max's face.

"The coffee is ready," Max diverted.

"Mugs are in the cabinet," Adams said.

Max poured two cups from the full pot. Adams accepted his, took a sip from the steaming mug, then set it aside to cool. He poured rice into a boiling pot and added a pad of butter.

"You used to be married?" Adams probed.

"Mm hmm," Max answered.

Naomi walked into the kitchen. "It smells wonderful, honey," she said, looking into the pan.

"It will be ready in just a bit," Adams answered, adding minced ginger and then a dark sauce.

"Seki and I will set the table," Naomi said, walking out.

Adams stepped back from the stove.

"I like you, Max," he said candidly, picking up his coffee mug. "I feel that we share the same goals, the same desires at heart."

"Which are?" Max asked.

"To push the boundaries of humanity," Adams said.

Max frowned. "I mostly just worry about getting paid," Max said.

"You are already a millionaire, Max." Adams said. "You can't be motivated by the money."

Max shrugged.

"What is your philosophy?" Adams asked. "What keeps you going?"

"I don't have a philosophy. The universe is vast and uncaring. It does not really matter what we think," Max said.

"It does matter," Adams said. "It matters because we are alive, and that is a gift."

"Worms are alive too. What philosophy do they need?" Max said.

"But you are not a worm, Max. Humans are capable of greatness," Adams said.

"Or humans are capable of going extinct. Even if we do not destroy the world ourselves, a super volcano could erupt, or an asteroid could impact and then all our effort will be for nothing," Max said.

"If everything is pointless, then why try?" Adams asked.

Max sighed and gazed out the window. A squirrel dug for acorns in the yard outside. Max watched it dig. Eventually it gave up and wandered away; its search fruitless.

"When I was young, my mother used to tell me that God was good. God made each of us to be special. God created each of us with a purpose. We might not know right away what that purpose was, but with faith we would eventually find out. When my mother got sick, I still believed. She died and I still waited for that sense of purpose. When my father got sick, I was starting to have some doubts, but I knew that people were tested, so I clung to my faith. Then my father died, and I was all alone. Finally, I understood. We are a cosmic accident. I work with rockets because I am good at rockets, so that's what I do. But there is no purpose to be had," Max said.

"I also lost my father when I was young," Adams said. "He was a pilot. He died in an accident when I was twelve years old. I was so angry, but loss is no reason to lose your faith," Adams said.

"Faith in what? Faith in God?" Max asked.

"Faith in God, or faith in humanity. You do not have to believe in God to believe in things greater than yourself," Adams said.

Naomi walked into the kitchen.

"Are we ready to eat? I am starving," she asked.

"I will bring the food to the table," Adams said. "Max, go on in and have a seat."

Naomi led Max into the dining room and seated him at their table. Their young daughter skipped into the room and slid into a seat across from him.

"I'm Seki," the girl said.

"Hi Seki. My name is Max. How old are you?"

"Eleven. My dad says you're a hero. You saved his life."

"I didn't do anything heroic. I just made a suggestion," Max said.

"What suggestion?" the girl asked.

"I had an idea about how to fly the spaceship."

"How did you know it was a good idea?" she asked.

"I did some math and the answer was in the numbers," Max said.

"I hate math," Seki said, making a face.

Naomi walked into the dining room bearing two full plates. Adams followed.

"Don't say that Seki, you are very good at math. Seki is in advanced classes in school," Naomi said. She set a plate of stir fry and rice before Max and another before Seki. Adams set down the last two plates and he and his wife joined the table.

"It smells good," Max admitted. He hesitated before picking up his fork, wondering if the family wanted to say a prayer or something, but Adams speared a piece of tofu and put it in his mouth.

"Please go ahead and eat," Naomi said. "Would you like anything to drink?"

"Just water would be fine," Max said. He had seen no alcohol in the house.

Naomi left and came back with a glass of water for Max. Max picked up a green bean with his fork.

"How are things at SpaceTech?" Naomi asked. "The private companies are growing so fast, it is hard to keep up with what the latest projects are."

Max swallowed a mouthful of rice before responding. "The Hawk rocket is promising. That's what they want to do crewed launches with. But when I first got there, they blew up some kind of supermassive test rocket. I don't know what that was all about."

Adams nodded. "That must have been their prototype Mars rocket," he said. "They have been teasing it for months. They say that when it is done it could take twenty or thirty people on each trip. I have not seen one fly yet."

"The rocket would fly all the way to Mars?" Seki asked. "How long would that take?"

"About seven or eight months," Adams answered.

"Wouldn't people go crazy cooped up that long?" Seki asked.

"Not necessarily. Sailors made long journeys in the age of sail and did not go crazy," Adams said. "But it is going to take more than just a fancy new rocket to colonize Mars."

"What would it take?" Max asked.

"A whole infrastructure. It would take a supply chain and a support system. It would take all of us working together. Not just a billionaire with big dreams," Adams said.

"Are you finished?" Naomi asked.

"Yes, thank you," Max said, handing her his empty plate.

"Dessert?" Adams asked, standing with his own dirty plate. "We have vanilla ice cream."

"Sure," Max said.

"Can I go play videogames?" Seki asked.

"Only for an hour," Naomi said.

Seki smiled and stood up. "It was nice to meet you, Max," she said. She skipped out of the room.

"Nice kid," Max said when Adams returned with bowls of ice cream. Naomi did not return, although Max could hear a dishwasher start in the kitchen.

"You ever think about having kids?" Adams asked.

"Not really," Max said.

"Why not?" Adams asked.

"I'm worried I'd screw them up," Max said.

"You have a low tolerance for mistakes," Adams observed.

"Don't you? In our field, mistakes get people killed," Max said.

Adams licked ice cream off his spoon. "Yet perfection is impossible," he pointed out.

"On the contrary, the physics is perfect. It is only humans that are flawed," Max said.

"I was prepared to die on Artemis," Adams said, shifting in his seat. "Before you called, I had figured out how to incorporate my body into the radiation shield. If my body absorbed enough ionizing radiation from the solar flare, the rest of the crew could have been safer."

"And then they would have needed to toss your irradiated corpse into space?" Max asked.

Adams nodded.

"Why do you need to be sacrificed though? What makes the other members of the crew more valuable? Do they deserve to live, and you do not?" Max asked.

"No person is any more or less valuable than another. I would have made the sacrifice because I was the commander. I had a responsibility to the crew," Adams said.

"Diving into the shadow of the moon was a better plan," Max said.

"I am not disputing that. My point is that sacrifices are sometimes necessary," Adams said.

"What about your family? What would they have thought had you died in space?" Max asked.

"I do not want to die, Max. I do not have a death wish, but I want you to understand my point of view. We are at the cusp of achieving great things. Humanity is ready to break from the bonds of this Earth and colonize the solar system. But in order to do that, we have to be able to tolerate risk. I want you to come back to the project. I want you working on Artemis, but you have to be able to compromise. You have to accept that you are going to lose sometimes," Adams said.

"Your altruism is blinding you. There is always another solution. Diving into the shadow of the moon was an idea borne from a simple calculation. Anybody could have thought of it. You would have thought of it too, had you not been planning suicide by solar flare," Max said.

Adams shook his head. "Not everybody has your gift, Max. Not everybody can visualize the orbital mechanics the way that you can. Perhaps if you had been the commander, then no sacrifices would have needed to be considered. This is why we need you. You need to come back to the team."

Max shrugged. He scooped the last of the ice cream from his bowl. Adams watched him in silence.

"I'll think about it," Max said finally.

"Stay with us tonight. We have a guest room with freshly laundered sheets. I am going scuba diving in the Florida cold springs tomorrow. You should come and join me," Adams said.

"Cold springs?" Max asked.

"Yes, north of Orlando there are hundreds of freshwater springs. They are connected by underground caves. I have been mapping them with a team of recreational divers," Adams said.

"Isn't that dangerous?" Max asked.

Adams nodded. "Cave diving can be dangerous, but I would not ask you to go into the caves. The open springs are quite safe. Deep, clear, cool water filled with fish. If you have never been, it is quite an experience," he said.

Max stood. "You have been very kind. It was a good meal, and you have a lovely family. I am going to have to decline on all counts. I want to find a bar and then find a cheap hotel to crash in."

Adams stood and extended his hand. Max reached to accept the handshake

"Do as you like. But I will never forget how you saved my life and the lives of my crew. I will never stop trying to bring you back," Adams said.

"I am sure that we will work together again," Max said. "There are always more projects."

Adams nodded and released his grip. He guided Max back to the front door. Naomi spotted them and came down the stairs.

"Max is not staying?" Naomi asked.

"I can't stay tonight," Max said. "But I do appreciate the offer. Really."

"Would you like a ride into town? Or I can call you a cab?" Adams offered.

"I can call for a car on my phone. I will be fine," Max said.

Adams offered his hand again and Max shook it. Adams' grip was firm.

"Thank you," Adams said.

"Sure. We'll talk again," Max promised. "I have to do some work with SpaceTech, but I haven't forgotten about you guys."

"Good," Adams said, releasing his hand. "See you later."

Max opened the door and walked out into the night.

CHAPTER TWENTY-FOUR

"Have you ever gotten drunk at Disney World?" Max asked, opening the passenger door of Georgy's rented car.

"No," Georgy answered.

"Me neither," Max lied, climbing into the car and closing the door.

Max reclined the passenger seat. With both hands he shaded his eyes against the morning Texas sun. Georgy negotiated the airport traffic and soon they were on the interstate.

"I thought you might be hungover so I got you some things. Look in the bag behind your seat," Georgy said.

Max reached around and found a brown paper bag. It contained a bottle of water, a gas station sachet of ibuprofen, and a pair of dollar store sunglasses.

"Thanks," Max said gratefully. He opened the water bottle and took a long drink, then put on the sunglasses and washed down four ibuprofens with the rest of the water.

"So, what's on the docket today?" Max asked. "Margaritas at the beach?"

"Not exactly," Georgy said. "There appears to be a situation."

"What kind of situation?" Max asked.

"How do you feel about having a co-pilot?" Georgy asked.

"That depends on the co-pilot. Are you offering to fly with me?" Max asked.

"If I flew with you, who would be your contact on the ground?" Georgy asked.

"Victoria could do it. She seems competent," Max said.

"She does," Georgy said. "But no, I'll have to pass on flying with you on this one."

"Get to the point, Georgy. What do you mean about a co-pilot?" Max asked.

"You might be getting one for this next mission," Georgy said.

"There are two problems with having a co-pilot," Max said. "Either they are somebody competent, that I like, then I will feel bad about getting them killed. Or they are somebody incompetent, and they might get me killed. It's a lose-lose situation."

"Have you ever liked somebody who was incompetent?" Georgy asked.

Max considered.

"No," he said, finally.

"Me neither," Georgy answered.

David was waiting for them when they pulled up to the SpaceTech corporate office. He stood on the curb and waved when he saw Georgy`s car.

"You guys got here just in time, the D.O.D.'s people are waiting in the main conference room," David said. He greeted Max with an effusive handshake.

"D.O.D.?" Max asked. "Department of Defense?"

"Yes," David nodded. "Follow me,"

David led them into the building. He took the stairs two at a time to the second floor. He walked them into a keycard secured hallway and then to an unmarked door. Inside was a brightly lit conference room with a large rectangular table and no windows. A ceiling-mounted projector shone the SpaceTech logo against the wall. Victoria sat at the table with a laptop computer open in front of her. On the other side of the table were three men. The leftmost was a thin, older man with graying hair and a severe, commanding expression. He stood impatiently with his arms crossed. The man in the middle wore a US Air Force Pilot's hat but no insignia, and he leaned nonchalant against the wall. The third was a small man in a blue suit and black sunglasses who sat calmly at the table.

"Finally," the gray-haired man said. "Now that they are here, we can get on with the mission briefing. Run the intel."

"Gentlemen I understand your impatience but there is yet time for introductions," David said. "These are my friends Georgy Kaverin and Doctor Maxwell Ardis. They are independent contractors from Thrust Solutions Incorporated."

The old man who had spoken grunted but did not respond. The athletic-looking man in the Air Force Pilot's cleared his throat.

"I am Pilot Robert Edwards," he said. "I am aware of your reputation, Max." He leaned forward and put both palms on the table, looking intently at Max's face. "I hope that we can work together."

An uncomfortable silence passed during which neither of the other men introduced themselves.

"And," David said, clearing his throat. "We have our colleagues from the Department of Defense. On your left is General Hector Williams," he said.

"Former Major General Hector Williams of the United States Air Force," the older man cut in. "Retired but acting as a consultant with the Department of Defense. I am Vice Chair of the Defense Appropriations Committee and acting lead Supervisor of the Division of Material Review," he said.

"And on your right is Mister John Doe. What department are you with again Mister Doe?" David asked.

The small man nodded. "I am affiliated with intelligence," he said.

"We know who one another are. Can we get on with it?" Former Major General Hector Williams said impatiently.

David nodded to Victoria. On the wall, the SpaceTech logo was replaced with black text on a white background.

"The situation was first brought to our attention with this email," Victoria said.

Max read the words on the screen.

Dear NASA and the United States Government,

I am a senior engineer of the People's Liberation Army Strategic Support Force. I will not say my name because this message may be interpreted as treasonous against the PLA/PRC. I am contacting you because two of our astronauts are in extreme danger. The PLA lacks the capability to recover them. They will die in space without assistance. I have included a trajectory plot of their spacecraft's orbit with this message. Please send a rescue if you are able.

"This message was sent to NASA's public email address, but was not noticed for several hours. It only came to our attention after NASA received a signal from orbit. The signal was a simple S.O.S. transmitted by tight beam microwave to three ground-based satellite dishes of the NASA network. The trajectory plot from the email attachment matches the source of the microwave signals in orbit," Victoria said.

"How do we know that this is genuine and not an elaborate prank?" General Williams demanded.

"The signals are genuine," said the quiet intelligence man. He pulled out a cell phone, touched a few keys, then nodded to Victoria. "You have a new email," he said.

Victoria clicked through screens on her computer and found the message.

On the projector screen a video played. Two people, an Asian man and woman, floated in the image. They wore blue jumpsuits with red Chinese flags on the left breast. In the background were the sterile white walls and hatches of a space station compartment. Both taikonauts were sweating profusely.

"Hello," the man said, waving at the screen. "My name is Zhao Ming."

"And I'm Lun Li," the woman interjected.

"We did not want to send this message," Ming said.

"But we really do not want to die either," said Li.

"We are the crew of a new top-secret Chinese space station. This is a different station from the public ones that you are aware of. This station is hidden from radar and optical detection with both active and passive stealth systems," Ming said.

"Which are the only systems on the station that are working right now," Li said.

"Right. Everything is broken," Ming said.

"Everything is broken," Li interjected. "We were only barely able to cobble together this transmission by hijacking a microwave array from a weapons system."

"And we were just lucky that this laptop still had battery left," Ming said. "Oh no, it's at eight percent power."

"It's okay," Li said, "We'll get the message out."

"Life support is failing, we have lost thruster control, the solar panels won't deploy, and the radiators are jammed. The temperature is rising,," Ming said to the camera.

"Everything is broken," Li agreed. "So, please, if you get this message, come to this orbit and rescue us. We will send a plot of our trajectory, but if that fails to go through, here is a diagram."

Li held up a whiteboard with a trajectory plot drawn out on it in marker. She held it close to the camera. Altitudes of periapsis and apoapsis, eccentricity, inclination and longitude of the ascending node, and semimajor axis were all clearly written. Max saw that it was a stable, mostly circular orbit.

Then the video ended and the screen went black.

"Exactly when was that message sent?" Max asked. He scrabbled in his pockets, searching around. "Do you have a pen? I need paper."

"The video is thirty-seven minutes old," John Doe said.

Georgy produced a ballpoint pen from his shirt pocket. Victoria blinked for a moment, then reached into a laptop bag and pulled out a creased legal pad. She slid it across the table to Max who began scribbling vigorously.

"This is all nonsense," General Williams barked. "They claim to be Chinese but they do not have Chinese accents. They sound like Americans."

"That does not mean anything," Victoria said. "Plenty of Chinese nationals go to college in America. Or they could have grown up here."

"Chinese spies then," Pilot Edwards scoffed. "The video may be a fake."

"They were definitely in microgravity," Georgy said. "Their movements were right. Their faces were plethoric. They were not hanging on wires. I can tell when somebody is truly in freefall."

"The stealth systems could explain why nothing is showing up on our radar or optical sensors," David said.

"They show up on *our* sensors," John Doe said quietly.

General Williams glared. "So it`s not a hoax then?" he demanded.

"I already said that it isn't," the intelligence man replied.

General Williams grunted. "It might still be a trap, but fine. If this is legit then we want their technology. Appropriations will find you the funds for the mission. Get us that spaceship."

"You mean rescue the crew?" Victoria corrected.

"Whatever," General Williams grunted.

"From this latitude there are two launch windows in the next eighteen hours," Max concluded, tapping his paper.

"We can launch the Hawk with our new crew capsule," David said.

"Your partially untested crew capsule," Georgy scoffed.

"And Robert Edwards will be flying the spaceship," General Williams said.

"Max is our capsule pilot," Victoria said. "He will be in command of the Hawk capsule."

"I don't care who you say is in charge, if you want us to pay for this mission, you'll seat Pilot Robert Edwards at the controls of the rocket ship," General Williams said.

"The crew capsule has duplicate controls," Victoria pointed out.

"They will both go," David offered. "Right Max?"

Max shrugged. "You can send your lackey along. As long as he stays out of my way," he said.

Pilot Edwards glared daggers at Max, but Max was insensible to his hostility. Max was busy calculating the amount of time until a cylindrical compartment approximately thirteen feet in diameter would become unlivable after its life support failed.

"If they have passive oxygen recycling, then heat dissipation would be the first problem," he said to himself.

"Okay," Victoria said, closing her laptop computer. "Let's get started."

CHAPTER TWENTY-FIVE

H ave you fixed the problem of the maneuvering thrusters getting stuck in the on position?" Max asked.

Victoria pursed her lips.

"An awkward silence is not a 'yes.' An awkward silence is closer to a 'no,'" Max said.

"We figured out what the problem was," she offered helpfully. "The thrusters are fine. They were just responding to conflicting signals from the autopilot system."

"But you haven't fixed the autopilot system yet," Max deduced.

"The engineers are going through the code," Victoria said. "But no, we have not fixed the autopilot system yet."

Max and Pilot Robert Edwards were strapped into the rocket and were wearing SpaceTech branded flight suits. Their reclined chairs were one hundred meters high in the Texas sky. The rocket was undergoing its final fueling on the launch pad. Victoria crouched next to Max, giving him final pointers on the new capsule controls.

"These look like Soyuz joysticks," Max said.

Victoria nodded. "On such short notice we decided to copy the system that you were already familiar with. This stick provides rotational control. This one is translational."

Robert jiggled his own set of control sticks.

"They are not activated yet," Victoria admonished. "The

capsule thrusters won't be operational until after the second stage decouples."

"Do you know how to fly one of these things?" Max asked his co-pilot.

"I have flown more than you have. I have flown F-35 fighters. I have flown attack helicopters and stunt planes and experimental hypersonic jets," Robert said.

"But do you know how to fly a spaceship?" Max asked.

"It can't be that hard," Robert said, poking at icons on his touchscreen.

"Are you able you disable his controls?" Max whispered to Victoria.

"Absolutely," Victoria whispered back.

"What are you two whispering about?" Robert demanded, glaring.

"I asked Victoria if she can disable your controls," Max said aloud.

Robert's eyes narrowed. He glared back and forth from Max to Victoria.

"I should get going. It is about time to launch," Victoria said.

Victoria crawled backwards, then clambered out the hatch. The airtight door pivoted closed behind her. Air hissed and the rubber seals compressed. Max and Robert were alone in the spacecraft.

"Hello, Max," Georgy's voice came the radio.

"Mister Ardis, I expect that you will not let us down," General Williams' basso rumble sounded.

"Daddy?" Max said.

There was silence on the line. Max chuckled.

"Say that again Ardis?" General Williams demanded.

"We are good to go General," Robert said. "Max seems to believe that this is an appropriate time for humor."

"I am not a man to disrespect, Mister Ardis," General Williams warned.

"And I am not a man to be intimidated," Max retorted. "Get off the radio if you have nothing useful to say. Put Georgy back on."

"I will not be spoken to like this by a civilian," General

Williams shouted. "I demand that..." his voice was cut off suddenly.

"We are T-minus ten minutes to launch," came Victoria's soothing voice.

"General Billy?" Max asked experimentally.

"Hi, Max," Georgy's voice answered. "David is taking the General on a brief tour around the command center."

"Darn, I was really enjoying our chat," Max said.

"I would beg you not to antagonize him, but I think I'll save my breath," Georgy said.

"If he plays nice, I'll play nice," Max said.

"Mmm," Georgy grunted skeptically.

"Why do you hate the military, Max?" Robert asked.

"I don't hate the military. I do not like bossy people, and General Willy sounds like he wears bossy pants to bed. I also hate telemarketers, anti-vaxxers, and fishers of dolphin-unsafe tuna," Max said.

"I hate telemarketers too," Robert agreed.

The rocket vibrated beneath them as the fueling process completed. The cabin vents blew cool air across Max's face. The Hawk capsule lacked an aerodynamic fairing, so the windows were uncovered. Outside of the rightmost window the Gulf of Mexico shimmered blue in the sun. A flight of birds passed lazily a few hundred meters away, drifting on the warm ocean breeze.

"T-minus five minutes," Victoria's voice said.

"Is it hot in here? I'm sweating," Robert said, wiping his face.

"It's normal to be nervous," Max said.

"I'm not nervous," Robert insisted.

"It helps to stay focused on the procedures. The timing of all the launch events is on the left of your screen," Max said, pointing.

"Okay," Robert said, looking at the screen.

"I also like to review the math. At the base of this rocket are five engines. When they ignite, they will produce 6 meganewtons of thrust. The vehicle has a thrust to weight ratio of 1.4. At liftoff, the G force will be low, but each engine consumes 200 kilograms of propellant per second. As the rocket gets lighter, the thrust remains the same and therefore acceleration increases. Acceleration for the first stage will build up to about 3G's before the main engine cuts off. We will be moving at Mach 10 when the second stage lights," Max said.

"These numbers help keep you calm?" Robert asked.

"They help to keep me present. The turbines spin at 20,000 revolutions per minute. Fuel and oxidizer react in the combustion chamber at 3,000 degrees and 100 atmospheres of pressure before blasting out the rocket nozzle at 2,500 meters per second. It is all made of physics and chemistry and mathematics and we ride the science to space so we can moon the moon and show the universe that nothing can hold us back. That is the whole reason that human beings exist. I am scared every time, but also never more alive," Max said.

Robert gave a weak smile. He turned away. "Is that smoke?" he asked, pointing out the window. White plumes drifted up from below.

"That's boil-off from the cryogenic liquid oxygen. It warms up and has to be vented to keep from over-pressuring the tanks. The extremely cold gas causes water vapor to condense out of the atmosphere and produces those white clouds," Max said. "It is normal. Have you ever watched a rocket launch before?"

"I've seen hundreds of missile launches," Robert said defensively. "And they've never vented gas before launch."

"Military missiles use solid propellants. Liquid rockets are a little different. Just relax. Georgy and I have done this many times," Max said.

Robert's jumpiness was starting to affect Max's composure. He closed his eyes and allowed his mind to clear. He pictured the rocket, a living thing, quietly breathing oxygen as it waited. He allowed his mind to zoom out, looking down at the rocket from above. He saw the coast of Texas, sandy barrier islands and blue-green bays stretching north and south. He pictured the rocket's flight, blasting upward into a cloudless sky over a brilliant ocean. A trail of water vapor would trace the rocket's path, connecting the concrete of the launch pad to black, limitless space above.

"T-minus two minutes," Victoria said.

"All green here," Georgy's voice came over the radio.

Max breathed out slowly, allowing his tension to drain away.

"We are ready," Max said.

"Ready," Robert agreed.

Georgy the Poet spoke:

"In rocket's blast I thawed my hands,
I turned my face Eastward again.
The night was long - It chilled my heart,
But in the flames, I smelled the dawn."

"Thank you, Georgy," Max said, smiling. He had nearly forgotten their tradition.

"You're welcome, Max," Georgy said.

"Vehicle switched to internal power," Victoria said.

Max closed the visor of his helmet. The SpaceTech flight suit was modern and slim. The visor was closer to his face than the Soviet design that he was used to, but stayed fog free. He checked that his gloves were properly fastened to the sleeves of the suit.

"T-minus one minute," Victoria said.

Max double checked all his readouts. The spacecraft was running on battery power now. All systems were nominal.

"The General is back in the command center," Georgy said with a sigh.

"T-minus thirty seconds," Victoria said.

Just like for a Soyuz launch, massive water hoses began spraying hundreds of gallons of water below the rocket to keep the acoustic blast of the engines from ripping the rocket apart.

"Engine start," Georgy said.

The Hawk was quieter than the Soyuz, but the sound of the rocket turbines was familiar. It started as a low rumble.

"T-minus ten," Victoria said.

The rocket began to shudder and vibrate, straining upward against its launch clamps, struggling to escape its shackles to the

Earth.

"Nine."

"Eight."

"Seven."

The sound of the turbines was rising in pitch. It rose and rose and rose from a hum then to a whine then to a shriek at the very edge of human hearing.

"Six."

"Five."

"Four."

Steam rose in massive clouds as heat energy from liberated chemical bonds boiled the cold water from the sprayers below.

"Three."

Thrust reached one hundred percent.

"Two."

Max glanced at Robert. The Air Force Pilot's eyes were closed. His lips were moving. Max realized that he was praying.

"One."

Max looked out the window and found himself grinning.

"Liftoff."

The launch clamps released, and the rocket shot into the air.

"Launch pad clear. Roll for azimuth alignment," Victoria said.

The horizon spun until Max's right hand window was looking north along the coastline. A pod of dolphins porpoised in the shallow bay below.

"Beginning gravity turn," Victoria said.

The rocket began to pitch over, nosing toward the horizon as its altitude and velocity increased. The G force steadily rose.

"Something is wrong," Robert said.

CHAPTER TWENTY-SIX

"Something is wrong," Robert repeated, more urgently this time. His eyes were wide as he mashed icons on his control panel.

Max's heart skipped a beat. His eyes flew over his display. All his readouts looked normal.

"What, what's wrong?" Max asked.

General Williams' loud voice came over the radio, "Soldier, report. What is happening?"

"I don't see anything wrong," Max answered, flipping through status screens.

"Something is wrong," Robert shouted. He was clawing at the visor of his helmet. Finally, he opened it. He was breathing fast.

"Georgy, give me a systems update," Max demanded.

"Something is wrong!" Robert screamed.

"My board is green, Max," Georgy said over the radio. "All systems look nominal."

"We need a full systems diagnostic," General Williams said. "Every team sound off. Prepare to abort launch."

"Abort! Abort!" Robert howled. He pounded on his console. He ripped one of his gloves off and smashed his finger into various icons on his touchscreen. He was fully panicking.

"Victoria, kill Robert's controls," Max said.

"Roger, Max. Robert's control panel is disabled," Victoria said.

"I am in command here. I demand a full and complete report.

Now!" General Williams demanded.

"Georgy, get General Idiot off the radio. Victoria, do you see any anomalies that would warrant an abort?" Max asked.

"Negative, Max I am seeing…" Victoria began.

"Mister Ardis, I order you to relinquish control to Pilot Edwards immediately," General Williams shouted, cutting Victoria off.

"Georgy, get the General off the radio!" Max shouted.

"I demand…" the General replied. His voice was abruptly cut off.

"The General's headset has been disabled," Georgy said.

"Thank you, Georgy. Victoria, what were you saying?" Max asked.

"Abort. Somebody, please," Robert pleaded.

"Shut up Robert!" Max yelled. "Victoria?"

"All systems are nominal. Max Q in ten seconds," Victoria said.

The whine of the turbines decreased as the rocket throttled down to pass through the point of maximum aerodynamic pressure. Max checked every system twice over. All five first stage engines were operating perfectly. The guidance system was nominal. Integrity sensors in the capsule and along the rocket fuselage were all reporting normal. Temperature and pressure sensors showed good values. Pressure in the fuel tanks and lines were exactly as expected. The capsule was airtight and life support looked good. Electrical voltage and battery power were at one hundred percent of expected.

The seconds went by and nothing untoward happened. The rocket passed through max Q and began to accelerate rapidly once again. The G-forces increased, and the rocket continued along its expected trajectory.

"Nothing is wrong. All systems are green. We are continuing with the mission," Max said.

"Roger that," Victoria said.

"Roger, Max," said Georgy.

Max turned to look at Robert. The pilot had stopped smashing his console and was sitting back in his seat. He whimpered slightly when he met Max's eyes.

"What did you see?" Max demanded. "Why did you say that something was wrong?"

Robert gulped hard. He pointed a trembling, hand toward the window.

"The rocket is leaning over," he said. "Can't you see that we're going to fall?"

Max glanced at the tilted horizon outside the window and then looked back at Robert's bloodless face.

"Of course we are leaning. We're pitching over for the gravity turn," Max said.

Robert's uncomprehending face gazed back blankly.

Max realized why Robert had panicked. Unfamiliar with orbital mechanics, he had expected the rocket to go straight "up" to space. When he had seen the rocket nosing down toward the horizon, he must have concluded that the rocket was going off course. Max shook his head in exasperation.

"From now on, just sit back and let me handle things, okay?" Max said.

Robert said nothing. Max returned his attention to his panel. "If I survive this," he promised himself, "I am never flying with a co-pilot again."

All this time, the G-forces had been steadily increasing, Max's arms were three times heavier than normal. His eyes were being gradually, but insistently, shoved into his skull.

"Approaching main engine cut off," Victoria said over the radio.

"How are things going up there, Max?" Georgy asked.

"All peachy," Max said. "You can tell David that his rocket is a smooth ride, in case he were ever thinking of bringing his mom along for a trip."

"I'm sure he will be glad to hear it," Georgy said.

"MECO in 5 seconds," Victoria said.

Max braced himself. The acceleration ceased. The elastic rebound of seat and cushion and human tissues threw Max forward against his restraints. Engine noise and rumble ceased.

They were in freefall, weightless, silently coasting through the upper atmosphere.

"Oh, God," Robert said sickly. His head had whipped forward when the engines had cut off. Now he looked positively green.

"It is too early in the flight to be sick," Max told him. "If you vomit, try and do it in the collar of your suit. Put your glove back on and close your visor. This whole rocket is still an experimental system. You never know when the capsule could lose pressure."

Reluctantly, Robert complied.

Max waited for the first stage to decouple. It was taking a long time. Finally, he heard it, a muffled grinding sound, like a large metal door sliding open. The Hawk used a hydraulic coupling system rather than explosive bolts like the Soyuz. Max was counting the seconds. Half a minute later, the second stage rumbled to life and acceleration returned.

"The delay between MECO and second stage ignition is longer than it needs to be. You probably lose between 100 and 150 meters per second of potential delta-v while the second stage is in free fall," Max commented.

"Roger that, Max. We will take note," Victoria said.

Acceleration, velocity, and altitude increased for the next seven minutes. When the second stage engine cut off, Max and Robert were in a stable low earth orbit, somewhat elliptical, with an inclination of 25 degrees and an altitude at apogee of 207 kilometers. They were traveling at 7,741 m/s.

"Before detaching the second stage, tell me how much propellant is still in the tanks," Max said.

"483 kilograms," Victoria said.

Max calculated that 483kg represented about 0.5% of the initial propellant mass of the second stage.

"That's too much," Max said. "If that propellant were moved instead to the Hawk's service module it could increase working delta-v by 30%." Such were the realities of rocket science that an inefficiency as small as 0.5% could have dramatic consequences for rocket performance.

"This is why you need Max you fly your rockets," Georgy

chuckled.

"Thank you, Max," Victoria said. "We will address that on subsequent designs. Decoupling stage two now."

With another grinding of hydraulic clamps, the second stage detached, freeing the Hawk capsule and its service module from the second stage of the rocket.

"The next maneuver is a circularization burn in twelve minutes," Georgy said.

"I see it," Max said. The large touchscreens displayed large and colorful graphics. The Earth was a blue-green orb. The spacecraft was a white icon on a black background. The projected orbit was a red dotted line. Max trusted none of it. He removed his gloves, opened his visor, and reached for his pen and paper.

The sound of retching made Max pause his scribbling. Robert was being sick. His helmet was off, and his apologetic eyes were watering. He had both hands, one gloved, one ungloved, pressed tightly over his mouth.

"Ooh boy. Hold on just one second," Max told him.

Max unstrapped himself. He pushed from his console and turned to the storage bags beneath his seat. In the second pocket he found what he was looking for. He took out a plastic vomit bag and passed it to Robert. The sick pilot accepted the bag gratefully.

"Nice job keeping it all in the bag," Max commended after a moment. "Take this," Max produced an antiemetic from the same storage pouch. "Put the pill in your mouth. Don't swallow, let it dissolve. It might make you feel a little sleepy, but it will help the nausea."

Robert did so, then gave Max a rueful grin. "Thank you," he said.

"Don't mention it. And we're in space now. We should try and work together if we can," Max said.

Robert nodded. "I'll do my best to help," he said. He looked out the window at Earth below. "It's beautiful," he said.

Max nodded. "It really is," he agreed.

Blue ocean and white clouds filled the view. They were still quite low, in space terms, and the horizon was a gentle curve. Max recognized the green shore on the left as the coast of Florida, receding quickly. Caribbean islands drifted by as the spacecraft raced eastward. Soon they would be over the deep ocean, crossing the equator somewhere above the Atlantic Ocean.

Max drifted back to his console, retrieving his pen and paper and pocket calculator. He resumed his work double checking their trajectory.

"What are you doing?" Robert asked.

"Math," Max answered. He showed Robert his paper and without stopping his busy calculations described the basics of orbital mechanics. He showed him how he could plot their trajectory including apoapsis, periapsis, period, eccentricity, and semimajor and semiminor axes.

"With just a bit more data, including inclination, longitude of the ascending node, and accounting for the Earth's rotation you can figure out exactly when you will be over any given point on the Earth's surface. It is a small step from that to plot maneuvers by imparting a change in velocity along a given vector to alter your orbit," Max explained.

"Isn't all of that taken care of by the computer?" Robert asked, pointing at his screen.

Max shrugged. "I like to double check."

"It all seems very complicated," Robert said.

"The math is simple. What is hard is getting your head around the concepts. Things seem illogical at first. Like how if you want to increase your altitude you don't burn radially outward, you burn prograde. Prograde and retrograde burns are often the most efficient way to alter your orbit. Efficiency is vital. Fuel is always limited," Max said.

Robert nodded but Max doubted that he understood. Max finished his calculations and confirmed that the circularization burn that the computer suggested made sense on paper. After that, they would alter their inclination to match the inclination of their target orbit. Then there would be the two burns of a Hohmann transfer needed to increase altitude and reach the rendezvous. Max gazed at the white icon of the Chinese space station on his screen.

"And then the mission truly begins," Max said.

CHAPTER TWENTY-SEVEN

"Burn in thirty seconds," Georgy said.

Max's hands hovered over his controls.

"Ten seconds," Georgy said.

The circularization burn was a simple maneuver, a mere few seconds of thrust prograde at apogee to raise their perigee.

"I'm going to try enabling the autopilot," Max said. With five seconds still to go, Max switched the system on.

The sound of thrusters filled the cabin, but he felt no acceleration. Max watched the propellant level tick down. The ship vibrated, but their heading and velocity remained unchanged.

"That is a no-go on the autopilot. Looks like the same problem as the last flight. I am switching to manual control," Max said.

Max switched off the malfunctioning autopilot system. The noise and vibration stopped. He ensured that the ship was oriented correctly, then he selectively ignited two small thrusters. There was a gentle forward acceleration which Max timed with a stopwatch. After the appropriate amount of time, he shut off the thrusters. Then, he checked and rechecked his trajectory.

"Looks good. Circularization burn completed," Max said, satisfied.

"Inclination burn at the ascending node in twenty-two minutes," Georgy responded.

"Everything is happening so fast," Robert said, blinking.

"Are you feeling any better?" Max asked.

Robert nodded. "I took another one of those nausea pills. I'm not sick anymore."

"Good. Just relax. You can unstrap from your chair if you want," Max said.

Robert unclipped himself and drifted out of his seat. He clung to his touchscreen's mount with both hands to steady himself.

"Moving around in zero G is a little tricky but you'll get used to it. There's no up or down anymore. Be patient and take your time. See those handholds above your head? See if you can pull yourself over to the window. There will be a sunrise soon," Max said.

Robert tentatively moved toward the window. He looked groggy but Max was glad that there seemed to be reduced risk of vomiting in the cabin. Max found a peanut butter and tortilla sandwich in a pouch and ate it while he thought about their mission. He replayed the distress call in his mind. The Chinese astronauts had said that "everything" was broken.

The US Department of Defense primarily wanted to recover the Chinese technology. A space station with stealth technology would be useful. The US did not have anything like that. But Max did not care about the technology or the Chinese space station. The Hawk capsule had two extra seats. Max planned to transfer the two Chinese astronauts over to the Hawk and return to Earth. The mission would be as simple as that.

Max finished his sandwich and drifted for a while. The land below was in darkness but splattered across the nighttime world was the yellow incandescence of humanity. City lights drifted, glowing in the shadow of the spinning Earth. Dawn rose, brilliant, over a blue ocean. The Sun blazed nuclear firelight into the quiet cabin.

"We will perform a short maneuver soon," Max said to Robert. The dazed pilot was gazing out the window, transfixed by his first sunrise in space. "You can strap in if you want, but the acceleration will be less than half a G."

Robert nodded and Max went to the controls. He had to

reorient the spacecraft to point "northward." They would burn parallel to the surface of the Earth but ninety degrees from their direction of travel. Their launch site in Texas was twenty five degrees north of the equator, but the Chinese space program operated from a launch site in the Gobi desert at forty degrees north latitude. Spacecraft launching due east orbited in an inclination equal to the number of degrees from the equator they started from. For Max to rendezvous with the stranded Chinese, he would have to match that orbit.

There was a soft hissing when the reaction control system thrusters engaged. Max used his control stick to swing the spacecraft's nose to the correct heading.

"Burning," Max said. He engaged the main engine on the service module. Max timed the burn with a stopwatch, then he cut off the engine. He checked and rechecked their trajectory.

"Looks good," he said.

"NASA has been contacted by the Chinese government," Georgy's voice came over the radio.

"Oh? Have the Chinese come out asking for help?" Max asked.

"Not exactly. Doctor Thompson reports that she got a call from one of the higher-ups in the Chinese space program. They said that if the United States was willing to break its policy of not working with the Chinese, they would be willing to discuss a mutually beneficial partnership," Georgy said.

"That's better than expected," Max said. "Any acknowledgement that they left two people stranded in space?"

"Nothing like that," Georgy said. "Apparently they made no direct reference to the current situation at all."

"Thanks Georgy. Let me know if they say anything useful," Max said.

"You got it," Georgy said.

The Hohmann transfer that Georgy plotted for him optimized time over fuel efficiency. The Hawk spacecraft had larger fuel tanks and used a higher energy propellant than the Soyuz. They would not be short on fuel. In fifteen minutes they would perform a prograde burn that would put his ship on a collision course with their target. The second burn, sixty-one minutes from now, would be to decelerate, placing the vessels side by side and motionless relative to one another.

Robert spoke little, gazing out the windows for a while, then returning to his console. Max wondered how much simulator training the pilot had gotten before the flight. Normally astronauts were extensively trained. They knew their spacecraft inside and out. Max was surprised by Robert's lack of competence, but now that the initial shock had passed, Robert was looking more confident. He seemed to be familiar with the systems displayed on the screen. He produced an electronic tablet and began referencing items on its display, making notes with a stylus as he did.

Both orbit maneuvers went as planned, but after the deceleration burn no Chinese space station appeared on the Hawk's radar. Max turned on the forward-facing docking camera. Space appeared to be empty.

"There is nothing on radar, Georgy," Max said into the radio. "Are we sure that we're in the right place?"

"The CIA spook says 'yes.' The stealth systems of the station are hiding it from your sensors. I am sending you the CIA's latest telemetry on the target," Georgy said.

Max received the beamed message. According to this data, the station should be 470 meters away, drifting toward them at about 0.5 meters per second. Max took the controls and rotated the Hawk to look out the window where the Chinese station should be.

There was nothing there. The illuminated Earth was directly below them. The midday sun was above. In between was nothing but stars. There was no glint of sunshine on metal, nothing that would indicate the presence of a station.

"Is it invisible?" Max asked.

"It could be painted black," Robert offered. "That would make it harder to detect optically. Some paints absorb radar too, like we use on stealth airplanes."

"If it's painted black then we need something bright in the

background to see it contrasted against," Max said.

Max took the controls. He activated the maneuvering thrusters. He made small adjustments, closing the distance while circling the expected target location. Soon he was "above" where the station was supposed to be. He turned the spaceship to look out the window.

And there it was. The station was a small black dot, dark against a bright background of white clouds below.

"I see it. Closing the distance," Max said.

Max reoriented toward the target and accelerated forward. He watched the dot grow in the forward-facing docking camera. The station was a cylinder, painted jet black, with unrecognizable protrusions on its surface. Max recognized a standard docking port on one side. The entire station was roughly equivalent in size to a single module of the ISS.

"Oh, no," Max said.

"What?" Robert asked.

"What's wrong?" Georgy asked.

"It's spinning," Max said.

The black-painted space station was tumbling along its long axis. Max pulled out his stopwatch. He timed it. The station completed a full rotation in a little over a minute. Max would have no way to dock the Hawk with the station. Max brought his spacecraft to a halt.

"That's not good," Georgy said.

"No," Max agreed.

The Hawk was equipped with a two-way radio set. He set the radio to transmit on a standard suite of maritime and aeronautical frequencies, including the international distress frequency. If the Chinese astronauts had a radio aboard, they should hear him broadcast.

"Chinese space station, this is Max. Can you hear me?" he said.

There was no response. Max turned the ship again so he could look out his window.

The station was about fifty meters away. It was dark. There were windows on its surface, but no light shone through them.

Communication antennae were retracted. No solar panels were deployed.

"No signs of life," Max said.

Max dug under his seat. He found a flashlight and pressed it against the glass. He played the light on the station, flashing it across the two windows that he could see. If there was anybody alive over there, he wanted to get their attention.

"Maybe we are too late?" Robert suggested.

From one of the station's windows a flashlight shone back. It moved and flickered in the dark.

"There is somebody alive over there," Max said. "But it must be hot in that tin can." The station was an all-black container with no power. There were no obvious heat radiators that he could see.

Max had done some calculations on survivability in an unpowered module in space. But he had assumed that the station would be painted white, or silver, some other sensible color. He had not calculated how fast a craft might heat up if it were painted pitch black, the worst possible color.

"Put your helmet on," Max said. "I'm going outside."

CHAPTER TWENTY-EIGHT

ax slid out of his flight suit and began donning an EVA suit. This was not the famous Soviet Orlan, but a new suit of SpaceTech's design: a slimmer, modernized version of the old NASA EVA suit. He strapped an oxygen mask on his face and breathed from an onboard supply of pure oxygen. By pre-breathing oxygen, he would lower his blood nitrogen level and reduce his chance of getting decompression sickness. This space suit operated at less than 1/3 of an atmosphere of pressure.

Removing his oxygen mask as infrequently as possible, he put on a layer of thermal, water-cooled underwear. He then put on the lower half of the suit, then the upper. Robert helped him with the connection between the two.

"Shouldn't you pre-breathe oxygen for forty-five minutes?" Robert asked. "That's what I was told."

"In a perfect world, I would pre-breathe for four hours," Max answered, "But we don't have time for that. I need to get over there. They must be cooking in that black coffin."

"So you're risking your life for them?" Robert asked.

Max grinned. "We both are. This isn't a desk job for you either."

Max sealed his helmet. His space suit was a tiny spaceship, self-contained for power and life support. The ventilation fans whirred to life, blowing cool air down his neck. Cool water pulsed through the thermal garment across his legs and torso.

"Ready for EVA," Max said into his headset.

"Roger, Max," Georgy said, his voice coming through the speakers in the helmet.

There was no airlock on the Hawk. The whole spacecraft would need to be depressurized in order for Max to exit. Robert sealed his pressure suit and sat at his console. He initiated an air purge from the cabin. Soon the atmosphere in the capsule was replaced by vacuum. Max opened the outer hatch and looked out into space.

The space station looked dark and foreboding. Max unclipped his tether and braced himself against the hatch.

"You're taking off your tether?" Robert asked over the radio.

"The station is spinning. A tether between the two would be a bad idea. We would wrap up like a ball of yarn," Max said.

"Okay," Robert said. "Remember to use your SAFER unit if you need it."

The Simplified Aid For EVA Rescue (SAFER) was a small jetpack built into a central belt on Max's suit. It only provided a few seconds of cold gas thrust, but it could keep Max from floating off into space in a pinch. Max preferred the Orlan, which had a more powerful life support system, but the emergency jetpack of this new spacesuit was nice.

"Close up and repressurize when I'm clear," Max instructed. Robert's simple pressure suit had ballooned when the interior pressure of the cabin was reduced to vacuum, which made extended work or delicate procedures difficult. "I might need you to push some buttons," Max said.

Max pushed off from the Hawk, aiming for one of the Chinese station's two hatches. A flashlight shone from one of the windows near the hatch, tracking him as he came. Max hit the hatch with both hands. He hooked his arm around a handhold and looked around. The hatch looked like it was built into a standard docking port. The Chinese must have decided to use the international shared design. The Hawk should be able to dock here if he can get the station to stop spinning. He wondered if there was an airlock, like on the ISS, or if opening the hatch would depressurize the interior of the station. There was a keypad nearby with Chinese characters. He did not touch any of the buttons.

Max knocked on the hatch. An answering knock came back. He touched his helmet to the bulkhead.

"Hey, can you hear me in there?" he asked.

"Yes. We hear you," replied a female voice. The vibrations of their voices were transmitted through the hard metal of the space station's hull.

"Can you open the door? Is there an airlock?" Max asked.

"There is an airlock, but we cannot open it," the voice answered.

"Why not?" Max asked.

"We need power to run the air pumps for the airlock and the power is out," the voice answered.

"How do I turn the power on?" Max asked.

"Check the solar panels. They won't deploy. They must be stuck," the voice answered.

Max could hear the desperation in the taikonaut's voice. She was trapped, helpless, in a powerless spacecraft. Rescue was mere inches away and they were unable to reach it.

"Don't worry. I'll get you out of there," Max promised. He lifted his helmet from the bulkhead.

"Solar panels," Max muttered to himself. He had a vague idea of where they should be. He pushed himself along the hull.

The rotation of the station was not enough throw him away from the station. It was, however, disorienting. Moving along the axis of rotation was not so bad, but the instant he reached for a handhold that was away from that axis, it seemed like the handhold twisted away from him.

"Alright then," Max muttered. He took the end of the coiled tether from his belt and clipped it to a nearby structural support.

Max's suit radio crackled. "I hear you, General," Robert said.

"What?" Max asked.

"Nothing, Max," Robert said. The radio went silent.

"What was that?" Max asked.

"What was what, Max?" Georgy asked.

"Is the General talking to Robert?" Max asked

"I'm not sure. I don't see General Williams anywhere. He must have left the control center," Georgy answered. "How is it going up there?"

"Not great. The taikonauts are trapped in a jet-black space station without power. It must be boiling hot in there," Max answered.

"That's not good," Georgy answered.

"No. I've got to get them out of there. But first I've got to turn the power back on to get the doors open," Max said.

Max found a way to solve his mobility problem. By stretching his space line between two handholds, he created tension that he could use to steady himself. With one hand on the station and the other paying out the line, he could keep himself oriented.

Max inched along the station's hull. Luckily, the station was dotted with protrusions to grab onto. He steadied himself against a LIDAR array, then pushed off, drifting to a microwave dish, then, passing his line between the two, drifted to a stop at a bank of missiles.

"I bet the military boys would be very interested in these," Max said. There were four missile banks, evenly spaced at 90-degree intervals around the cylindrical hull of the station. Each missile bank contained six missiles. Each missile was about two meters long and eight centimeters in diameter. Their nosecones were transparent, and Max could see lenses inside.

"And that must be a solar panel," Max said. He spotted the distinctive thin supporting rods, closely hugging a broad, flat section of the hull.

Max judged the distance for his next push, raising an arm to steady himself against one of the missile mounts. When he did, he noticed that his glove was covered in black goop.

"Did I touch some grease?" Max asked. He looked down. Any part of his suit that touched the station was covered in black. He touched a patch of the dark substance on his left leg. It was the consistency of a thick glue. With a sinking feeling, Max realized that he was smeared in the station's black paint.

"That can't be good," Max said. He gazed about the hull. In places where the paint was in direct sunlight it was glossy and liquid. In places where it was in shadow the paint it was matte and powdery.

"Georgy, the black paint that they used on this station is really messy and sticky," Max said.

"Maybe it jammed up the deployment mechanism for the solar panels?" Georgy responded.

"My thoughts exactly," Max said. He pushed away from the missile launchers, trailing his tether behind him. He snagged the protruding horizontal of the solar panel and swung himself around.

Black goop was clogged into the space between the panel's horizontal and the bulkhead. Max thrust a gloved finger into the space and tried to dig the goo out. It was thin and sticky at first, but then the station rotated away from the sunlight. In shadow, the temperature plummeted. The paint thickened, hardening beneath Max's fingers until he could no longer scoop it out.

Experimentally, he tugged on the horizontal. No dice. The panel was stuck fast. He waited. One minute later the sun shone again. The paint thinned. He pulled, but the panel remained stuck. Max scooped as much paint out as he could. He went into shadow again and he had to wait. He had removed just a hands-breadths of wet paint from the meter-long panel.

Max felt vibrations through the hull. He realized that somebody was pounding on the wall inside the station. He put his helmet against the bulkhead.

"American!" he heard the female voice say. "American!" it demanded.

"Yes," Max answered. "I can hear you."

"There are less than ten minutes of daylight left and we are low on oxygen," the voice said. "Hurry!"

Max looked up. They were orbiting fast toward a dark terminator. His heart skipped a beat.

CHAPTER TWENTY-NINE

The solar panels would not generate any electricity in the Earth's shadow. If Max failed to deploy the panels soon, it would be forty-five minutes until the sun shone again. He would be unable to restore the power and open the door; unable to help the trapped, dying taikonauts inside.

Trying to dig out the solar panels from the cloying muck was too slow. Max tucked into a ball and braced both feet against the station. He shoved the fingers of one glove into the space he had already cleared. He thrust the other into the goop nearby, pushing through the muck to as best he could to get purchase on the brace.

It was dangerous to exert oneself too hard on a spacewalk. Exhaustion could be fatal. Generating too much carbon dioxide could overload the space suit's life support system. But Max was watching the darkness approach. He pulled with all his might.

The solar panel would not budge. He heaved again, straining his back, his vision narrowing.

Suddenly the resistance was gone. His hands had slipped. He was floating away into space. He grabbed the tether to reorient himself. It was also covered in the black goo. He pulled himself back toward the hull, but the spinning of the station was causing him to drift sideways.

Max engaged the emergency jetpack and flew back to where he had been working. The solar panel was in shadow again and the paint had hardened. Max centered himself, planted his feet, found his grip on the solar panel, and waited.

The station rotated and the sunlight shone down. Max watched the sticky black paint turn from matte and solid to glossy and liquid. He took a deep breath and pulled on the panel. He grunted with the strain, feeling his glove begin to slip.

Finally, the panel moved. It broke free of the black gunk. Max could feel the resistance of the unpowered electric motors as he lifted it higher. The photovoltaic array emerged, unfolding as it extended from the bulkhead.

Max lifted as high as he could, expanding the panels to his full standing height. Bright sunlight shone on the black photovoltaic cells.

The space station gave a lurch and Max was thrown into space. Max was spinning, launched tangentially from the surface of the hull. He stopped his spin with the emergency maneuvering unit. Using judicious puffs of gas to reorient himself.

The space station was no longer tumbling. It had stabilized itself and sat motionless relative to the Hawk spacecraft, which floated nearby. Lights were coming on across the station's hull. A flashlight winked from one of the station's uncovered windows.

"The gyroscopes activated. Power must be restored," Max breathed. He flew back to the station's hatch, re-coiling and stowing his tether along the way. He knocked on the door, touching the bulkhead with his helmet.

"You did it!" the voice inside exclaimed. "The power is online."

"Can you open the door?" Max asked.

"Yes. Cycling the airlock now. Wait a moment," the voice answered.

Max felt the vibrations through the hull as the air pumps ran. Soon there was silence again. Max pulled on the hatch and the round door swung open.

Inside was a small airlock. The inside door had a small round window set in its center. An Asian woman's face filled that window. Max recognized her as Lun Li, the taikonaut from the distress call. She looked anxious and gestured for Max to enter the station.

Max floated in and closed the outer door behind him. There was a hissing noise as the airlock repressurized. The interior door opened.

A wave of moist air entered the airlock. Max's helmet fogged as water condensed on the outside of it. He removed the helmet and was shocked by the heat inside the station.

"Thank goodness you made it," the Chinese taikonaut said. Her face was a picture of exhaustion and relief. "We thought that we were going to die here." Her clothes were soaked with sweat.

Max took in his surroundings. The station's interior was similar to the compartments of the ISS. Removable white panels covered the walls. A laptop computer floated in a corner. Chinese characters ran across lit touchscreens. There was a man floating nearby, stripped to his underwear. It was Zhao Ming. His eyes were closed.

"Is he okay?" Max asked.

Li shook her head. "He has heat stroke. We need to cool him down," she said. She floated over and dabbed water from a pouch on his face and neck.

"How hot is it in here?" Max asked. Even just breathing was tiring in this hot air. He was grateful for the cooling garment within his space suit.

"Sixty one degrees Celsius," Li answered, glancing at a nearby instrument. "And increasing. The vents are blowing, but they are only blowing hot air. Can we get him over to your ship?"

Max went to the nearest vent. It was emitting a constant blast of hot, dry air.

"The life support system is on, but it's failing to throw off the heat. Are there radiators on the hull?" Max asked.

Li nodded. "There are, but they will not deploy," he said.

"They're probably just as gunked up as the solar panels," Max said, shaking his head. "You're right. We need to abandon this ship. Do you have EVA suits?" he asked.

"No," Li answered. "We were not expected to do any spacewalking during this mission."

"That's fine. We can just dock my ship and get the heck out of here," Max said. He found his floating helmet and put it on.

"Robert," Max said into his helmet radio. "Depressurize the Hawk. I'm headed back over."

"What is the plan?" Robert asked.

"We need to dock and transfer over two Chinese taikonauts. One has heatstroke and the other is not far off," he said.

"You don't need to EVA for that. I can dock the Hawk to the station," Robert answered.

"You can?" Max asked.

"Of course I can," Robert said, sounding insulted. "I did the simulator training."

"But the autopilot is not working. The docking needs to be done manually. Don't turn the autopilot on. It will just waste fuel," Max said.

"I did the simulator training for docking," Robert said again. "You think that I'm an idiot, but I'm not."

"I never said out loud that I think you're an idiot," Max retorted. He looked out the window nearest the docking port.

The Hawk was visible, framed in the setting sun, floating between the station and the distant horizon. Jets of gas emitted from the Hawk's RCS thrusters.

"Orienting docking ports," Robert said.

Max watched the Hawk turn, slightly overshoot, then correct. The nose of the spacecraft hunted around before centering.

"Beginning approach," Robert said.

The maneuvering thrusters gave a brief burst of gas. The Hawk drifted closer.

"Georgy, are you monitoring this?" Max asked.

"Yes, Max," Georgy answered over the radio. "Closing speed is 0.18 meters per second. Docking camera feed shows that the alignment is good."

"Robert, don't mess this up. Even a small alignment error could be bad. A collision can result in a catastrophic hull breach," Max said.

"I know that," Robert answered, sounding irritated.

"Just watch your docking camera. There are alignment targets on the docking port," Max said.

"I know," Robert said.

"If the target drifts, correct with the translational controls on the left control stick," Max said.

"I know, Max," Robert shouted. "Shut up and let me do this!"

Max shut up. He watched the Hawk drift closer. It was fifty meters away and approaching slowly. It would take almost five minutes to reach the station at its current speed.

Ming groaned. Max turned to look at the ailing taikonaut. His eyes were still closed but he was grimacing now. He pulled away from Li who was trying to hold a wet cloth to his forehead. The taikonaut opened his eyes, uncomprehending. Max touched his arm. His pulse was thready. His skin was dry and pale.

"We need to cool him down. Help me out of this spacesuit," Max said.

Li helped Max remove the top section, then wriggle out of the pants. He removed the cooling undergarment, instantly sweating in the sauna heat of the overcooked station. Together he and Li slid the thermal pants over Ming's legs. Ming gazed around but did not resist. Max and Li put the upper and lower parts of the space suit together around him and engaged the onboard power supply. The small water pump hummed, and the cooling fans whirred. Ming closed his eyes.

Li and Max looked at one another. Max could tell that she was near to physical collapse herself. Every breath in this sauna was exhausting.

"It's going to be okay. We are going to get you home," Max promised. He retrieved his radio headset, fitting it on an elastic cap that he wore beneath the helmet.

"Home?" Li asked. "We are traitors to China now. We can't go home."

With a thud the Hawk made contact with the station.

"I have docked with the station. I have a good connection," Robert said into the radio.

"Great. Open the door and get us out of here," Max responded.

Nothing happened.

"Can you hear me Robert? Is there a problem with the door?" Max asked.

"Order received," Robert said.

"Yes, open the door," Max said.

"Understood," Robert said. "Understood. Coordinates received."

"Robert, who are you talking to?" Max asked with a sinking feeling.

Robert did not respond. The Hawk's thrusters blasted to life and the ship and docked station accelerated forward.

CHAPTER THIRTY

In the sudden acceleration Max fell toward the door. He landed heavily, bruising his shoulder. With a thud the two taikonauts landed in the airlock beside him. The laptop computer smashed into the bulkhead and shattered into pieces. Li supported Ming's unconscious head.

"Robert!" Max yelled.

There was a small window in the hatch. Through it he could see Robert in the command chair. His mouth was moving, but Max's radio was not picking up what he was saying. The pilot's hands manipulated both control sticks.

"Robert!" Max said again, he pounded his fist on the hatch.

"Max?" Georgy said over the radio. "What's going on?"

"Robert hijacked the Hawk. He is using it to push the station into another orbit," Max said.

"Apogee is increasing," Victoria said. "390 kilometers and climbing."

"Robert is talking to somebody. Who is he talking to?" Max asked, glaring through the window at the busily working pilot.

"It's got to be General Williams," Georgy growled. "Where is he? I will handle him."

"Victoria, shut off his controls," Max said.

"I can't. Somebody has hacked into our system and locked me out," Victoria said.

Max swore. He pounded on the door, "Robert, what are you

doing?"

"I am doing my duty, Max. I am carrying out the mission," Robert said over the radio.

"Our mission is to rescue these taikonauts," Max said.

"No, our mission is to recover enemy technology," Robert said.

"There is no enemy," Max said. "Stop this. Let us into the Hawk. Its boiling in here."

"I'll let you in when we reach our destination," Robert said.

"Where is that? Where are you taking us?" Max demanded.

"To a rendezvous. There is an X-37 waiting in orbit," Robert said.

The Boeing X-37 was a top secret robotic spaceplane operated exclusively by the US Department of Defense. There were usually one or two in orbit at any time, and nobody without special government clearance would know what secret business they were up to.

"Except..." Robert muttered. He tapped on his screen. "This ship isn't going the way that I want it to go." He made an adjustment with his left control stick and the acceleration increased. Max pushed himself to his feet and went to the side window.

"What's happening with our orbit, Victoria?" Max asked.

"Apogee 470 km, perigee 308 km, inclination 41 degrees," Victoria answered.

Max could see that the Earth was now behind the spaceship. Robert was attempting to increase apogee by flying directly away from the ground.

"He's burning radial-out," Max said. "Robert you need to stop right now. You don't know what you are doing." He mopped sweat from his streaming face.

"You just want to undock the ship and go home. I won't let you abandon the mission," Robert said.

"You don't understand orbital mechanics. You'll never reach a stable transfer orbit burning like this," Max said.

"Apogee 550 km and climbing," Victoria said. "Perigee dropping."

"Shut up, Max. You can't lie to me. I can see a rendezvous predicted on my screen. Rendezvous distance is decreasing," Robert said.

Max returned to the hatch. He looked through the small window. "You're burning radially. You're just increasing your eccentricity," he said.

Robert dropped his eyes to glance at Max. He shook his head, lips pursed in disapproval. It was clear that he did not comprehend what Max was trying to say.

"You can't just plan an encounter and fly to it. You have to match your target's orbit and perform a transfer. What does the computer say that relative velocity will be at the closest approach with the X-37?" Max demanded.

Robert touched his screen, then frowned. "Negative three hundred and… hmm. That's not right."

Robert shut off the thrusters. Weightlessness returned.

"Finally," Max said. "Let us out of here Robert."

"I can fix this," Robert said. "If our relative velocity is negative, then I just need to go faster. I'll burn prograde."

Robert tilted his right-hand control stick. The ship and station rotated through ninety degrees. He restarted the thrusters and acceleration returned.

"Stop doing this! Let me in!" Max shouted.

"I don't take orders from you, Max," Robert retorted.

The radio crackled. "I found the General," Georgy said. "He's conspiring with the spook. Get off that computer!" Georgy shouted.

"I don't take orders from a Russian," the General could be heard to say. "You're in league with the communists. I should have known."

"Tell your idiot pilot to transfer control back to Max," Georgy demanded.

"Robert, you have your orders. Get to that rendezvous," the General said.

There was a dull thud and the sound of a hand hitting an unprepared face. A headset clattered on a hard surface.

"The General won't be a problem anymore," Georgy said, breathing hard.

"Perigee stable at 250 km. Apogee 717 km and climbing," Victoria said.

Despite the overwhelming heat in the station, Max felt a sudden chill of fear. In desperation he pounded both hands on the hatch.

"Robert, you have to stop. You'll put us into the Van Allen belt," Max said.

"Oh no," Li murmured. Her eyes were wide. Ming stirred in the space suit. He was beginning to come to.

"But the rendezvous is so close," Robert said, gazing at his screen. "After two orbits we will be less than a kilometer from the X-37."

"Your orbit is very eccentric. You are taking us too high. The radiation from the inner Van Allen belt will kill us," Max said.

The Van Allen radiation belts are two bands of ionizing radiation that circle the Earth. The Earth's magnetosphere captures high energy particles from cosmic rays and the solar wind and holds them there, protecting the Earth, but posing a hazard to any interplanetary explorers. It was currently extra dangerous, having been hypercharged by the recent CME.

"Spacecraft are shielded against radiation," Robert argued.

"Not against the Van Allen belts! Not in the condition that they are in now! You have to go around them. You can't go straight through them," Max said.

"They had to fly through them when they went to the moon," Robert shot back.

"We have no time for a history lesson, but that's not true. The Apollo and Artemis astronauts plotted courses to minimize their exposure to the Van Allen belts. Victoria, isn't there anything that you can do?" Max said.

"I can't shut off his controls. I think that CIA spook interfered on this side and locked me out," Victoria said.

"Can you engage the autopilot? Drain his fuel. Don't let him push us above 1,000 km," Max said.

"I can try," Victoria said.

A new vibration pulsed through the interlocked hulls of the two vessels. Both yaw thrusters of the Hawk blasted on at once, diametrically opposed.

"The autopilot is engaged," Victoria said.

"It won't change anything. I have more than 10% fuel left and only 100 m/s to go," Robert gloated.

"Victoria!" Max yelled.

"I'm sorry, Max. I am trying to get back in," Victoria said.

Max slumped forward. The acceleration went on and on. He considered trying to turn the Chinese station's missile weapons on the Hawk, but any damage to the docked ship would certainly compromise the integrity of the station as well. The heat was starting to wear him out. His breathing was labored. He turned to look at Ming and Li. Ming's eyes were open now, but he looked confused, uncertain. Li, who understood exactly what was happening, gazed at Max with fear in her eyes.

Max shook his head. There was nothing that he could do.

Eventually the acceleration stopped.

"Bingo fuel," Victoria said.

"Victoria, what can you tell us about our orbit?" Max asked quietly.

"Your current altitude is 321 km. You will reach an apogee of 1,180km in a little over one hour. You will enter the inner Van Allen belt in fifty minutes," Victoria answered.

Max sighed. He turned to Li and Ming.

"I'm going to need my spacesuit back," Max said.

CHAPTER THIRTY-ONE

"**Is** there another airlock?" Max asked.

"Yes," Li answered. "On the opposite side of the cabin. It is identical to this one." She pointed to the end of the compartment opposite from where the Hawk was docked.

Max helped Ming squeeze out of the suit, then he put it back on himself. Tugging on the fabric of the undergarment was hampered by Max's body being sticky with sweat. He struggled into it, trying not to exhaust himself before the real work began.

"This station doesn't have any thrusters, does it?" Max asked.

"No," Li answered.

"I didn't think so. I didn't see from the outside. When the power came on, the station stopped its spin. That was from gyroscopes?" Max said.

"Yes," Li answered. "Three control moment gyros. They are on trusses built into the exterior hull."

"They must be pretty large to stop the spin so quickly," Max said.

"Fifty kilos each," Li answered.

Max whistled. "That is big. Almost as big as the ones on Skylab. That's good. We can use them." He put his helmet on. "Can you tap into my radio? I want to be able to talk to you guys when I'm floating outside."

"What are you going to do?" Li said.

"I'm going for a walk," Max said.

Li floated to a nearby computer screen. She pulled out a keyboard and touched a series of keys. "I see your radio frequency. I can talk to you no problem," she said.

"We're only on 2% battery power now. We are in the Earth's shadow. The solar panels are dark," Ming warned.

"Thanks for the reminder," Max said. "I can get you some extra power too."

Max glanced around him, identifying a promising section of wall and floating to it. He ripped a covering panel away, revealing an electrical panel with a mess of wires.

"Which of these wires would you say are the least important?" Max said.

Li floated over and gazed at the mess. "The purple ones are for the radar set. The red ones are backup for the life support system," he said.

"Great. I'll take them all," Max said.

Max wrapped his gloved hand around the bundled wires and pulled. The lights flickered and there was a shower of sparks as he ripped wires loose. Li looked shocked. The lights stabilized. Max pocketed the lengths of wire and pulled himself into the airlock.

"Cycle the airlock and open the door," Max instructed, sealing his visor. His spacesuit was airtight. A refreshing stream of cool air blew at the back of his neck. Cool liquid pulsed along his thighs.

"Can you hear me?" Li's voice came through the speakers in his helmet.

"Yep," Max answered. The airlock cycled and the outer door opened to space.

"Max, the spook admitted to hacking the Hawk. Victoria has full access again," Georgy said.

"That's great, Georgy. A little too late, but that's great," Max said. He floated into space.

The nighttime Earth drifted below. A halo of deep blue trailed the western sunset. City lights flamed in organic filaments of sodium fire. Max took a deep breath of his recycled air. His eyes took in the sleeping, waking, joyful and burdened humanity below, and he exhaled as the universe turned above. A million-million stars burned in the brilliantly lit blackness. He might die soon, but at least he was home.

"What are you going to do?" Georgy asked.

"As long as there is potential delta-v I'm not done," Max said. "Li, tell me about the missiles."

"There are twenty four of them. Four banks of six each. They are anti-satellite weapons, designed to reach anywhere in Earth's orbit," Li said.

"Do they have warheads? If so, could I disable their fuses?" Max asked.

"They do not have warheads. They are kinetic kill vehicles," Li answered.

Max drifted across the station, taking in the four missile banks. They were large and evenly spaced.

"How much do the missiles weigh? About two hundred kilos apiece?" Max asked.

"240 kg each," Li answered.

"You are not going to shoot them, are you?" Ming asked, voice shaky over the radio.

"Tell me about their motors," Max said.

"They have solid fuel motors that develop 25 kilonewtons of thrust for the duration of a four-second burn time," Li said.

Max was doing the math in his head. He had a good feeling about this.

"We are almost out of power," Ming warned. "The solar panels are in shadow."

"That is easily fixed," Max said.

Max floated to the solar panels. He clipped their thin power lines with a pair of wire cutters from his tool belt and spliced in the loose lengths of wire he had taken from inside the station. He pulled himself toward the Hawk, spotting the lithium-ion battery packs exposed on the spacecraft's service module.

"If the missiles have solid fuel motors, their specific impulse is probably about 250 seconds?" Max asked.

"I do not know exactly," Li said. "I am sure that is secret information."

"Georgy, can you shake the spook? Maybe he knows?" Max said.

"I'll see," Georgy said.

"And what is the mass of the station?" Max asked.

"14,500 kilograms," Li answered.

"Is that including the missiles?" Max asked.

"Yes," Li said.

Max uncovered the Hawk's battery terminals and connected the wires, splicing the station's electrical system into the Hawk's battery supply.

"The station is receiving electrical power," Ming said.

"We will need it," Max said. He gray-taped the connections in place. He began to move back toward the missiles, then paused when he noticed the radiators, stuck fast to the surface of the station beneath a layer of black goo. He dug one out. It gave a slight resistance, then unfolded on its own, spreading white panels laced with copper heat pipes. He floated over and freed the other, which spread open in the same way.

"The radiators are working," Ming said with relief. "We are finally getting cool air through the vents."

Max's mathematical mind added up the situation. He had a welder at his belt, and he considered cutting the Hawk free, but as much as he hated Robert, he did not want to kill him. Besides, the Hawk's battery power would be useful for running the station's control moment gyroscopes. The mass of the Hawk, tightly docked, would have to be accounted for as well.

"The spook says that solid rocket motors on Chinese military rockets typically have specific impulses ranging between 250 and 270 seconds," Georgy said.

"Thanks Georgy," Max said. That was good information.

The Hawk spacecraft massed 10,300kg without fuel. Added to the 14,500kg mass of the station, that made a total of 24,800 kg for the two vessels docked together. The missiles contained approximately 200 kg of solid fuel propellant each and there were twenty-four of them. That gave Max 4,800 kg of propellant to play with and 20,000 kg of dry mass that needed to be moved. The rocket equation appeared in his mind:

$$Delta\ v = Isp\ x\ g0\ x\ ln\ (mwet/mdry)$$

Therefore:

$$Delta\ v = 250s\ x\ 9.806m/s^2\ x\ ln\ (24,800kg\ /20,000kg)$$

"Georgy, what is the natural logarithm of 1.24?" Max asked. "I left my slide rule in my other pants."

"0.215," Georgy answered.

"Awesome," Max said. He finished the math, simplifying the numbers for easier calculation.

$$Delta\ v = 250s\ x\ (approximately\ 10m/s^2)\ x\ 0.2$$

$$Delta\ v = approximately\ 500m/s$$

"We can do this," Max said to himself. "This is going to work."

Max took a breath then explained his plan to the team. "The missile launchers are all pointed parallel to the hull. If I can fix the missiles firmly into their mounts, Li can point the whole station with the control-moment gyroscopes and then fire the missiles in sequence. They will act like little booster rockets. We have 500 m/s of delta-v. That should be enough to drop our apogee safely below the inner Van Allen belt," Max said.

There was a moment of silence as the various listeners considered his words. Victoria was the first to respond.

"The delta-v requirement to stay below the Van Allen belt changes depending how soon you burn. It would only take 150 m/s of acceleration retrograde to drop your apogee if you burn right now. But, in ten minutes it will take 230 m/s. In twenty minutes, it will take 500 m/s of delta-v to stay beneath one thousand kilometers apogee. After twenty minutes, you will not have enough thrust to keep out of the dangerous regions of the inner belt," Victoria said.

Max grinned. He unclipped the laser beam welder from his belt.

"I guess I had better get to work then," he said.

CHAPTER THIRTY-TWO

The clamps that held the station's missile launchers in place were made of steel. That was good because steel was easy to weld. Max began by fusing together the decoupling mechanism of the nearest launcher. The weapon mounts were strong enough to carry the heavy missiles all the way from launch pad to orbit. With just a bit of extra attention Max guessed that they would be strong enough to hold the missiles in place when ignited in their holders.

"I want to apologize," Robert said.

"Oh?" Max said.

"Victoria has been explaining to me what I did wrong," Robert said.

"Your ignorance of orbital mechanics should not be a death sentence. Your malicious disregard for workplace safety, on the other hand…" Max said. He held on with one hand while he added a weld to the articulating mechanism of the missile launcher.

"What can I do to help?" Robert asked.

"Open the door and turn up the life support system in the Hawk. Our new friends are quite warm," Max said.

"It is now fifty-five degrees Celsius in the station," Li said.

"Okay," Robert agreed.

Max felt the vibration as the door between the Hawk and the station opened.

"Wow. That is hot," Robert said.

"You can also turn off the gyros on the Hawk. They are negligible compared to the ones on the station. We can let the station take over orienting," Max said.

"I can do that," Robert said.

Max floated back and admired his handiwork. All six clamps for the solid-fuel missiles of one of the launchers were solidly fused. The mount itself was reinforced with choice welds at potential weak points.

"How many missiles do you think that we can set off at once?" Max asked. "Can we shoot them asymmetrically or will that cause too much torque on the station?"

"I think that we should only fire symmetrically and only two missiles at a time. The hull is designed to handle compressive forces and linear acceleration, but it is not reinforced for torsional stresses," Li said.

"Can we do more than two at a time?" Max asked.

"Altogether the missiles can impart 517 meters per second of delta-v to the station. They have four-second burn times. 517 meters per second divided by four seconds equals 129.25 meters per second per second of acceleration," Li explained.

Max whistled. "That would be an acceleration of 13G's. You are right. Let's stick to just two at a time," he said.

"Which would still be an acceleration of a little more than 1G for four seconds," Ming said.

"Is there any way to decrease the thrust and increase the burn time?" Max asked.

"No," Li answered.

Max checked his watch. He had been working for four minutes. He went to the missile launcher opposite the one he had just welded and repeated the process, firmly fusing the missile clamps and weapon mount in place.

"Alright let's get oriented and fire it up. The earlier we get burning, the better," Max said.

He had been working for nine minutes. By ten minutes, the delta-v requirement jumped to 230m/s. At twenty it would take

500m/s of delta-v to stay out of the deadly Van Allen radiation.

"Don't you want to come back inside first?" Li asked.

"No. Cycling the airlock takes time. We need to get burning. And there may be some emergency repairs I need to make from out here. I can hang on for 1G for four seconds," Max said.

"I understand. Orienting retrograde," Li said. The station was now acting like a bulky spaceship with a front and a rear. The front was where the Hawk was docked. The rear was the direction in which the missiles' rocket motors would blast.

Max clung to a ladder situated equidistant between the first two launchers. From here he would be clear of the exhaust of the rocket nozzles. Silently, the station rotated 180 degrees as Li took control of the gyros. The nighttime Earth was to Max's left and the star-strewn blackness of space was on his right. Max clipped his tether to a ladder rung. He gripped a rung with both gloved hands and positioned his feet on another.

"For optimal trajectory adjust orientation seven degrees declination from retrograde," Victoria said.

"Understood. Adjusting," Li said. The station turned slightly, nosing down toward the Earth.

"Firing missiles number one and thirteen," Li announced.

Max tightened his grip. He watched the launchers, half afraid that one of his welds would fail, possibly ripping a hole in the hull as it did.

With a roar and a sheet of white-hot flame the two missiles ignited. The ladder attempted to pull itself out of Max's hands. His feet slipped off the rung. His body weight plus 50 kg of spacesuit yanked on his arms and shoulders. He grit his teeth, clinging to the thin aluminum handhold. The sound of his involuntary whimper was lost in the roar of the missiles, blasting their vibrations through the hull of the station. Four seconds later the acceleration stopped.

"It worked!" Li exclaimed. "Hull integrity is good."

"Your projected apogee has dropped from to 1,180 kilometers to 1,145 kilometers," Victoria said.

"Are you okay, Max?" Georgy asked.

"Yeah, I'm okay," Max said. He suppressed a groan of pain. His arms ached and he had bit his tongue. He tasted coppery blood in his mouth. The rung he had been holding had bent, pulled nearly flush with the hull by his sudden weight on the thin aluminum. He shifted his hands and replaced his feet. He would spread the strain out over four separate rungs.

"We don't have much time. We need to keep burning. Li, fire the next two missiles," Max said.

"Firing missiles two and fourteen," Li said.

The twin flames blasted into space and the acceleration slammed on again. Max was more ready this time. His feet stayed on the rungs. The vibration rattled his teeth. After a seeming eternity, the acceleration stopped.

"Apogee 1,111 kilometers," Victoria said.

"The Hawk wobbled around a lot that time," Robert said. "Are we sure that the docking collar will hold?"

"The clamps look fine. We are not losing any air pressure," Li said.

"We need to keep firing. Li, do the next two," Max said.

"Firing missiles three and fifteen," Li said.

The weight came on Max again. He clung for four seconds of agony.

"Apogee 1,078," Victoria said.

"Max?" Georgy asked.

"I'm fine. Keep going," Max said.

"Firing missiles four and sixteen," Li said.

Halfway through the burn there was a high-pitched shriek. It came from all around, resonating through the hull of the station.

"What was that noise?" Robert asked.

"I do not know. The hull is intact," Ming said.

"Apogee 1,046 kilometers," Victoria said.

"Everything looks okay out here," Max said, looking around from his precarious perch. There were scorch marks on the hull of the station behind the two launchers. "Keep going."

"Firing five and seventeen," Li said.

The acceleration came on and Max made the mistake of looking down. He hung over an infinite abyss that was trying to pull him in. His head was swimming.

"Apogee 1,016 kilometers," Victoria said.

"We only need one more burn," Max said.

"Firing six and eighteen," Li said.

Three seconds into the burn there was a massive bang and a flash of light. The station jerked sideways. Weightlessness returned.

"We are losing atmosphere," Li said. "We have a hull breach."

One of the launchers had ripped itself from the hull. It was nowhere to be seen, presumably pulled with the missile out into space. Max unclipped his safety tether and flew to the place the launcher had recently been.

"It is a small hole," Max said. Between two broken bolts was a ragged tear less than a centimeter across. A jet of condensing air could be seen leaking out. Max pulled out his roll of gray tape and pressed a length of tape across the hole.

"I see it," Li said. "Placing a patch now."

"Pressure stable," Ming said.

"That could have been worse," Max said. "Victoria, how did we do?"

"You did it. Apogee 991 kilometers. You will fly clear of the Van Allen belt radiation," she said.

Max breathed a sigh of relief.

CHAPTER THIRTY-THREE

The Boeing X-37 spaceplane caught up with them twenty orbits later. By that time Robert had progressed from chastened, to defiant, to sulky. Max had managed to refrain from hitting him, but Li had shown no such restraint. She had hit him twice. The first was a punch on the jaw soon after the adrenaline had drained from their narrow escape from death. The second physical assault was ten orbits later with a heel kick that split Robert's lip and endeared Li indelibly into Max's heart.

Max watched the X-37 approach. There was no crew cabin in the automated drone, but the propellant it carried would refill the Hawk's fuel tanks and allow them to return home.

"Are you sure that I don't need to do an EVA?" Max asked.

"Victoria says that the propellant transfer procedure is entirely automated," Georgy said over the radio.

"I did not know that they already had this technology," Max said.

"Me neither. Apparently SpaceTech has been working with the military for some time," Georgy said.

The X-37 was crabbing across space, drifting sideways on pulses of propellant gas. It was about ten meters long, with a wing-shaped body and cylindrical payload bay. It looked like a miniature version of the Space Shuttle, but without a cockpit. The clamshell bay doors were open now, revealing a white-painted fuel tank and two solar panel arrays. A robotic arm was folded up inside.

Once less than a meter away, the drone spaceplane brought itself to a stop. It was centered over the docked Hawk spacecraft. The robotic arm unfolded itself to connect two flexible hoses to ports on the Hawk's hull. Soon there was the vibration of pumps as the Hawk's propellant tanks began to fill.

"I feel like we are living in the future," Max said.

"We are," Li said, giving Max a smile.

When the refueling procedure was complete, the X-37 retracted its hoses. It used its arm to grapple directly to the Chinese station.

"What do you think they are going to do about the station?" Ming asked.

"I don't know, and I don't care," Max said.

"Maybe the US and Chinese space programs will finally start working together," Li suggested.

"Maybe," Max said. "Let's go home."

Max closed the airtight door and decoupled from the station. He took command of the spacecraft and plotted their aerocapture and descent trajectory. Two hours later the deceleration pressed them into their seats as they struck the atmosphere. Max watched the reentry plasma flicker through the window. It glowed red then green then a brilliant purple. The dark of space gave way to a blue sky as the parachutes opened. The capsule drifted, twisting on the long nylon strands, then splashed down onto the gentle Gulf swell.

"The D.O.D. has politely requested to talk to you," Georgy said.

Max and Georgy sat on a park bench in Corpus Christi, Texas. The museum ship USS *Lexington*, a massive Essex-class aircraft carrier, sat at the end of the pier. Morning sunlight slanted across the bay, glinting on the calm blue water.

"That is not going to happen," Max said. He took a sip from a paper cup of black coffee.

"I did not think so," Georgy said. He wore a Hawaiian shirt and khaki shorts. He was fiddling with a sealed envelope with both burly hands.

"Are you in trouble for hitting the general?" Max asked.

"Victoria was able to smooth things over. The official report tells of a flawless operation. If it became public that a civilian contractor struck a former general, people might wonder if the operation was as flawless as they claim," Georgy said.

"How are our Chinese colleagues?" Max asked.

"Li and Ming are happy to be alive. The Chinese government is pretending they don't exist, which is as good an outcome as any could have hoped. NASA put them up in a hotel," Georgy said.

Max finished his coffee and looked at the cup. It had been so full of promise, but now it was empty. He thought he knew how it felt. He tossed the cup into a trash can and Georgy handed him the envelope.

"What is this?" Max asked.

It was addressed to him from Naomi Leverrier.

"That is an invitation to a funeral," Georgy said.

Max opened the envelope and unfolded the handwritten letter inside.

"A funeral for Adams?" Max asked, incredulous.

"He went cave diving," Georgy explained. "A member of his group got lost. Adams went back for him and died trying to save him. They recovered both bodies yesterday."

"What a stupid way to die," Max muttered.

"I think that you should go to the funeral," Georgy said.

Max stared at the letter for a long time.

"I think so too," Max sighed.

The sun shone in an inappropriately blue sky. Birds sang and swooped from tree to tree. Adams was buried in Arlington with the honors of a veteran. His child and sobbing widow stood in a crowd of friends and family while Max stood at the edge in a borrowed black suit.

Doctor Thompson gave Max a friendly smile. Naomi never met Max's eyes. An elderly woman held her while she cried. Her daughter, Seki, looked confused and scared. A disrespectful squirrel buried nuts beneath a tree nearby.

Max shuddered at the abyss. Adams was gone. His consciousness had disappeared into nothingness. Max had never learned to accept death with equanimity. He knew that he would go into his own death screaming, with the raving terror of one who knew that nothing lay beyond. He wondered if Adams had accepted his death with stoicism. Bowing to fate gracefully as the oxygen in his scuba tanks ran out.

Somebody, a priest perhaps, was speaking. A coffin was lowered into a grave. Two men with shovels began filling the hole. Dirt rained on the wooden box where a dead hero lay.

Max sat on the edge of a hotel bed in Washington, DC. He dialed a familiar number on his phone.

"Max?" Doctor Thompson said, answering his call.

"I want to come back to the project. I want to help with Artemis," Max said.

There was a long silence.

"The job is yours if you want it. Adams would want you to fly on Artemis 3," Doctor Thompson said finally.

"I'll do it. But I have one condition," Max said.

"What is it?" Doctor Thompson asked.

"I want Lun Li to fly with me," Max said.

CHAPTER THIRTY-FOUR

Max found himself back in Florida, doing what he should have been doing all along.

"We are expanding the mission profile," Max announced.

The auditorium was packed with the team leaders of the Artemis program. Doctor Thompson and the NASA administration sat to his right. The flight team and engineers, including Javid, sat on his left. Georgy sat front and center, alongside Victoria. SpaceTech was a close partner to the Artemis program now.

"The original mission called for two Space Launch System flights. The first to place a lunar lander into low moon orbit. The second to launch the Orion spacecraft carrying the crew," Max said.

Graphics appeared on the display screen beside him, depicting first an orbital diagram of a lunar lander being orbited around the moon, then the launch of an Orion capsule, docking with that lander in lunar orbit.

"But now that SpaceTech is onboard, they can use their smaller Hawk rocket to ferry the lunar lander. That frees up an SLS launch for something bigger," Max said.

The display changed. A large object orbited over the gray surface of the moon.

"The next SLS launch will place a space station into lunar orbit.

It will have four docking ports, deep space refueling capability, residential accommodations, and capability for modular expansion," Max said.

A murmur of approval filled the room.

"We will establish a permanent human presence in the solar system, and the lunar station is the first step on that journey," Max said. He put down the remote.

Doctor Thompson rose and went to the podium.

"Thank you, Max," she said. She turned toward the audience. "We need to restructure our teams to optimize workflow and promote cooperation with our new commercial partners."

The conference continued, but Max left the auditorium. Georgy rose and followed him.

"You seem different," Georgy said, catching up with him. "Have you been drinking?"

Max shook his head. "The opposite."

"Humans are going back to the moon for the first time in fifty years," Georgy said.

"Or for the first time if you believe the conspiracy theorists," Max said.

"Conspiracy theorists would claim the ocean was not real while they were drowning in it," Georgy said.

"That is wishful thinking," Max joked.

"The lunar lander's engineering team is struggling with the lander's autopilot system," Georgy said.

"That is fixable. Have they asked Victoria for help?" Max asked.

"Not yet," Georgy said. He pulled out his phone and began composing a message.

"We can always land manually. We don't need autopilot," Max said. He opened the double doors and went into the warm Florida summer.

The sun was past the zenith in a sky dusted with high cloud, and the grass was green and damp from a recent rain. Max crossed the street as Georgy walked beside him and a daytime moon hung pale in the blue sky.

The high bay doors of the Vehicle Assembly Building were open. The Space Launch System rocket was inside, stacked and undergoing final checks. The rocket was enormous, twenty-six stories tall and bright orange with insulating foam. Two massive solid rocket boosters were strapped on either side of the central core. The Orion spacecraft was a tiny thing perched at the apex of the titanic launch vehicle.

"In the age of reusable rockets, it seems ridiculous that ninety percent of this rocket is going to fall into the ocean," Georgy said.

"The SLS is just a stepping stone," Max said. "Just like the moon is a stepping stone to the rest of the solar system."

"Somebody is going to have to make space travel profitable for things to really take off," Georgy said.

"Not my problem. I'm just a mechanic," Max said. "And the SLS is as good as the SLS is going to get. Let's go look at something more interesting."

Max was an excellent pilot in the black of space. He had developed an eye for relative motion and a sense for the immutable laws of orbital mechanics. Fighting a slippery lunar lander in a gravity well, on the other hand…

"I can't do it," Max grouched. He released the controls and the simulated lander crashed into the lunar surface. The screens reset and Max was once again coasting low over the gray, cratered landscape.

"You overcorrected," Li said. "Let me show you."

There were two sets of controls in the lunar lander simulator. Li took hers in her hands. She rotated the lander sideways and the screens rolled. She stopped when the moon's surface was vertical in the screen and activated the main engine. The simulator vibrated to simulate the rumble of the engine but could do nothing to change the 1.0 G of acceleration of the Earth's gravity well.

Max watched the orbital velocity decrease. Altitude was dropping and Li canted the vehicle upward, using engine thrust to counter the pull of gravity toward the moon. She maintained a constant distance from the lunar surface as she bled off orbital speed. Soon the craters were sliding by at a slower and slower pace. Li watched the radar, registering surface scatter as she sought a good place to land. She aligned the vehicle's axis of thrust with a summative vector that would ease their descent and counter remaining transverse velocity. Once the transverse was eliminated, they fell straight down. The surface rose. Li adjusted the thrust in minute increments, and they touched down softly. There was plenty of fuel left in the tanks.

"Show off," Max said.

"I have thousands of hours of flight time in helicopters," Li explained.

"But can you land on Mars though?" Max pulled a keyboard out from under his seat and typed in a series of commands. The screens changed to show them whizzing over the red planet. The simulated vehicle vibrated as it was buffeted by the simulated atmosphere.

"Probably, but that is not what we are here for," Li said. She unbuckled and stepped out of the simulator, climbing a short set of stairs to the test center's concrete floor. Max turned off the computer screens and followed. The building bustled with activity. They walked past a simulator for the Orion spacecraft and a full-scale mock-up of the lunar station.

"I'm doing more training for this mission than I've ever done for a mission before," Max admitted.

"Really? In China we do even more. Everybody knows how to do everybody's job. I could fly the Shenzhou with my eyes closed," Li said.

"I could fly a Soyuz with my eyes closed, but that's because I'm really good," Max said.

"Or it's really easy," Li said.

"Do you miss China?" Max asked.

"I miss my niece. I don't really miss the rest. My parents and I were never close," Li said.

"Is the Chinese government going to punish your family for your defection?" Max asked.

"Defection? This isn't a spy novel. No, they don't care. The government only cares if you criticize the government. There have already been a dozen fake articles in the state newspapers where I sing the PRC's praises. They claimed the mission was a success, remember? And now China and the US are cooperating like never before," Li said.

"Politics," Max snorted.

"As long as I don't complain China won't bother me, and I don't intend to complain," Li said.

Li left the building and went to a car in the parking lot. She got into the driver's seat. Max climbed into the passenger seat.

"Thank you for agreeing to come with me to the moon," Max said.

Li put on her seat belt and backed out of the parking spot. Max did not bother with his seat belt, he assumed that the car's warning beeps would stop eventually.

"I want to go to the moon. I would never turn down a chance like that. My question is why you picked me. You hardly know me," Li said. She spared Max a glance of her dark brown eyes. She put the car in drive and left the parking lot.

"It was because of how you responded when under pressure. You never panicked," Max said.

"I was half-conscious for most of that. I had heat exhaustion," Li said.

"Exactly. Even when you were disoriented you never hesitated," Max said.

"I just wanted to survive. I did what I had to do," Li said.

"Everybody wants to survive, but not everybody can. Some people go into denial or get angry or panic or shut down. You didn't. You have good instincts," Max said.

Li considered that. "Do you have trouble trusting people?" she asked.

"Always," Max answered.

"You never asked me why I want to go to the moon," Li said.

"Why do you want to go to the moon?" Max asked.

"I want to know that I could do it," Li said.

"You just want to prove that you can?" Max asked. "Let's be honest, the rocket is doing most of the work."

"No, I want to be able to say that I took the leap. I never want to look back at my life and wonder what could have been," Li said.

"So you are risking your life because you don't want to have regrets?" Max asked.

"You only live once," Li said.

"YOLO is something teenagers say ironically," Max explained.

"Well I'm serious about it." Li glanced at Max. The beeping of the seat belt warning alarm had never stopped. "You should put your seat belt on," Li added.

"Why? We aren't going very far," Max said.

"Because you only live once," Li said.

"Fine," Max said, complying. The seat belt clicked, and the beeping finally stopped. In a few more minutes of driving the airfield runway came into view.

Computer simulators were fine, but nothing could beat the real thing. Maneuvering while thrown against the restraining straps and the hard concrete came racing upward was its own special challenge.

The Lunar Landing Practice Vehicle would be instantly recognizable to any Apollo astronauts. It was a direct successor to the Lunar Landing Training Vehicles that they had used. Four large landing legs extended from an aluminum scaffolding. In the center of the spiderlike vehicle was a swiveling jet engine, gyrostabilized to be always pointing down. The jet was programmed to output a thrust equal to five-sixths of the weight of the craft. Thus, to the vehicle's pilot, it always felt as though the vehicle were falling in a steady one-sixth gravity of acceleration, the same as that of the moon. On other parts of the frame were pressure-fed hydrogen peroxide monopropellant rocket thrusters. The vehicle mimicked the expected behavior of the lunar lander.

Li fitted her helmet and tightened the harness. She grabbed the twin sticks of the LLPV and nodded to the flight controller. Max pushed earplugs into his ears and took a step back.

The turbofan jet engine roared to life, blowing away dust and scattered leaves from the concrete runway. The suspension of the four landing legs extended, but the vehicle did not leave the ground until Li triggered the rocket motors. The vehicle leapt into the air.

Li turned, banked, and spun the small machine. She flew low, zooming at high speed, nearly scraping the concrete. She soared up to three hundred meters then fell. Seconds from striking the ground Li blasted the rockets at maximum thrust, catching the vehicle at a perfect stop. The landing legs kissed the ground. Her eyes were shining as she powered the jet engine down.

"If they finalize the lunar lander's autopilot, the computer could just handle the moon landing for us," Max said, removing his earplugs.

"What would be the fun in that?" Li retorted, grinning.

CHAPTER THIRTY-FIVE

Max hated the underwater training. NASA called this facility the Neutral Buoyancy Laboratory.

"How many more solar panels do you need me to replace?" Max asked.

"Just two," came the manager's voice through his radio.

Max was in a space suit, ten meters deep in a big swimming pool. A mock-up of the lunar station was submerged in front of him. He sighed as he went to work on the seventh of nine solar panels, jutting in a linear array from the station's hull.

A scuba diver hovered at the edge of Max's vision. The man looked completely at peace. He sat cross legged with eyes closed at neutral buoyancy in the column of water. As the scuba diver breathed in, he floated up slightly, and as he exhaled, he settled downward. He looked comfortable and Max envied him.

Max was very uncomfortable. When fully inflated, the spacesuit floated to the surface, and thus it had to be weighted down with metal bands that added significantly to the effort needed to move. To an outside observer, the suit had the appearance of weightlessness, but Max was anything but. He flopped around inside the suit at 1.0 Earth gravity. When upright, his full weight came down on his crotch, with no possible way to readjust when sensitive things got pinched. When he rotated his body forward, his chest fell against the front of the suit, and he had to crane his neck back to keep his forehead off the visor.

When he had to rotate upside-down it was even worse, as his body weight came down on his shoulders and neck. He was sweating profusely, and the face shield fogged with his hot breath. He struggled with a stuck bolt, cursing the test mechanic who had overtightened it. He had been in this pool for four hours today.

"Let me give you a hand," a voice said.

Max looked up to see a space suited figure approaching. The calm, smiling face of Albert Puck was visible through the clear visor.

Albert Puck had been Adams Leverrier's backup. He was a veteran Navy pilot, and he would have been the commander of the moon landing mission, had not Max come along and taken the position. Max had only met him a couple of times before, but he seemed to harbor no resentment about his demotion. He seemed a genial and easygoing man.

"Max is supposed to complete this stimulation alone," said the simulation manager.

"But Max is not alone," Albert said. He came level with Max and peered into his fogged visor. "Why don't you go back up? I can finish up here," he said.

Max knew that Albert had no need to do any more training in the Neutral Buoyancy Laboratory. Albert had logged more underwater hours than anybody.

"How about a compromise? I'll fix this panel and you get the next. That way we'll be done in half the time," Max said.

"Teamwork makes the dream work," Albert said cheerfully. He pulled out a wrench and went to work.

Max was glad to be finally pulled from the pool. Wordlessly, he climbed out of the space suit and went to the locker rooms to shower. Afterward, he changed into slacks and a t-shirt then walked to the break room, rubbing sore shoulders.

"You were in the Neutral Buoyancy Laboratory today?" Miranda asked.

Doctor Miranda Santos, MD, PhD was the final member of their four-person crew. She was a dark-skinned woman in her late forties with prematurely gray hair and a perpetually sympathetic expression. She was the crew's medical officer and the most highly educated of the four astronauts. Max had no qualms at admitting that her PhD dissertation on theories of quantum mechanics was entirely beyond him. She was sitting on the couch in the astronaut break room when he walked in, reading a paperback book.

"Today. And yesterday. And if anybody asks, I've completed all my mandatory hours in the underwater simulator," Max said. He went to the cupboard and retrieved a package of dried ramen. He filled it with water from the tap and put the Styrofoam cup into the microwave.

Miranda chuckled. "I'll be sure to tell Doctor Thompson," she said. She closed and put down the book.

Albert and Li walked into the break room. Max had not expected to see the rest of the Artemis crew here tonight. It was late evening and most people had gone home.

"Please don't tell me that this is an intervention," Max said.

"The four of us haven't had much of a chance to talk together," Albert said. He pulled a plastic chair up to the small table and sat down.

"I don't have enough noodles for all four of us," Max said. The microwave dinged and he pulled a set of disposable chopsticks from a drawer nearby.

"That's okay. I ordered pizza," Albert said, waving a hand.

"What kind of pizza?" Max asked. He went to the table and sat down. He removed the paper lid and dipped his chopsticks into the ramen, savoring the familiar salty smell.

"I don't resent your sudden inclusion on the mission," Albert said, ignoring his question.

"I do," Miranda interjected. "We had a well-oiled team. We all knew each other. We had been preparing for this for months. Now, you and Li have leapfrogged to the front of the line. Olivia Satcher and Melvin Dwight should have been on this flight with us. Now they are on backup."

Albert shot Miranda a disapproving look. She met Albert's eyes defiantly then looked back at Max. Lun Li, uncomfortable, folded her arms and leaned against the door frame.

Max raised the cup noodle to his lips. The hot broth burned his lips, but he slurped it anyway.

"This isn't about Olivia and Melvin," Max said when he put the cup back down.

"Yes it is. They don't deserve to be sidelined," Miranda said.

"I don't care about Olivia and Melvin, and neither do you," Max said.

"What?" Miranda challenged.

"Olivia and Melvin don't matter," Max said.

"Of course they matter," Miranda retorted.

"If you really cared about Olivia or Melvin, you would give one of them your seat. This is not about them. You're upset because your personal sense of justice has been offended. You feel like this isn't fair," Max said.

"And what is wrong with that?" Miranda asked.

Max shook his head. "Nothing. But the world is not fair. It never has been, and it never will be," he said.

"You don't believe in justice?" Miranda asked.

Max shrugged. "I believe in cause and effect," he said.

Albert's phone buzzed. "Pizza is here," he said. "I will be right back," he stood and strode out the door.

Li crossed the room and stood at the table. "I'm sorry that we cut to the front of the line, Miranda. But I want to be on this mission. I want to go to the moon. Doctor Thompson invited me to go, and nobody is going to stop me. What is your reason for wanting to be here?" she said.

"I am going to the moon because I earned it. My whole life I've been fighting uphill. I was the only half-black, half-Hispanic woman in my medical school class. I was the only one who had lived on food stamps through grade school," Miranda said.

"So you deserve to go because of hardship? Or for minority representation?" Li asked.

Miranda shook her head. "No. I deserve to go because I am qualified to do the job. But I want to go because somebody like me should. People need role models to relate to. To see people like them doing great things. Marginalized people need to know that greatness is possible for them, or else nothing will ever change," Miranda said.

"There are more than fifty minority groups in China," Li said. "Life can be very bad if you are not in the majority."

"People are racist," Max shrugged. He twirled his cooling noodles around his chopsticks.

"Societal structures can be racist. The people are just victims," Miranda said.

"People are inherently self-interested," Li said. "They're selfish."

"People are neither selfish nor selfless. They are just people. They live as they are raised. They are products of their environment," Miranda said.

"No politics, please," Albert said, reentering the room with a stack of pizza boxes.

"We were talking sociology, not politics," Miranda said.

"Close enough," Albert said, setting the boxes on the table. He opened the top one and helped himself to a greasy slice.

Max finished his noodles and set the empty cup aside. He picked out a slice of pizza and took a messy bite.

"Cheesy pizza," Li said, reaching into the box. "I love it. It reminds me of my time at Caltech."

"You went to Caltech?" Albert asked. "Me too. When were you there?"

"Oh-eight to twenty-twelve," Li answered. "For undergrad. You?"

"Oh-nine to twenty-fourteen," Albert said with a smile. "But, I am a few years older than you. That was for my doctorate."

"Tsinghua University. PhD in Electrical Engineering twenty-sixteen," Li said. "But they don't have as many good pizza places in Beijing as they do in Pasadena."

Max rubbed his left shoulder, aching from the exercise of the underwater simulator.

Miranda noticed his pain. "The underwater simulator hurts. It is when we have to go upside down that gets me. I can't stand it.

All the blood goes to my head, and my arms feel like they are on fire," she said.

"An actual spacewalk is easier," Max said.

Li took a seat at the table. She glanced from Albert to Miranda. "Neither of you have been to space before, have you?" she asked.

Miranda shook her head. "No," she answered.

"No," Albert said. "But I look forward to seeing Earth from space. I've heard that no photo or video can do it justice."

"I'm sad to say that on my flight I didn't get much of a chance to look out the window," Li said.

"For the whole flight?" Miranda asked, surprised.

"I was pretty distracted," Li said. "Lots was going wrong."

"How many flights have you had, Max?" Miranda asked.

Max squinted while he munched on a pizza crust.

"More than ten," he guessed.

"Max has flown to space thirteen times," Albert answered.

"That must be more than anybody alive," Miranda said, astonished.

"And yet nobody will honor my frequent-flier miles," Max said.

"Personally, I am honored to be flying with you," Albert said.

"I trust Max," Li said.

"We're a team. We are going to work together. We might as well like each other too," Albert said.

"All right," Miranda sighed. She sat at the table and took a slice of pizza. "To being in the same boat," she said, raising her slice.

Max waved his stub of crust. "And to hating the Neutral Buoyancy Laboratory," he added.

"Cheers to that," Li said emphatically, helping herself to the final slice.

CHAPTER THIRTY-SIX

Launch day was finally upon them. Two other launches had preceded. The first had placed the new lunar station into orbit around the moon. The second had sent the lunar lander along after it. It was time to join them and put human boots on the lunar surface.

Max had practiced for missions before, but never like this. The team had gone through months of rigorous training. They had spent hundreds of hours in the simulator. They had flown the entire mission countless times.

"Can I recite some of my poetry tomorrow?" Georgy asked.

"Can I stop you?" Max asked.

"Probably not," Georgy said.

The astronaut dormitory at Cape Canaveral was a spartan suite of bedrooms and a small kitchen. Georgy's home cooking was settling comfortably in Max`s stomach.

"I'm not scared about the launch tomorrow," Max said.

"Isn't that a good thing?" Georgy asked. He carried their dirty dishes to the sink.

"Fear is useful. Fear tells you when you're doing something stupid and need to stop," Max said.

"So, maybe you're not doing something stupid?" Georgy offered.

"Flying on the largest rocket ever made to land on the moon is a little bit stupid. There are a thousand things that can go wrong,"

Max said.

"So why aren't you scared? Fortune favors the bold?" Georgy said. He put on rubber gloves and washed the pan he had brought from home.

"Fortune favors those who do their homework," Max corrected him. "I think we've just practiced so many times that it feels routine. It feels like another practice."

"I bet it will feel different tomorrow," Georgy said, drying the pan with a dish towel. "When you're on top of the rocket and the countdown hits zero; when those two solid rocket motors light up, you'd have to be dead to not be excited."

"Don't jinx me," Max said with a grin. "But you're right. I'm sure I'll be terrified tomorrow."

But Max did not feel terrified. Not even when strapped in. Not even after the rocket's fueling was done and the final countdown began.

"T-minus five minutes," said Doctor Thompson's voice over the spacecraft's speakers.

There were four chairs in the Orion spacecraft and all four were filled. They were reclined ninety degrees from the vertical, so the occupants looked straight up toward the sky. In the top right chair was Max, the commander. To his left was Lun Li, the lunar lander pilot. "Below" their feet were the other two seats. The top of medical officer Miranda Santos's helmet almost brushed the bottom of Max's pressure-suit boots. To her left was Albert Puck, mission navigator. All four were reviewing their final countdown procedures. Their helmets were closed and locked. Their pressure suits were sealed. They were ready to go.

"All systems green," Javid said over the radio.

"Looks like we are fully fueled," Max said. "First stage engines are ready for ignition."

"Navigation is internal," said Albert.

"Life support systems nominal," said Miranda.

Max scanned his screen. He went again through the familiar checklist. There were over a hundred items on it, most of them checking on something that the computer had already confirmed.

The Artemis first stage was entirely automated. Sometimes he wondered if NASA made the checklists just to keep them busy. He went in sequence through thirty-five more items before the next callout.

"T-minus four minutes," Doctor Thompson said over the radio.

"Automated abort system is ready," Max said. "Let's hope that we don't need it."

"Roger that," Albert agreed.

"Solid rocket boosters are a 'go,'" said an unfamiliar voice over the radio. He must have been the representative from the military contractor Northrop Grumman, the manufacturer of the solid rocket motors.

"Of course they are. The solid rockets have been sitting in storage and ready for a decade," Max muttered under his breath.

Strapped to either side of the first stage hydrolox propellant tanks were the two largest solid rocket boosters ever made. They used the same technology as intercontinental ballistic missiles, filled with a thick glue-like propellant that could be stored for years. Once they were lit, they provided constant thrust until they were out of propellant. They could not be throttled or shut down. Solid boosters were inefficient, getting a specific impulse of only 242 seconds (much less than the 452 seconds of the hydrogen-oxygen main engines). This meant that for a given mass of fuel they could impart only a fraction of the delta-v as the efficient liquid engines could. But the boosters were big, powerful, and cheap. Max hated them, but they would help get this underpowered and overweight rocket off the launch pad. Then the main engines would take over.

"T-minus three minutes," Ohemaa said.

"I haven't heard much from Georgy. Are all of his systems green?" Max asked.

"I'm here, Max," Georgy said. "How are you doing?"

"Solid as a rock, Georgy. Do you have any parting words for us?" Max asked.

"I have prepared something, actually," Georgy said. He cleared his throat and spoke.

"What do you call that poem, Georgy? An ode to hubris?" Max asked.

"*Hope,*" Georgy answered.

"Vehicle is on internal power," Albert interjected.

"T-minus two minutes," Ohemaa said. "We are 'go' for launch."

If there ever existed physical evidence of man's power over its own destiny, it was embodied in this machine. Rockets existed at the intersection of chemistry, physics, computer science, materials science, high mathematics, and nearly every other scientific field known to man. They were made possible only by the tireless work of tens of thousands, themselves working atop the efforts of forgotten multitudes that came before. The SLS was jointly funded by the citizens of a nation. It was created by the power of cooperation and represented sublimation of the human will. Perhaps, Max thought, there was good to be said of hubris after all.

"T-minus sixty seconds," Ohemaa said.

"Can't we just launch already? I'm sure we're all quite ready to go," Max said.

"I'm for sure ready," Miranda responded nervously.

"Sixty seconds isn't very long. What's the big rush?" Li said.

"Fifty seconds," Ohemaa said.

Max felt his heart beat faster. He took a deep breath, reveling in the adrenaline that surged through his body. He grinned.

"Forty seconds," Ohemaa said.

Max wished he could see out, but the Orion spacecraft was protected by a full aerodynamic fairing, blocking all the windows.

"Thirty seconds," Ohemaa said.

Max knew that there were exterior cameras that he could switch to on his screen, but decided that was an unnecessary luxury. His screen was displaying a plethora of engineering data. He had personalized it to be exactly the way that he liked it.

"Twenty seconds," Ohemaa said.

Just launch already, Max thought. *This is taking forever. This is an eternity of seconds.*

"T-minus ten," Ohemaa said.

Max was gripped by an incredible urge to press the abort button. He could stop the countdown, unbuckle from his seat, and walk away. He could leave rockets forever and never look back.

"Nine," Ohemaa said.

Max did not press the abort button.

"Eight," Ohemaa said.

He gripped the armrests of his seat.

"Seven," Ohemaa said.

"Main engine start," said Georgy.

All four RS-25 main engines ignited.

"Six," Ohemaa said.

The main engines spun up, turbines accelerating.

"Five," Ohemaa said.

The thrust of the main engines shivered the tall stack, tightly held by the launch pad's sturdy clamps.

"Four," Ohemaa said.

Max breathed in through his nose.

"Three," Ohemaa said.

Max breathed out through his mouth.

"Two," Ohemaa said.

His screen showed him that the chamber pressures on the first stage engines looked good. All four rocket engines were at maximum thrust.

"One," Ohemaa said.

The rocket strained against its restraints.

"Launch," Ohemaa said.

The twin massive solid-fuel rockets ignited. The restraining bolts exploded, and the rocket leapt into the air.

CHAPTER THIRTY-SEVEN

Max was crushed into his seat. It felt as though a giant hand had seized him and was shaking him. The solid rocket boosters made this a bumpy ride.

"Liftoff!" came Georgy's exultant voice through the radio.

Max blinked hard, trying to focus on his vibrating screen.

"Everything looks good. Azimuth roll complete," Max said, squinting.

"Copy that. All systems green," Javid said over the radio. Cheering could be heard in the background.

Max studied the numbers in front of him. Acceleration and velocity looked good. The rocket nosed over as it began its gravity turn toward the east. They quickly passed through the speed of sound and approached max Q.

"Vehicle throttling back for max Q," Max said. His hands were on the controls, ready to abort should the rocket fail at this crucial moment. Everything continued to stay green.

"Passing through max Q. Throttling back up to one hundred percent," Javid said presently. The G-force began increasing.

Max glanced at the mission clock. It had already been two minutes since liftoff.

"Albert? Miranda? You greenhorns still good?" Max asked.

"No complaints from me," Albert said.

"Doing great Max. It's the ride of a lifetime," Miranda replied.

Max turned his head to glance at Li. She gave him a thumbs up and a confident grin through her closed visor.

"Prepare for booster shutdown," Ohemaa said.

Ten seconds later the solid rocket boosters burned out and the acceleration dropped. With a thump the boosters detached and fell away.

"Phew," Max said. "I'm glad that we are done with those." The flight was much gentler now.

"Agreed," Li chimed in. "The solids were a rough blast."

On its four hydrolox main engines, the rocket continued to pick up speed. Thrust was constant, but the vehicle became lighter as the fuel burned away, therefore acceleration increased. It was a quiet ride, nearly vibrationless due to the dampening effect of the long fuel tank between the spacecraft and the engines.

"There are elevated temperature readings on engines two and four," Max noticed.

"We see that, Max, but the engines are still within tolerance," Javid responded.

"Chamber pressures in both engines are low. Oxidizer consumption is up. Javid, have somebody review the camera feed of the launch. There must be a hydrogen leak again," Max said.

"I will look at it myself. Georgy will take over for me here," Javid responded.

"The escape tower is scheduled to jettison in thirty seconds," Georgy said. "Unless you need to abort?"

"Go ahead with the tower jettison," Max said.

Max watched his screen closely. Temperatures in engines two and four continued to climb. Oxidizer consumption ticked up again as the computer adjusted the mixture in an attempt to keep the thrust constant. The aerodynamic fairing fell away and bright sunlight filled the capsule.

"You're right Max. There were bright flashes in the engine bells of engines two and four. I think I can see hydrogen leaks on the footage. Injector pins in both engines must have come loose. Do we need to use abort mode three?" Javid said

They were on a suborbital trajectory. Under abort mode three they would shut down the main engines and coast through the thin upper atmosphere. Their spacecraft would fly in a parabola, detach from the booster at the apex, and land under parachutes in the south Atlantic Ocean.

"Don't abort yet, but watch these engines," Max said.

The golden injector pins had been used to deactivate bad injectors. Without the pins, there was a risk that the injector plates could crumble. Engine heat continued to rise. Combustion chamber temperatures were approaching dangerous levels.

"I'm changing the mix ratio," Max decided. "I'm going to pump the engines hydrogen rich to cool the engines back down."

"But that will reduce your thrust. You might not make orbit," Georgy said.

"We may not make orbit on the first stage, but we can go as far as we can then make orbit on the second stage. I'm going to pitch the nose up to gain altitude. It's less efficient, but it will give the second stage more time to work. Javid, let me know before I pitch up too far. If this doesn't work, we will need to keep reentry within survivable G's," Max said.

"I understand," Javid said.

Max overrode the computer's automatic hydrogen/oxygen adjustment in engines two and four. He increased the proportion of hydrogen to run the engines fuel rich. Engine temperatures dropped from dangerous levels, but there was a noticeable decrease in acceleration as the thrust from the engines decreased.

"Pitching up," Max said, taking the right-hand joystick.

With a lurch, the capsule slewed and the blue green horizon beyond the windows tilted away.

"That looks good. Hold it there at five degrees inclination," Javid said.

"Holding," Max said. The rocket's acceleration passed three G's. He glanced at Li. She looked nervous but nodded her approval.

"Okay you can pitch up another degree," Javid said.

"Got it, pitching up," Max said.

"Good. Hold it. Hold it there," Javid said.

"Roger," Max said.

Max had never manually flown a spacecraft on ascent. Getting from ground to orbit was usually the domain of computers and giant booster rockets. It required extreme precision and thousands of man-hours of calculation. Now, Max was winging it, but he felt good about it. His gut told him that this was going to work.

"We trust you, Max. Get us into orbit," Albert said.

"We'd be there already if there weren't all this darn gravity in the way," Max said.

Max wondered why Doctor Thompson had not chimed in. He knew that she must be there, standing in the control room, headset microphone at her lips. He half-expected her to take over at any moment, to order an abort, to stop their wild caper and bring her wayward children back home before they hurt themselves.

"It's looking good, Max. It's looking real good. At apogee it should only take a few hundred extra kilos of fuel from the second stage to make orbit," Javid said.

Acceleration was nearing 4G's and velocity was 5.9 kilometers per second. Less than ten percent of the propellant was left in the first stage tank. Soon they would ditch the first stage and fly the rest of the way to orbit on the second. Max was grinning.

But suddenly, engine number two shut down. Engine four shut down half a second later. Engines one and three were still burning, but the rocket's acceleration dropped by half.

"That did not feel right," Miranda said.

"Engines two and four turned off automatically. Chamber pressures crumped. The injector plates must have let go and the computer shut them down before they could blow," Max said.

"So, what now?" Albert asked.

"We keep going. We can still make orbit, right, Javid?" Max asked

"If you burn all of the fuel in your second stage you will reach an slightly eccentric LEO with a perigee of 300 kilometers," Javid said.

"But we need the second stage to send us to the moon. If we burn up all the fuel getting into orbit, we won't have enough fuel left to perform the translunar injection," Albert said.

"Let's focus on one thing at a time. Let's just get to orbit first," Max said.

The last of the fuel drained from the first stage tank and the first stage engines burned out. They were briefly weightless, but not yet in orbit. Max could see on his screen that the parabola of their flight now terminated in the Indian Ocean. He punched in the command to manually decouple the first stage of the rocket. There was a shudder as the explosive bolts fired. Max waited an agonizing second, then he fired up the second stage's twin RL-10 motors.

The RL-10 hydrolox engine was an extremely efficient rocket motor, but it was weak. Each of the two engines only provided 110 kilonewtons of thrust, a pittance compared to the 8 meganewtons of thrust provided by the four RS-25 engines of the first stage. Max throttled the second stage up to maximum and the gentle engines burned in the silent vacuum. A soft acceleration held him in his seat.

Max studied his screen. "Javid upload an optimal course trajectory to LEO for me, will you?"

"Yes Max. Uploading now," Javid said.

Max allowed the computer to take over and sat back in his chair. Javid's course corrections arrived, and the spacecraft began steering itself automatically. This would be a nearly four-minute burn while gravity tried to drag them back down to the Earth.

"Could we at least do a moon flyby with the fuel in the service module?" Li asked.

Once the 26,000 kilograms of hydrolox propellant in the second stage was used up, they would still have the 8,600 kilograms of dinitrogen tetroxide/hydrazine propellant and hypergolic engine of the Orion's service module.

"No. It won't be enough. Translunar injection takes about 3,000 meters per second of delta-v. The service module can only provide about 1,200," Max said.

Their vehicle was skimming the Earth's atmosphere as it strove for space. Its nose was pointed upward by thirty degrees from the horizon, trying desperately for those last few hundred meters per second needed to reach a stable orbit. It was a race between the fiercely striving spaceship and the implacable pull of gravity.

"We can't make to the moon by ourselves," Max said. "But maybe we can ask for help. Georgy, can you get David Steins on the phone?

"Sure. He gave me his mobile number, just one moment," Georgy said.

Twenty seconds later the CEO of SpaceTech was on the radio. "Hi Max! I was watching the launch. It looks like your first stage gave you some trouble," David said.

"Yes, we are using the second stage to make orbit, but we will be too short on fuel to make translunar injection. Do you have anything that could give us a hand?" Max asked.

"I might have just the thing. Remember Big Test Rocket One?" David asked.

"You mean that big thing that blew up on the launch pad when I first arrived in Texas?" Max said.

"Yes. That's the one," David said.

"I remember it exploding," Max said.

"Well we have two more just like it ready to go. Give me thirty minutes and we can launch one," David said.

"Then what? Our spaceship can't do fuel transfer," Albert interjected.

"We don't need fuel. We need a tow. Or a push. Can you make that happen, David? Can you set up a pusher plate on your rocket?" Max asked.

"I think we can. Let me put some people on it," David said.

"Are you okay with this Doctor Thompson?" Max asked.

"A change this drastic adds risk for the crew. What does your team think?" Ohemaa responded.

Max glanced at Li. She nodded. "Let's give it a try," she said.

"I agree with Li," Miranda said. "We can also spend some time in low earth orbit and assess our options."

"I'll do whatever gives us the best chance of getting to the moon," Albert said.

The second stage engines shut down. Max checked his screen. They had made it to orbit. It was a somewhat lopsided orbit, with a perigee of 200 kilometers and an apogee closer to 300, but it was stable. The hydrolox propellant in the second stage was at zero percent.

"All right," Max said, removing his helmet. "David, give it a shot."

CHAPTER THIRTY-EIGHT

Thirty minutes later ground control was on the radio again.

"We're piping in a live video feed from Texas," Doctor Thompson said.

Max had shifted out of his pressure suit and was in polyester shirtsleeves. The Orion was more spacious than any spaceship Max had flown, but with four people crowding the single cabin, it felt cramped. Max floated in the small space behind the four seats, cataloging and organizing his tools while Albert worked his way free of his suit in the center of the cabin.

"Thanks Doctor Thompson. We're excited to see it," Miranda answered.

All four screens now showed a rocket sitting on a launch pad. Max put his tools away to watch. The vehicle that sat on the pad was a tapered silver cylinder. It looked more like a grain silo than any traditional rocket that Max had ever seen.

"We call it 'Big Test Rocket Two,'" said David Stein's voice over the radio. "We believe that it can act as a pusher tug by grappling with your second stage then accelerate you to TLI."

"The second stage is just dead weight now. Shouldn't we ditch the second stage and then you could grapple directly to the service module?" Albert said.

"The extra weight won't be a problem. The BTR has plenty of extra delta-v and we don't want to risk damaging the service module engines by grappling to them directly. The extra weight of the second stage will also keep the acceleration within tolerable levels. We aim to keep the acceleration at 1G for the duration of the push," Victoria said.

"Is that rocket made of stainless steel?" Max asked.

"Yes it is. Steel is heavy but it's also stiff and cheap. We hope that by upsizing the rocket we can compensate for the weight penalty," David answered.

"How big is that thing anyway?" Max asked. It was hard to estimate size on the video feed. The coastal marshes surrounding the pad were perfectly flat. There were other launch pad structures in the foreground, but Max could not estimate how large they were either. There was nothing in the image to give the rocket scale.

"The rocket is one hundred meters tall, ten meters in diameter, and masses four thousand tons," Victoria answered.

Max whistled. "That's pretty big. Think it'll fly?"

"We hope so!" David answered enthusiastically.

"How's it going to reenter the atmosphere? I don't see a heat shield or anything," Li asked.

"We haven't figured that part out yet. We'll probably add ablative tiles eventually. But this one doesn't need to reenter, it just needs to give you a push," David said.

"And how is it going to do that exactly?" Miranda asked.

"Keep watching the screen," Victoria said.

The screen switched to a zoomed-in view of the top of the rocket. The massive rocket's nose was a dome of smooth, shiny steel. Welded onto the apex was a lattice of steel supports and four robotic grabber arms.

"Did you attach commercial-grade robotic grabber arms?" Max asked.

"Yes. We took them off our assembly line," Victoria answered.

"Our spaceship in its current state masses twenty thousand kilograms. Are those arms going to be able to handle that much weight under acceleration?" Max asked.

"Not alone. That's what the steel lattice is for. The arms will settle the engine bells into the steel supports. Our simulations show that this lattice structure can handle six hundred kilonewtons of force if applied linearly," Victoria said.

Max did the math in his head. The second stage of their spaceship had two engine bells, each one 2 meters across. That gave each nozzle an area of about 6.3 square meters for a total area of 12.6 m^2. The vessel weighed 20,000 kilograms. It would require 200 kilonewtons of force to accelerate at 10 m/s^2, which meant that any vehicle pushing the spacecraft at 1G would experience 200 kilonewtons pushed back into itself; a force that would be experienced as linear compression between the pushing engines and the mass of the Orion spacecraft. 200,000 newtons divided by 12.6 square meters equaled 16,000 pascals of pressure. Fortunately, that was a number well within the bounds of structural steel, assuming it was properly supported. Max knew that his math was not perfect, especially since the stresses would be focused on a narrow band just at the circumference of the engine bells. The second stage engine bells would probably compress somewhat, but they would not be needed for the rest of the mission. The proposed plan to push the Orion seemed grossly reasonable from an engineering standpoint.

"Let me see the welds," Max said.

"I can do that," Victoria said.

There was a moment of quiet, then the video feed from a flying drone camera appeared on the screen. It panned around and zoomed in, focusing on the structure atop the BTR. Max saw a latticework of steel supports, shaped like a figure eight.

"Can you zoom in more?" Max asked.

"Sure," Victoria answered. The camera zoomed in, focusing on the joints between structural members.

Max squinted, studying the waves of crystallized metal in the hand-welded structure.

"Those welds look good," Max said. "This should work."

"Great. We will launch in two," David said.

"Two minutes?" Li interjected. "That's so quick!"

"We were already fueling for a pressure test when you called," Victoria explained.

"Fast is good," Albert said.

"Agreed," Victoria responded. The screen switched back to a wide view of the launch pad. A cloud of gas that Max guessed was condensing vapor due to venting liquid oxygen drifted from the top of the rocket. There was no supporting tower. The massive rocket stood alone, dwarfing the scattered water towers and fuel silos that surrounded it.

"T-minus sixty seconds to launch," said Victoria's voice over the radio.

There was no countdown. Max timed sixty seconds on his wristwatch. At zero seconds the base of the rocket erupted in orange flame. The rocket rose and began accelerating, slowly at first and then faster. It began nosing over for the gravity turn.

"Uh oh," Max said. The rocket was leaning too much. It leaned farther and farther until it was pointing its nose more toward the ground than toward the sky.

"BTR is going off course. Initiate the flight termination sequence," Victoria said with a sigh. The rocket exploded as its onboard pyrotechnics detonated, igniting the fuel and oxygen, and triggering a rapid unscheduled disassembly. A cloud of black smoke blossomed, and a shower of debris fell toward the marsh below. The crew of the Orion groaned aloud.

"Darn," said Li.

Nobody spoke for a moment. Max turned to the computer and began plotting reentry trajectories. It would be a short trip back home.

"We do have one more prototype," David said hopefully.

"It looks like the problem was a simple computer navigation error. We can fix it for the next flight," Victoria added.

"How soon can you have the next prototype ready?" Doctor Thompson asked.

"We can have Big Test Rocket number Three ready to fly in twenty-four hours," Victoria answered.

Max glanced at his crewmembers.

"We can wait twenty four hours," Li said. "We've got plenty of power, food, water, and oxygen. What do we have to lose by waiting?"

"Let's give them one more chance," Albert added.

"Ground control, we want to see BTR Three fly," Max said.

"Alright team. Good work today. You're in a stable orbit and all systems are green. Get some rest and we can try again tomorrow," Doctor Thompson said.

The next day on Earth came sixteen sunrises and sunsets later for the Orion crew. Max organized his tools, slept for eight hours, and relieved himself twice in the curtain-shielded zero-gee lavatory. Feeling certain that they would be returning, defeated, to Earth within a couple more orbits, Max and the crew gathered to watch the launch of the SpaceTech rocket.

"Here we go, Big Test Rocket Three, launching in three… two… one," said Victoria.

The smoke and flame from the rocket's engines bloomed across the computer screen. The camera feed shook with the acoustic vibration of rapidly combusting propellant and the stainless-steel rocket rose into the air.

Miraculously, this rocket did not explode. It did not veer off course. It rose gracefully, passed through the sound barrier, and leaned over for a gravity turn.

"Your ride is on its way," David announced triumphantly.

"Let's not clink our glasses yet. The rocket has to make orbit first," Victoria said.

"But it is looking good so far," David said.

Max watched the numbers climb. The BTR was on an aggressive ascent trajectory. The rockets nose was already parallel to the horizon and it was accelerating fast. This rocket was efficient and powerful. If SpaceTech could successfully mass produce this new rocket, it would make many older rocket designs obsolete.

Within three minutes the rocket was above the Kármán line. Three minutes after that the rocket was in orbit. Its engines shut down and it drifted, serene, waiting for its next command. There were no staging events the entire way.

Max whistled. "A single-stage-to-orbit vehicle," he said.

"And this is just the prototype!" David exclaimed happily. "The shareholders will be so impressed."

"Okay team," Doctor Thompson said, getting everybody's attention. "The SpaceTech BTR is going to perform all rendezvous maneuvers to conserve fuel on the Orion. We will continue to upload the feed to your computer so that you can monitor its progress."

"Thanks Doctor Thompson. We're not going anywhere," said Li.

CHAPTER THIRTY-NINE

The approach of the BTR went according to schedule. Obeying its commands from the ground station, the automated rocket burned twice. The first burn was to accelerate, raising its apogee to create a rendezvous. Then, arriving at the rendezvous, it flipped one hundred and eighty degrees and burned for the second time. It slid onto the spacecraft's radar and matched the Orion's orbit.

All four of the Artemis astronauts were wearing protective spacesuits and were strapped into their command chairs. Max watched the radar blip move across his screen, closing the distance rapidly.

"It's big," Li commented.

"Yes," Max agreed. He flipped through the exterior cameras to watch the remotely piloted spaceship approach.

The stainless-steel cylinder gleamed in the sunlight. Max was glad for the filter of the camera's lens because the reflected glare would have been painful to the naked eye. Gas jets pulsed as the BTR decelerated.

"We are patching through the camera feed from the BTR," Victoria said.

An icon appeared on Max's screen and he activated it. The camera on the BTR's nose showed the Orion floating in space, framed in blackness. The big rocket maneuvered behind the spacecraft and a targeting reticle appeared on the screen.

Max's hands hovered above his controls. He was ready to dump the second stage and run if things started going wrong. The BTR drifted closer. It grasped the second stage's engine bells with its grabber arms and settled them into its welded framework supports.

"Looks fine from up here. The BTR has us," Max said.

"Looks good from down here too," Victoria confirmed.

"We will be in the correct window of our orbit for translunar injection in ten minutes. Let's align and get blasting," Albert said.

"Roger that. Artemis you are go for TLI" Doctor Thompson said.

"Works for me," Li added.

The moon appeared over the horizon of the blue-white Earth. Max watched it rise, pale-gray against black space. The spacecraft turned until it appeared to point toward its target.

"Engine ignition," Victoria said.

Even at low thrust on just one of its five massive engines, the power of the BTR was considerable. The crew were pressed into their seats by one full G. It was a long burn – five minutes of steady acceleration. Max scanned his instruments continually for any sign of structural failure or weakening, but the jury-rigged contraption held. Finally, the engine shut off. They had increased their velocity relative to the Earth by 3,200 meters per second. The BTR un-grappled and floated free. Albert detached the empty second stage.

"Trajectory looks good," Albert said.

"All systems nominal," Miranda added.

"Nothing broke," Max said. "That's a bit of an anticlimax, isn't it?"

"No," said Li with a smile. "Something doesn't have to go wrong for the journey to be exciting."

"Congratulations, Artemis. You are on your way to the moon," Doctor Thompson said.

Max unbuckled from his seat. Li followed his example. Albert helped Miranda unclasp her helmet.

From Earth, the moon may look close by, but appearances were deceiving. Even though they were moving at thirty times the speed of sound, it was still going to take their spaceship three days to reach the moon.

Max input a short command and two RCS thrusters briefly fired. The spacecraft began spinning on its axis at a rate of one degree per second, a spin designed for even surface heating in constant sunlight. Max gazed out the window. The Earth, massive and close, rose and then set in his view. Two minutes later the moon appeared, small and pale gray.

"Time for a systems-check and inventory," Albert announced.

"Sure," Max said, turning away. There was work to be done.

There were no days or nights in the empty space between the Earth and the moon. There was only the interminable sunlight and the star-strewn blackness. The journey would have seemed timeless except for the steadily shrinking Earth in the window. In all his years of spaceflight, Max had never left low Earth orbit. When in LEO, Earth felt close enough to touch. It was a constant presence, blocking out the sun and filling the entire view. Now, the whole Earth floated in a single windowpane.

The crew was on a rest period after six hours of checklists and systems diagnostics.

"The Earth looks so fragile," Miranda said.

She put the lens of a video camera against the glass, capturing the view of the Earth as it slid from left to right, seemingly orbiting the spinning spacecraft.

"It looks lonely," Li said.

"It looks like it's just waiting to be smashed by a comet," Max said.

"Or blown up by a super volcano," Li said.

"We don't need to wait for a natural disaster to destroy the planet. Human industry is messing it up with pollution and global warming," Albert said.

"Way to be a bummer, Albert," Li said.

"Artemis team, this is Houston," Doctor Thompson's voice came over the radio.

"Present," Max said.

"I know that you are on a break, but we would love if you could send us something to release to the press," Doctor Thompson said.

"We can do that. Watch the feed from handheld camera three," Miranda said.

Miranda panned the small camera over the crew, who waved in turn.

"Hi from space!" Miranda said cheerfully. She then aimed the camera out the window. They all shared a moment of silence as they watched the Earth drift by.

"We'll be back soon, Earth," Miranda said. She floated to the opposite window. "We're going to go visit your neighbor," she said, framing the moon in the camera lens.

CHAPTER FORTY

After an eight-hour sleep period, a gentle wakefulness alarm buzzed in the cabin. Yawning and stretching, Max accidentally kicked Albert in the small of the back.

"Sorry, Albert, they need to start making these things bigger," Max said.

"I think it's cozy," Albert said with a grin.

"The lunar station will give us some elbow room," Miranda said.

"Are you awake too, Li?" Max asked. Shades covered the windows. Except for the pleasant green and blue glow of indicator lights on the control panels, the spacecraft was dark.

"Yes. I'm awake. I slept great. Is it always this comfortable to sleep in space?" Li asked.

"Always," Max said. He floated to the nearest window and drew back the sunshade. A waxing moon drifted beyond the glass. It appeared bigger than ever before.

More light flooded into the cabin as Li went to the opposite window and removed the shade. She gasped, drawing Max's attention to the view beyond.

"It's even more beautiful," she whispered.

Earth was smaller now, just a blue-white beach ball, hanging alone in infinite blackness. They all gazed for a reverent moment, until the view rotated away.

Self-care was the first act of the new day. They washed

themselves in turn, using a small, curtained area of the cabin for privacy. Max brushed his teeth and breakfasted on a tube of yogurt and a package of dried banana. There were no alerts on his terminal. Everything was business as usual. The telemetry data in the navigation computer was corroborated by the readings from the onboard star-tracker. The communication link with NASA mission control was operating with good bandwidth and the deep space network was operational as a backup.

Max checked the other systems. Fuel tank pressure looked good. Primary and secondary electrical systems were working. Current from the solar panels was at expected levels. Life support was operating within capacity. Cabin pressure was nominal. Spacecraft external temperatures were well within tolerance.

"It looks like it's going to be a boring day," Max.

"Don't jinx us," Albert chuckled, emerging clean-washed from behind the privacy curtain.

"You don't really believe in jinx, do you?" Li asked.

"Oh, no. Not really," Albert said. "Superstition is just the brain attempting to reconcile all the chaos."

"Chaos is a fiction of the mind. In a deterministic universe, nothing is random," Li said.

"How do you account for probability then?" Albert asked. "Science is useless without good statistics."

Li shrugged. "Statistics is a crutch for when you lack enough data to elucidate precise cause and effect. You have to admit that if you had enough information about any given system, you could predict future outcomes with absolute certainty," Li said.

"Where does that leave free will?" Albert asked.

"Where indeed?" Li answered drily.

"If it's going to be a slow day, we can make a video for NASA to release to the press," Miranda interjected.

Albert nodded. "Sure, but I don't have anything prepared," he said.

"Me neither," Li said.

"You could start, Miranda. You could talk about what we are doing now and what we're going to do next," Max offered.

"That's a good idea," Miranda said.

Miranda bound her hair with an elastic tie and retrieved her video camera. She Velcroed the camera to the wall and sent the feed to a monitor nearby so she could watch herself while she spoke. She floated for a moment, composing her thoughts, then began recording.

"Hi Earth!" she said cheerfully. Then she stopped and shook her head. "I didn't like the way that I said that." She deleted the video and started again.

"Hi Earth!" she began again. "This Doctor Miranda Santos, calling from the Orion spacecraft of the Artemis Moon mission. Our voyage is going quite well. There was a little bit of excitement on ascent. We had some issues with our first stage engines, but with some quick thinking and the help of our partners at SpaceTech we were able to get a boost toward the moon. We are now coasting, with our engines off, and we will reach the moon in two days. Our mission has nine big events coming up."

Miranda began counting on her fingers.

"First, we will brake into lunar orbit and dock with the brand-new lunar space station, which is waiting for us in a polar orbit. Second, Max and Li will board the lunar lander and undock from the lunar station. Third, those two will go down to land on the moon while Albert and I wait for them aboard the station. Fourth, they will leave their spacecraft and walk on the surface, scouting out the area for the scientific base NASA hopes to start building there soon. Fifth, once done with their moon walk, they will blast off from the moon's surface and make it back to lunar orbit. Sixth, they will pilot their lander back to rendezvous and dock with the lunar station. Seventh, all four of us will board the Orion spacecraft and undock from the lunar station. Eighth, we will fire up our engines and fly back to Earth. Just like the trip to the moon, the voyage home will take three days. And finally, ninth, we will reenter the Earth's atmosphere and parachute into the ocean, where a boat will be waiting to pick us up. Nine major mission events to keep an eye on!"

"Well said, Doctor Santos," Albert said. He floated upside-down into the frame and waved at the camera. "A pathfinder mission like ours is laying the groundwork for many more trips just like it. Once we get the infrastructure in place and all the equipment tested out, a trip to the moon and back will be easy-peasy!"

"If you have any questions about our trip to the moon, please submit them to the NASA dot gov website and we will try to answer as many as we can. We have another day of travelling in front of us, and we would love to spend some of that time talking to you," Miranda concluded. She waved goodbye to the camera, then stopped the recording.

"Thanks team," Doctor Thompson's voice came over the radio. "We're going to publish your video right now. Well done."

"You guys did well. I don't think I'd be good at talking to the public," Max said.

"We will get you some practice," Miranda replied.

Miranda was true to her word. She assigned Max twenty video-recorded questions from the bank of public submissions that NASA had uploaded to the spacecraft's computer. Many of the questions had been submitted well in advance of the launch of Artemis, and about two thirds of them were from children. The ones that Miranda chose for Max regarded spacecraft systems and propulsion. Li was given questions about landing on the moon and about the lunar surface. Albert took questions about spacecraft navigation, and Miranda responded to questions about health and the human experience in space. They spent the day taking turns with the camera and coaching each other. Max was nervous in front of the camera, but the joy of science took over and he finished feeling energized. When the time for sleep came, he slept deeply and dreamed about rockets.

The next day was the final leg of their coast. They talked to mission control, reviewed their safety plans, and sent more videos back to NASA. The entire time the moon came closer, growing by every revolution of their slowly spinning craft.

After a final sleep period, the buzzing alarm woke the crew. It was time for lunar orbital insertion. The moon was massive now, filling the space beyond the windows with its cratered surface. They were diving down toward it, aimed to pass close above its North pole.

"We burn in one hour," Albert said.

The lunar insertion burn, the maneuver that would slow the speeding spacecraft down to lunar orbital velocity, would be the first maneuver performed with the Orion's service module. The service module was attached directly "behind" the Orion capsule. It was the same diameter as the Orion, but about 25 percent taller. It contained the hypergolic propellant tanks (hydrazine and dinitrogen tetroxide), a main rocket engine, maneuvering thrusters, and the attachment points for the solar panels.

Max checked the Orion's trajectory and the orbit of the lunar space station. If this burn went as Albert had planned, it would both put them into lunar orbit and create a rendezvous with the lunar station. Everything looked good.

The moon's surface grew nearer, and the shadowed craters were sharp in the vacuum of space. The team went through their checklists again.

"Maneuver begins in five minutes," Albert announced.

All four crewmembers strapped into their acceleration chairs. Max hovered his hands above the controls, but the automated system performed its job before he could take over. Small attitude control thrusters pulsed, and the spacecraft swung around, pointing its nose back toward Earth. A second pulse stopped the rotation.

The main engine ignited. To achieve lunar insertion orbit they needed to adjust their velocity by 900 meters per second. Their vehicle weighed 26,000 kilograms and their engine, coincidentally, had an output of 26,000 newtons of thrust. This meant that their acceleration began at 1 meter per second per second, climbing gradually as they burned off fuel, and would take 900 seconds.

Max scanned the numbers with satisfaction. It was pleasing how round the figures were. The gentle acceleration of the small, efficient engine was just enough to allow him to rest his head back against his headrest, watching their velocity steadily drop as they made a perfect orbital injection.

"The lunar station is on close range radar," Li announced.

Max watched the radar blip slide across his screen. The engine shut off and the blip stopped moving. They were less than 5 kilometers away from the lunar space station and had matched its orbit perfectly.

"Nice rendezvous, Artemis," came Doctor Thompson's voice over the radio.

"Don't look at me, the computer did it," Albert said.

"Good computer," Li said, patting her console.

"All right, let's take her in to dock," Albert said.

Albert took the controls and the spacecraft swung around, pointing toward the station. Electric motors in the nose of the capsule hummed, swinging an aerodynamic cone of aluminum alloy out of the way and revealing the docking port underneath.

The thrusters pulsed as they drifted toward the lunar station. The alignment looked good and Albert let the automated docking system take control.

It was not hard for Max to imagine ordinary civilians taking this journey, especially if spaceships could be made with more elbow room. There was some G-force to endure on the way to orbit, but no more than that of a good roller coaster. The autopilot systems, if perfected, could do all the complicated work. Piloting a spaceship was not a difficult task for a computer. With a few of the bugs ironed out, a round-trip ride to the moon could be something that anybody could do.

With a gentle bump the spacecraft docked to the lunar station. The docking ports connected and clamped home. A green light on his screen showed Max that the seal was good. Max unfastened his belt and floated to the hatch. A digital readout showed that the air pressure was equalized on both sides. The darkened interior of the lunar station could be seen through a small window. Max turned the handle and the hatch swung inward. The station lights came on.

In its current state the lunar station was a series of three rooms. This first room was a cylindrically hallway with four docking ports. The next cabin was a spacious living quarters, and the third room was for storage and energy management. The station was modular and expandable. The whole place had a fresh, plasticky smell.

"I guess this is home for the next couple days," Miranda said, floating past Max and into the living quarters.

"For you guys maybe. Max and I are just visiting," Li said. She floated to the opposite docking port. Through the window the interior of the lunar lander could be seen. "In half of an orbit we're out of here," she said with a smile.

The space station was in an orbit designed to minimize losing communications with Earth. To do this, the orbit was somewhat eccentric, dipping close to the north pole and rising high above the south pole. For the most efficient lunar landing, they would undock the lander and burn retrograde at apoapsis, dropping their periapsis to skim the surface for landing. They would be halfway through the lunar orbit in six hours. There had been talk of putting the station in a higher orbit, something called a "near-rectilinear halo orbit," which would place the station such that it was never in the shadow of the moon relative to the Earth, but that would have put the station in an orbit with a seven-day period, which would be a long time to wait for a rendezvous window when blasting off from the lunar surface.

"I can't wait to go," Max said, gazing at the lunar lander.

CHAPTER FORTY-ONE

The six hours flew by. Max and Li inspected their lander. All its systems were at 100%. It had survived its own journey to lunar orbit and automated docking with the lunar station without a blemish.

"We would have been here days ago if we had ridden in the lander," Li said. She floated in the command seat, waiting eagerly for the time to undock and begin the next leg of their voyage. Max floated in the hatchway, sipping on a bag of fruit juice. Both had slipped back into the pressure-ready flight suits in which they would make their descent.

"You're braver than me. That would have been a trip with no escape system. There would have been no way to abort if something had gone wrong," Max said.

"Soon space travel will be so safe and routine that nobody will need abort systems," Li said.

"I hope you're right," Max said.

"I am," Li said.

"Away team, are you ready?" came Georgy's voice over the station's speakers.

"Are we called the 'away team' now? Did we decide on that?" Max asked.

"No. I did," Georgy said with a chuckle.

"I like it," Li said.

"We are ready, Georgy. How long to apoapsis?" Max asked.

"Twenty minutes," Georgy said.

"Great. Let's do it," Max said. He finished his juice, stuffed the empty pouch into a trash bag against the wall, and pushed himself into the lander.

The lunar lander was spacious. It had even more interior volume than the Orion spacecraft. There were four seats but enough space for several more. The lander could afford to be big and bulky. It would only ever have to deal with lunar gravity, and it did not need to pay any consideration to aerodynamics. It was shaped like a long rectangle, with a textured aluminum floor beneath upright chairs. A large airlock graced the far end, and the compartment was big enough to stand upright to don or doff a bulky EVA space suit.

"Safe travels," said Miranda. She and Albert waited in the doorway, watching as Li and Max strapped themselves into their seats.

"We'll be back soon," Li promised.

Albert closed and sealed the hatch and Max turned his attention to the computer.

"Will you be our primary contact for the lunar landing, Georgy?" Max asked.

"Yes," Georgy answered over the radio.

"How did that happen?" Max asked.

"I asked nicely," Georgy said.

"I'm not complaining," Max said.

"The lunar lander is on internal power. Undock when you are ready," Georgy said.

"You got it," Li answered. She would be the primary pilot for this phase of the mission.

Li punched a command into her terminal and the docking clamps released. She pulsed the maneuvering thrusters and the lander drifted away from the station.

"Do you think that the lander's autopilot will work? They had been having trouble with it," Max asked.

"I hope not," Li answered.

"You want to land this thing manually?" Max asked.

"Duh," Li said.

"We heard that," Georgy said.

"Fix the autopilot, then," Li said.

"They assure me that they are working on it," Georgy said.

The lander drifted farther away from the station.

"Apoapsis in five minutes," Georgy said.

They were approaching the highest point of their lunar orbit. Out the right-side windows the moon hung. Its surface was partly illuminated craggy landscape and partly darkened mystery. The lander rotated and brilliant sunlight flooded into the cabin. Through the opposite window the lunar station's shiny metal gleamed against the infinite night.

"Initiating retrograde burn," Li announced.

Valves in the lander's pressure-fed main engine opened. Hydrazine and dinitrogen tetroxide flowed into the combustion chamber. When mixed they ignited spontaneously, generating heat, pressure, and thrust. The acceleration was just under 1G, but it was not for long, only long enough to bring their periapsis down from 100 kilometers to 5 kilometers. The motor shut off and the acceleration stopped. The moon looked no different, but Max knew that they were diving down toward it now, on a course that would intersect with the north pole, 180 degrees away. The lunar station receded, shrinking to a point of light before disappearing into the darkness.

Over the next six hours the moon grew. They rode the terminator, the line between light and dark. Mountains, ridges, and crater edges cast sharp shadows below.

"The north pole is a good place to land. The sunlight's angle will be low. It will be easy to see boulders and other obstructions," Li said, gazing at the rocky surface.

"The moon's landscape is surprisingly diverse. It's not just a round surface covered in craters. I can see mountains and valleys and plateaus everywhere," Max said.

"There used to be volcanoes too, billions of years ago when it was crystallizing from a magma ocean. Since then, it has been frozen in space," Li said.

"In that case there must be valuable resources in the crust," Max said.

"Same as on Earth. The moon is an ejected chunk of the Earth after all," Li said.

The surface continued to expand. Mountains and ridgelines appeared suddenly over the approaching horizon, passed close below, and disappeared behind.

"Landing burn in five minutes," Li said, fastening her helmet onto her pressure suit. Max did the same.

The camera feed was as large as life on their LCD screens. Li watched her instruments and waited. At the right moment she engaged the lander's engine.

This was a long maneuver, as they had to scrub off nearly 2,000 meters per second of orbital velocity. The deceleration burn took 3 minutes. All the time the ground came closer and closer.

"We are on final approach," Li said finally. ""Orbital velocity is less than 100 meters per second. Let's test the landing autopilot."

Li activated an icon on her screen and the engine shut off. The ground continued to drift closer. The lander's orientation did not change. No thruster fired. She waited five seconds, then turned the autopilot system off.

"The automated system does not seem to be working. I am taking manual control," she said.

Li engaged the engine at minimum thrust. This engine had deep-throttling capability, allowing her to reduce their acceleration to 0.25 G without causing combustion instability. She scanned the video feed for a place to land.

Max's heart was pounding. They were drifting sideways and down. His heart skipped a beat when Li shut the engine off again. They were falling.

"If we drift a little farther, we can make it closer to this clear spot," she said, tapping her screen.

"Sure," Max said breathlessly. They were travelling at 57 meters per second and accelerating downward. His instruments showed that they would smash into the lunar surface in less than 30 seconds. He gripped his armrests.

"I can fly us a little laterally," Li mused aloud. She was perfectly calm as she slewed the lander 90 degrees and pulsed the main engine twice. "That looks better," she said.

"Yep," Max gulped.

"Prepare for landing," Li sighed. She turned the lander upright again and hovered her hands over the main engine controls. The lander continued to fall, picking up speed as it hurtled toward the lunar surface.

At what seemed like the last possible moment, Li engaged maximum thrust. Max was shoved into his seat by the acceleration. The lander's four legs touched regolith. Li shut the engine off.

Cheers erupted from the radio. "Nicely done, Li," Georgy's voice said.

"We watched that from here. Great landing!" Miranda's voice came over the radio.

Max had to remove his helmet to wipe the sheen of sweat from his face. He commanded himself to breathe.

"Yes. Good job," Max said finally. Li took off her helmet and gave him a wink.

Max looked out the window. They had landed on the moon.

CHAPTER FORTY-TWO

An eight hour rest period was the next item on the schedule.

"Or we could go for a walk instead," Li offered.

Max considered. They had been awake for thirteen hours, but he doubted that he could sleep right now. He was too excited.

"I would like that," Max said. He directed his voice at the microphone built into his console. "Would that be alright, Doctor Thompson?" he asked.

"Doctor Thompson is nodding. She says go ahead," Georgy said. "There are no EVA tasks scheduled. Don't worry about doing any science or surveying. Just focus on getting accustomed to moving around in lunar gravity. Make it a short walk, less than an hour. Your sleep time starts soon."

"Thanks," Max answered.

Max unstrapped from his seat and stood. The moon's gravity was one sixth that of Earth's. Max felt light and a little unsteady. His body seemed to move in slow motion.

"I'm glad they made this cabin tall," Max said. He bounced when he tried to take a step. His stiff hair brushed the high aluminum ceiling. "Low gravity is a weird experience," he said.

"I love it," Li said, balancing on her toes. She bent and did a handstand, then tucked into a forward flip, landing gracefully on her feet.

"I don't think I'm going to try that. I would kick the computer screen," Max said.

"Someone should definitely build a big moon base. If only because it would be fun," Li said. She jumped and hung by one finger from a handhold on the ceiling.

"Need help with your EVA suit?" Max asked, going to the large compartment against the wall.

"Please," Li answered.

These were brand new spacesuits, designed by NASA for maximum mobility on the moon. They had hard joints at the waist and shoulders, places where previous suits would struggle to articulate when fully inflated. Their life support systems were the most advanced ever designed. Li removed her flight suit, then climbed into her EVA suit through the hatch on the back and Max sealed her in. The suit could be made ready by one person alone, but it was easier with two.

"Comms working okay?" Max asked.

"Yep," Li answered. Her voice was broadcast over the lander's speakers.

Max climbed into his own suit and Li helped him seal up.

"Testing," Max said into his helmet microphone.

"I can hear you," Li responded over the radio.

"We can hear you too, Max," Georgy said.

"Us too," said Miranda from lunar orbit.

"Let's take a walk," Max said.

Max and Li entered the airlock. They sealed the inner door behind them, and the airlock pumped itself empty of atmosphere. A green indicator light shone, and Max opened the outer airlock door.

The sun touched the horizon of a silent world. The Earth was a blue and white ball, cupped in the rim of a massive crater.

"It's beautiful," Li breathed.

A desolate landscape stretched before them. A field of gravel gave way to dusty plain. A mountain ridge stood tall to the south. There was a fissure to the east, cut deep into the rocky ground. Li had landed them on a flat plateau, somewhat elevated from the land around. She walked down the ramp.

"It is easy to walk in these suits," Li said.

Max followed, taking cautious steps down the smooth ramp. His boots kicked up puffs of dust when they hit the moon's surface.

"Should we say something special?" Max asked.

Li did not answer. She crouched low, then jumped straight up. She flew two meters high. She spun, seeming to hang at the apex of her jump while she looked all around before drifting back down to the ground.

"Let's see what's over there," she said, pointing. Max followed her finger to a place where the plateau abruptly ended.

"I will follow you," Max said.

Li began walking. Max found it easiest to travel with a gliding stride, bounding in slow leaps over the dusty ground. Li switched from a walk into a skip, stopping once to take a high leap over a one-meter-tall boulder in her way.

They arrived at the lip of a shallow crater. It was hard to estimate its size exactly, but it looked to be at least two or three kilometers across. Li judged the angle of the slope, then started down it and Max followed after.

A few meters down, the low-angle sunlight was blocked by the opposite crater lip. Li turned on her helmet-mounted lights and continued onward while Max stopped and looked up.

"Woah," he said aloud.

On a world with a negligible atmosphere to scatter sunlight, being in shadow was the same as being in total darkness. The nighttime universe opened above him. A million billion untwinkling stars scattered across the blackness. The dusty trace of the Milky Way galaxy stretched from horizon to horizon. It was the grandest night sky that Max had ever seen.

"Look at what I found," Li's voice came through Max's radio.

Max looked down. Li squatted on the ground a little farther down the slope. Her outstretched arm touched something that shimmered in her helmet's light.

Max walked to her. He squatted and saw that a delicate film of crystalline frost covered the ground.

"I think that this is ice," Li said.

"That's incredible," Max said.

"We knew it would be here. Satellites have seen ice in craters at the poles, but it's amazing to see it in person," Li said.

"We can see your camera feed," Georgy said. "That looks like water ice."

"This could be useful for future colonists," Li said.

"Very. We have noted its location. That crater doesn't have a name yet. What would you like to call it?" Georgy asked.

Li looked up at Max and shrugged. When he looked down at her, he could see the entire starry universe reflected in her helmet's visor.

"Leverrier's crater," Max decided.

"Leverrier's crater it is. He would be proud of what you are doing here," Georgy said.

"Adams would just be glad that it's finally getting done," Max said.

"It's almost bed time. You kids should be getting home," Georgy said.

"Roger that, Georgy," Max said.

Max and Li retraced their steps back up the slope. They emerged blinking into the sunlight. The four-legged lander was a haven. It was a piece of gleaming manmade familiarity in an alien wasteland. They returned to their ship and climbed the ramp to the airlock.

"Wipe your feet," Li said.

"It's going to be hard to avoid getting moon dust into the cabin," Max noted, knocking dry dust from his boots on the outside door.

"We need to bring doormats next time, Houston," Li said. "Nice thick ones."

"Bring doormats. I am writing it down right now," Georgy responded, a touch of humor in his voice.

Max and Li cycled the airlock and reentered the cabin. The LED lights shone cheerfully from the high ceiling. Max climbed out of his space suit and Li climbed out of her own, a broad smile on her face.

"I think I will sleep well tonight," Max said with a sigh.

They stretched out on hammocks and slept for eight, blissful, uninterrupted hours. Max dreamed that he was floating on a warm sea, cool nighttime wind in his face and starry sky wheeling above.

When they woke the next day they bathed, brushed their teeth, and reviewed the day's schedule over a meal of reconstituted bacon and eggs and plastic pouches of black coffee.

"We are primarily here to do survey work," Max commented.

"Yep. NASA is looking for a place to build a moon base, but there is a limit to what can be seen from orbit. Boots on the ground is the best way to get the lay of the land," Li said.

"How do you want to divvy this up?" Max asked, looking at the list of to-dos.

"I can start with sample collection. NASA wants drill cores to understand subsurface conditions. Why don't you start with the laser scanners? We can switch jobs after a few hours," Li said.

"Works for me," Max said.

They climbed into their space suits and exited the lander onto the lunar surface. Li carried a large drill and several sample-collection tubes. Max brought three laser-surveyors, each already mounted on its own tall tripod.

Li began her first collection with the ground at the base of the ramp. Max placed his first surveyor nearby and turned it on. It would capture a detailed image of the landscape. He looked around and started toward a rise to the northeast. He mounted the gentle upward slope with an easy stride.

"I think that this spot will be in constant sunlight all the time," Max said once he arrived at the top of the hill. He stood at the crest of a broad dome that might have been part of an ancient shield volcano.

"Yeah?" Li responded.

"This is a high enough spot that I think the sun will never be blocked. There are no ridgelines that cast shadows here. The sun will just travel three hundred and sixty degrees around the horizon. This would be a good place to install solar panels," Max said.

He opened the second tripod and switched on the surveyor. He stepped back to give it a good view of the surrounding landscape. In the distance he could see Li working. She had walked about half a kilometer from the lander. She drove her drill into the ground in the middle of a flat, open plain.

"Where I am standing might be a good place for future landings. The ground is hard and seems to be pretty dense. There aren't many big rocks around here," Li said.

"I'll come down and set up a surveyor," Max said.

Max made his way to Li and set up his third laser machine. It blinked orange while it performed its task, sweeping invisible laser light in all directions to create a digital map of its surroundings. He knew that the laser surveyors were also talking to each other, triangulating features to create a composite image for the engineers to review back home.

"If we start landing really big space ships, we will need to build a hardened landing pad. Something free of any debris that could get kicked up into rocket engines," Li said, leaning on her drill.

"You landed just fine and it's mostly gravel on the plateau," Max said.

"We are in a small ship, but there's always some risk of rocks getting bounced somewhere you don't want them to go," Li said.

"Do you need a hand with that?" Max asked, indicating the drill.

"Please," she said, stepping back.

Max took over the drill and put his weight on it. He floated upward a bit, then steadied himself and put his boots back on the ground. The drill bored slowly downward until it seated at its metal stop. Max withdrew the drill and unloaded the drill core into the long cylindrical container Li had set nearby.

"When you're done with that, come and see this," Li said.

Max set down the drill and turned around. Li had walked off. The lander was visible on the plateau. He could see the blinking green light on the laser surveyor he had left on the dome-shaped rise, but Li was nowhere in sight.

"Where are you?" Max asked.

"From where you are standing walk directly away from the lander. I am about three hundred meters away and down a slope. You can't miss me," Li said.

Max walked and the ground fell away at the edge of the plain. He crested a rise and saw Li standing on a round boulder. She was shining her light into a dark cave that rose from the ground.

"Is that a lava tube?" Max asked, walking toward her.

"Looks like it," she answered.

Max stood at the base of the boulder and shone his own headlamp into the darkness. The cave was roughly cylindrical and as large as an airplane hangar. It led into the hillside and dead-ended in a wall of smooth rock.

"Something like this would be perfect for a residential habitat. You would only have to seal up the open end. It would be easy to make it airtight and it would work great for thermal regulation and radiation protection," Li said.

"We see it," Albert's voice came over the radio. "Good find. We are orbiting above you now and can pinpoint your exact location. We've got the cave marked for later."

"Thanks, Albert," Li said.

There was no day or night on the lunar north pole. The sun would creep slowly around the horizon each day but never set. Max and Li worked for six hours, exploring the landscape, taking measurements, and bringing back samples.

"Our job is just about done, I think," Max said.

"Don't say that. I don't want to leave," Li said.

"I'm getting hungry. Want to meet me back at the lander?" Max asked.

"Sure. I could use a bite," Li said.

They returned to the lander, climbed out of their suits, and had a meal of warm vegetable soup. Max spread hummus on a tortilla and Li gazed out the big window. Max went to his console and checked the to-do list on his screen.

"You didn't give us enough work to do, Houston. We've finished all our chores already," Max said.

"Sorry, Max. They wanted to keep this mission simple," Georgy's voice came back over the radio.

"Oh, well. If we are done then I guess we can go home," Max said. He stood and went to the window. The now-familiar lunar landscape lay beyond. He touched the cool glass with his hand.

"Soon coming to the moon will be routine. People will be landing here all the time," Li said.

"Maybe we will come back again," Max said wistfully.

"Maybe," Li said.

Max sighed and returned to his seat. The lunar station completed its orbit every 12 hours. That meant that a launch window for rendezvous only came twice per 24-hour day. Their next launch window would be in 5 hours. The next one after that was in 17.

"The responsible thing to do would be to use the next launch window to blast back to the station," Max said.

"You're right," Li said sadly.

"That's right," Doctor Thompson's voice came over the radio.

"You're listening in, Doctor Thompson?" Max asked.

"You've kept your radio on continuously. Of course I'm listening. Everybody is listening," Doctor Thompson said.

"I don't want to go home," Max said.

"I understand, Max. But we all have jobs to do," Doctor Thompson said.

"Li, do you have any last words from the surface of the moon?" Max asked.

"I can see the whole Earth through this window," Li said. "But I've never felt more at home."

"Yeah," Max said. "Me too."

CHAPTER FORTY-THREE

Max and Li strapped themselves into their seats. They sealed their flight helmets and waited for the launch window.

"Bye, moon," Max said.

"Ignition in five seconds," Li said.

"See you soon," Miranda said over the radio.

Li touched her screen and the lander lifted off. Max was pressed into his seat by 1G of acceleration. The engine rumbled as it converted fuel and oxidizer into heat and pressure, directing the exhaust into downward thrust. There was a hum of electric motors as the boarding ramp retracted into the hull.

Then, everything went wrong.

The spacecraft went suddenly and completely silent. There was a hiss of escaping air, then Max's pressure suit ballooned, turning from a pliant garment into a stiff airbag.

"We have a hull breach. Atmospheric pressure in the lander has dropped to zero," Max exclaimed. "Are you okay, Li?" He turned his head to see that she was still manipulating her controls. Her movements were awkward as she fought against the suddenly rigid suit. Acceleration still held Max in his seat. The lander was still flying.

"I'm fine. We've lost atmospheric pressure, but we are okay. Engine thrust is good. Navigation is online," Li said. Her voice came over Max's helmet speakers.

"What happened? What caused the breach?" Max asked.

"I'm not sure, but I think our comms are out too. Houston? Cape? Can you hear us?" Li said.

Only silence greeted her words.

"Albert? Miranda? Are you receiving us?" Li said.

No response.

"Trajectory looks good though. I have both maneuvering and main thruster control," Li said.

"Keep us on the path to orbit. I'm going to find that breach," Max said.

Max craned his head around, but the cabin interior that he could see from his seat looked intact. He unstrapped and stood in the steady, vibrating acceleration. When he looked behind his seat, he saw the damage.

"The hull breach was caused by a rock. It must have been kicked up at takeoff," Max said, looking at the big hole in the floor right behind his seat. A chunk of lunar breccia the size of a closed fist sat next to the breach. The rock must have been bounced upward by the hot exhaust gases from the rocket nozzle.

"The hole is too big. I can't patch it," Max said. The hole was half a meter across and jagged.

"We have another problem," Li warned. "Main engine oxidizer pressure is dropping."

Max glanced at his screen. Fuel oxidizer levels were plummeting. There must have been damage to an oxidizer tank or the engine plumbing. He turned back to the hull breach and went to his hands and knees. He peered through the hole and could see orange gas escaping from a damaged metal conduit. The lander's glowing engine bell and the receding lunar surface was visible in the background.

"I can see the leak. A dinitrogen tetroxide line is damaged," Max said.

Max took a roll of gray tape from his tool bag beneath his seat. He laid prone and thrust his head into the breach. The leak was coming from where the oxidizer line met a large cylindrical tank. The jointed plumbing was flexed to allow gimballing of the engine below.

"Keep the ship as steady as you can," Max said.

Wary of tearing his pressure suit on the sharp edges of the opening, Max carefully reached into the breach with a length of gray tape. He wrapped the tape around the place the orange gas was escaping but it did not stop the leak. The corrugated joint did not offer enough flat surface for the tape to seal. He left the first piece of tape where it was and wrapped more around the offending area. Orange gas spilled out past his makeshift patch.

The lander shuddered violently and Max was thrown against the edge of the jagged hole. Sharp aluminum cut into the right armpit of his pressure suit and he heard the hiss of escaping air. Max rolled onto his back and found the hole in his suit with his left hand. Fortunately, it was a small hole. He covered the hole in his suit with a length of tape and the air leak stopped.

"We are losing thrust," Li warned.

"I can't stop the oxidizer leak," Max said, sitting up. They were accelerating at less than half of a G now. The oxidizer was escaping into space. He put another length of tape around his arm and pulled himself to his computer screen.

"What's our altitude and velocity?" Max asked.

"Altitude 7,000 meters and velocity 1,200 meters per second," Li said.

"That won't be enough to reach orbit. Put everything you've got into getting us altitude. We need to buy some time," Max said. Fuel level was at 50% but oxidizer level was at 5% and dropping fast.

Li pitched the lander upward. She punched up maximum thrust, but their acceleration continued to fall. Seconds later, the engine shut off. They were weightless.

Max's screen told him that they were in a ballistic parabola. Their spacecraft would rise, coasting to a peak of 9 kilometers in altitude, then fall back toward the moon. They would smash into lunar regolith in about two hours.

"That's it. We're out of oxidizer," Li said.

"How much hydrazine do we have?" Max asked.

"We still have half a tank, but we can't use it as monopropellant. The main thruster does not have a built-in catalyst bed," Li said.

The lander's big main engine combined hydrazine fuel and dinitrogen tetroxide oxidizer in a hypergolic reaction. One could use hydrazine alone as a monopropellant, but that required a hot metal catalyst to heat the hydrazine and initiate decomposition. Compared with the hypergolic reaction of hydrazine and dinitrogen tetroxide, hydrazine decomposition was inefficient. The specific impulse of monopropellant hydrazine was only 220 seconds. The hypergolic reaction of hydrazine with oxidizer raised specific impulse to 290 seconds and dramatically increased thrust. Their main engine was designed for bipropellant efficiency and power.

"What about the maneuvering thrusters? They use the hydrazine as a monopropellant," Max asked.

"Yes, but they have less than 20N of thrust altogether and they are not designed for sustained firing. They don't have the thrust to make orbit before we crater and they would melt if we even tried," Li answered.

"But they do have hot metal catalysts to ignite monopropellant hydrazine," Max mused.

Max drummed his fingers on the screen. He and Li were sitting on 0.5 metric tons of good rocket fuel. There was plenty of potential delta-v on this spaceship. There must be a way that he could use it.

"I'm going to try something," Max said, pushing himself away from his computer. He floated to the airlock door.

"If you want to get out and push that sounds good," Li said. She tried to laugh but her voice was strained.

"We're not going to die here," Max promised.

Li took a deep breath, steadying herself. "Yeah. We're still alive. We can figure something out," she said.

"We have usable rocket fuel. Our main engine is intact. We just have to put the two together," Max said.

Max opened the interior airlock door. It was already cycled to vacuum, so it opened easily. He locked it open and manually opened the exterior door. Red lights flashed to indicate that it would normally be a bad idea to leave both airlock doors open but given that there was a big hole in the ship's hull, Max did not care. He put the strap of his tool bag around his body and floated into space.

The space suits that he and Li were wearing were not EVA suits. They were just emergency pressure suits. They were designed to keep them alive if the cabin lost pressure. They were not optimized for moving around. Compared to an EVA suit, they were made of a much thinner material. They ballooned in a vacuum, making it difficult for Max to move his shoulders and bend his elbows. His gloves had become bloated and ungainly. He rotated around a handhold on the exterior of the spacecraft, stiff legs protruding out toward the receding lunar horizon.

Max squinted in the harsh sunlight. The visor of the pressure suit was not as deeply tinted as that of a proper EVA suit and the shining aluminum of the lander was near blinding until his eyes began to adjust. Eight clusters of maneuvering thrusters extended from the surface of the lander. Each had four nozzles, pointed in such a way to allow thrust in any direction during landing or take off.

"Which of these maneuvering thrusters would you say is the least important?" Max asked.

"There's a lot of redundancy in the maneuvering system. If you're scavenging a catalyst, you can take it from any of them. Nothing is as important as the main engine," Li answered.

"I'll just cut the closest one then," Max said.

Max took his laser welder from his bag. He dragged himself to the nearest thruster cluster and aimed the welder's aperture at its base. Setting the laser to maximum power, he began cutting.

The thin aluminum melted easily, and he inclined his welder downward, uncaring of the damage he did to the lunar lander's thin skin. He found the plumbing for the hydrazine propellant and melted through it, then located the two small electrical wires running toward the catalyst coil and followed them up into the thruster. He found the coil, a small spiral of gleaming metal, and sliced it away from its housing. He pulled it clear of the ruined thruster, careful to preserve the two wires that protruded from one side. He cut into the lander's skin again and pulled as much wire free as he could. Then he cut the wires at their base and put his welder away. He held a small iridium catalyst and several meters of loose wire.

"Houston? Miranda? Albert? Can anybody hear me?" Li said into the radio. There was only silence in response. "Still nothing on comms, Max," Li said.

"Even if they could hear us, they would not be able to help us anyway," Max said.

Max rotated his stiff body until he faced toward the lander's main engine. Every movement in the awkward pressure suit was tiring. He pushed himself in the direction of the engine, floating from handhold to handhold.

"Apoapsis in twenty minutes," Li said.

The most efficient window for an orbital injection burn would be right at apoapsis. Once they were past apoapsis they would be falling faster and faster downward. Past a certain point, no amount of thrust would save them.

"Thanks Li. Keep me posted," Max said.

"Can I help you out there?" Li asked. "I can't do much from in here."

"Yes. Find the main electrical box. It should be behind one of the panels beneath your seat," Max said.

"Okay," Li said. Max heard Li grunting as she fought against the tight pressure suit.

The peak of a tall mountain whizzed by danger close. He ignored it. He could see ruptured bulkhead ahead. He was almost to the underside of the lander, where the rock had punched through the hull.

"I found the electrical panel," Li said.

"Great. Leave the panel open and come to the hull breach. I'm going to pass you two wires," Max said.

Max gingerly picked his way around the sharp metal edges

surrounding the dark hole. He peered up and saw Li's space-suited form against the cabin lights.

"Catch," Max said. He pushed the loose ends of the wires toward Li. They uncoiled in the weightless vacuum.

"Got them," Li said, catching the ends.

"Great. Go back to the electrical panel and find the emergency backup circuit for the life support system. That circuit should be one hundred and twenty volts, DC current. When I tell you, patch these wires directly into the circuit," Max said.

"Okay," Li said. Her shadow disappeared back into the cabin.

Max took the coil, still attached to its long wires, and floated over to the main engine bell. The rocket nozzle was a dark circle two meters across. It still radiated dangerous heat, but the engine bell provided his only access to the engine's primary combustion chamber. He fished a set of vise-grips from his tool bag and clamped them to the nozzle's rim, careful not to touch the hot metal with his gloves. The heat would melt the thin fabric of his pressure suit. He took another pair of vise grips and did the same a few centimeters away. He experimentally tugged on the rubberized grips of his clamped tools. They held in place. He now had two relatively safe handholds on the hot engine nozzle. He used them to pull himself around and peered directly into the engine's heart.

The rocket nozzle was about two meters deep. He took a length of gray tape and wrapped it around the wires where they left the coil. He put another length of tape across the first, leaving a sticky length of tape exposed. He laid the loose strands of wire carefully across one of the insulated vise grips, protecting the stretched wire from the hot engine. Holding the partially taped coil in his right hand, he took a metal wrench in his left and, using the vise-grips, pushed himself into the engine.

The walls of the bell closed around him as he floated toward the engine's throat. He could feel the heat on his face, radiating infrared energy from the black nozzle. His aim was good, and he arrested his momentum with his outstretched wrench. No part of his delicate suit touched the hot metal of the nozzle. He pressed the wire and tape against the nozzle near the throat. The tape melted when it touched the wall, and he withdrew his hand before his glove could be burned. The coil catalyst hung into the engine's throat, dangling by its two thin wires.

Using his wrench, Max carefully pushed himself back out of the engine. The wire had stayed intact, protected by the rubber handles of Max's vise grips. Max steadied himself by gripping the other set of vise grips.

"Ready to wire the coil into the electrical panel?" Max asked.

"I'm ready," Li said.

"Go ahead," Max said.

Max waited. He knew that some of the copper in the wires had probably melted when they touched the hot engine, but melted copper was still a pretty good conductor. He hoped it would be enough.

"It's wired in. The circuit is closed. I got a nice spark when I made the connection," Li said.

"Great," Max said.

He squinted into the dark engine bell. The heating coil began glowing cherry red. In seconds it was a brilliant white.

"It's working," Max said with relief.

"Want me to turn it back off until we're ready to blast?" Li asked.

"No, leave it on. We want it to generate as much heat as possible," Max said.

Max pushed himself from the engine and floated around the spacecraft's hull. He grasped at handholds and began dragging himself back toward the airlock door.

"You just taped the coil directly into the engine bell?" Li asked.

"I had no other way to do it," Max said.

"Won't it get blasted loose when we turn the engine on?" Li asked.

"Yes, but if we can get the hydrazine up to 600 degrees Celsius, the reaction should be self-sustaining," Max said.

"But it was not self-sustaining on hydrazine when we ran out of oxidizer," Li pointed out.

"We had the thrust turned up too much. The flame front was blown out of the engine. I think that we can maintain spontaneous exothermic decomposition if we have the thrust turned all the way down to minimum," Max said.

"I hope you're right," Li said.

"Me too," Max said.

Max was breathing hard. He was tiring. His arms and shoulders complained, fighting against the stiff suit. He finally reached the airlock and pulled himself in. He was glad that he had left both doors open. He wondered how efficient his pressure suit was at removing exhaled carbon dioxide. Pressure suits like this were not built for extensive periods of strenuous exertion.

"How is our trajectory?" Max asked, floating into the cabin.

"We passed apoapsis fifteen minutes ago. We are at eight thousand meters altitude and falling," Li said. She was at her console, hands on the flight controls.

"Punch it," Max said.

CHAPTER FORTY-FOUR

Li took manual control of the lander's engine. She opened the hydrazine valves at minimum thrust.

Nothing happened.

"I don't think it's working," Li said.

Max opened his mouth to speak, then the floor rose up and slammed into him. His nose struck the inside of his visor and his eyes filled with tears. Had the engine exploded? He lifted his head, blinking. Then he realized that they were under constant acceleration.

"It's working!" Li exclaimed. "We are getting 1.51 meters per second per second of acceleration. I have a good vector plotted for orbital insertion."

Max rolled onto his back. He tried to sit up, but the torso of his suit was too stiff, and he was too tired. He laid back, enjoying the reassuring vibrations coming through the hull.

"Good job. Keep it at minimum thrust," Max said.

"We're going to make it," Li said

"Of course we are," Max said.

They continued that way for some time, laboriously working their way out of the lunar gravity well. Max imagined their course through space, theoretical periapsis rising from a point deep within the moon's crust to a safe orbit in empty vacuum. His breathing slowly returned to normal.

"We are approaching orbital velocity," Li said.

"Keep burning as long as you can. No reason to save any fuel," Max said.

"Orbit achieved! Velocity 1,675 meters per second. Periapsis 7,900 kilometers. Apoapsis 9,000 kilometers," Li said.

Suddenly, the vibration stopped. Max floated up from the lander's floor. They were weightless again. He twisted his body until he could see Li's face.

"We are out of fuel," Li explained.

"That's fine. The fuel did what it needed to do," Max said.

"It sure did," Li sighed. She closed her eyes. "We are in orbit," she breathed.

They shared a moment of relieved silence. Max could hear her steady breathing over the suit radio.

"Now we just need to wait for Miranda and Albert to come rescue us," Max said.

Li opened her eyes. "Let's see if we can fix the comms," she said.

"The antennae looked intact when I was outside," Max said.

"I just initiated a system diagnostic on my terminal. It will take a few minutes to run," Li said.

Max floated to his console. He wondered if any other communication links were working. There were radio bands for navigation links, microwave data links, and the radio link to the deep space network. If any of them were working, he could send a signal of some sort. He flipped through the different screens.

"It's hard to move in this suit," Li complained. "I'm amazed that you were able to do an EVA in this thing."

"I have a lot of experience doing EVAs, but it was not easy," Max said.

"It was adrenaline keeping me going before. Now, everything hurts," Li said. Max glanced at her. Her thin, stiff pressure suit wanted to pull her arms and legs straight, like she was performing jumping jacks. Li was floating in that position, taking a break from inspecting an electrical panel on the wall.

"You could try squeezing into the moon EVA suit. We can

probably pressurize the airlock," Max suggested.

"Yeah. That's a good idea. Can you help me wrestle the suit in there?" Li asked.

"Sure, just a moment. Let me finish looking through the comms panels," Max said. He swiped through the screens one final time.

The deep-space network link was not working. He could not send or receive any packets of data. The technical data link showed zero bandwidth. He had instructed the computer to force a signal through, but nothing happened. He checked the navigation panel. The onboard star tracker was working. The computer showed a good trajectory plot of the spaceship based on its own guidance system, but no navigation data could be uploaded to or downloaded from ground control. He swiped away from the navigation panel...

But something was not quite right about their trajectory.

Max flipped back to the navigation panel, heart pounding.

Their orbit was degrading, and Max suddenly knew why. It was because of the mascons. The moon's crust was not uniform in density. There were places in the lunar crust that were much more dense than lunar average. These "mass concentrations" were the remnants of huge, ultra-dense asteroids that had crashed into the moon billions of years ago. They created gravitational anomalies that pulled spacecraft off course. The effect was worse if you were lower in the lunar gravity well, and their spacecraft was flying extremely low. There were only a few inclinations that allowed for stable low lunar orbits. They must not be flying in any of them.

Max plotted their orbit forward in time. There were mountain ranges on the moon 5 kilometers tall. They would drop below a periapsis of 5 kilometers in 1.5 orbits. Max estimated that they had only approximately 3 hours left to live before they would smash into a lunar mountain.

Max felt numb as he floated away from his console. He helped Li wrangle her bulky moon suit into the airlock while he silently wrestled with the problem. She closed both airlock doors and used the control panel to command the airlock to pressurize.

"The airlock is working," she said.

Max watched her puffy pressure suit collapse as the gas pressure inside and outside the suit equalized. She removed her helmet and climbed out of the pressure suit, breathing deep of the clear air and wiping her sweating face on her polyester undershirt. She smiled and waved at Max through the window. She climbed into the EVA suit and sealed it.

"This is so much better. Can you hear me?" Li asked.

"Yes. It seems like the suit radios are working fine," Max answered.

"Too bad they are too short-ranged to reach Albert and Miranda," Li said. She flexed her gloved hands and moved toward the airlock controls.

Suddenly the cabin lights went dark. Max saw the blue flash of an electrical arc reflected in the airlock window, then everything was pitch black.

"Li! Are you okay? Can you hear me?" Max asked.

"Yes. I can hear you. We must have had a short," Li said. She switched on her helmet light. She pressed the buttons on the airlock touchpad, but nothing happened. She pulled on the interior door handle, but it did not move.

"You won't be able to open the doors without pumping out the air. The pressure differential is too great," Max said.

"I'm trapped in here," Li said, sounding alarmed.

"Not for long. I will get you out," Max said. He glanced around. Even the emergency lights, which should have been self-contained and battery powered, were out. The short circuit must have arced into the cabin hull. Max wondered how much damage it had done.

Max found that his tool bag was still loosely looped around his body. He located a handheld flashlight and switched it on. He then found his laser welder. A green indicator on the side showed that it still had 85% charge.

"Get back from the door," Max said.

Max picked a point in the corner of the door and made a small hole. Immediately a torrent of air burst out. It roared through the cabin, vibrating his suit, but it did not hang around for long. The air found the rent hole in the spaceship exterior and rushed out into space. Max let the air drain away.

"Try the handle now," Max said.

Li tried, but the door would not budge. She turned and tried the exterior door, it opened easily. Starry blackness lay beyond.

"I can get outside now at least," Li said.

"I'm not done with this door," Max said.

Max turned his laser welder on maximum. He sliced away the attachments of the aluminum door on both sides. Burning rubber from the air seal produced black soot that coated Max's gloves.

"Give the door a good kick," Max said.

Li braced herself in the airlock and thumped the door with her heavy boots. It moved outward by several centimeters. Max floated out of the way and Li kicked it again. The door flew inward, bouncing against the cabin wall.

"We're spinning," Li commented. Max joined her in the open doorway. The moon's surface was directly in front of them now, and he could see the horizon coming into view. The ship's stabilizing gyroscopes were dead. The outrushing air from the airlock had caused the ship to tumble.

"Is it just me, or is the moon's surface closer than it should be?" Li asked.

Max sighed. "It is closer," he said, and he told her about their degrading orbit.

CHAPTER FORTY-FIVE

The computer screens were black. The lights were out. All
energy in the batteries had discharged at once and none of
the backup systems worked. The ship was dead.

"We have only three hours to live?" Li said. "I can't believe it.
After everything we've done?"

Max did not answer. His flashlight played over the fused and
blackened lump that had once been the primary electrical panel.

"I would say we should have a drink, but we can't even do
that," Li said.

"Whiskey would be my choice," Max said. He gazed at the
moon rock which had caused all their problems. It was such a
small thing.

"I would want a vodka mule. Or a nice, minty rum mojito," Li
sighed.

Max heard a sucking sound over the radio. Li's moon suit had
a drinking tube for clean water. He felt thirsty, but his pressure
suit had no such provision.

Max floated to a storage locker that carried life support
supplies. He replenished the half-empty oxygen bottle of his suit.
He offered her a bottle.

"I have plenty of oxygen," Li said. She checked the readout on
her arm. "Three hours' worth actually," she scoffed.

Max checked the lithium hydroxide canister that scrubbed his suit's carbon dioxide. It looked good and he plugged it back in.

"Do you have any other vices?" Max asked.

"Gambling. It is illegal in China, but I used to travel to Macau whenever I could. I love it all. Cards, slots, horses. I have lost so much money, but I can never stay away. The thrill is… there's nothing like it. Not even flying."

"I never gamble. I hate not knowing what is going to happen," Max said.

"That's the best part," Li said. "Sometimes I lose too much, and that hurts. But then you get a big win and it's all worth it."

"Rockets were my vice. And rockets have killed me," Max said.

"You're talking in the past tense, Max," Li said.

"I might as well. We are doomed," Max said.

Max floated in the doorway to space. The Earth was straight ahead, bathed in brilliant sunlight.

"You don't know that. Miranda and Albert might find us," Li said.

"In three hours? We have no radio. No radar. No lights. We're just a floating piece of debris," Max said.

Li joined him. "What if we jumped off? The ship is useless anyway. If we jumped really hard, maybe we could clear a mountain? Buy ourselves some time?" she asked.

Max shook his head. "We would only get two or three extra meters per second of delta-v. It wouldn't be enough to make any difference."

Max looked into the spacecraft's cabin. It was a dark hole. A coffin. He looked away.

"Even if we die, we will be remembered forever because of this mission," Li said. "Many more will follow in our footsteps. That's not a bad way to die."

The moon hung close. Max felt an urge to push away from the dead spaceship. He could float down toward the silent world. He would still die, but he would die untethered, free. Tears were in Max's eyes, but he had no way to wipe them away.

"I don't want to die," he said defiantly.

Max took his welder from his bag. Grabbing a handhold on the edge of the airlock, he pushed himself outward. He rotated around stiffly around until he was clinging to the hull. He saw the solar panels nearby and he pushed himself to them. Laser set to maximum, he sliced off a chunk of the nearest photovoltaic panel and threw it into space.

"What are you doing?" Li asked, floating in the airlock.

"We are just a hunk of metal. We are a single, small radar signature. But every extra piece of debris that we generate will increase our radar signature. It will increase the chance of Albert and Miranda finding us," Max said. He sliced another chunk from the solar panel and threw it over his shoulder.

"That is a good idea. The panels inside just clip on. I'll start by throwing them out the airlock."

Li disappeared into the darkened ship; helmet light switched on. One by one, metal panels and other junk began flying outward through the open airlock. A field of shiny detritus began to blossom from the tumbling spacecraft.

Max continued cutting pieces from the solar panels. "More pieces should be better," he muttered to himself.

He cut the next panel into quarters.

"But what is the best size and shape?" he asked himself.

Probably big squares he thought. The bigger the better. As the pieces tumbled, they would be more likely to reflect the Orion's onboard radar.

But bigger pieces meant fewer pieces. Max tried to remember the mathematics that governed radar. He cut the next two pieces in half. That made twice as many pieces. Max cut the last solar panel in half, then in half again and in half again. He tried to cut a three-centimeter piece of solar panel in half, but struggled to manage it with his balloon-fingered gloves and gave up.

Max cut out a round section of bulkhead. He took it in his other hand and started to cut it in half. He suddenly realized that he was floating away. He had no lifeline. In panic he rotated and threw the whole heavy piece of aluminum into space. The equal and opposite reaction carried him back to the spacecraft's hull. He thrust his awkward legs beneath a horizontal support and kept cutting.

Max was fighting against time. He was fighting against the stiff, awkward flight suit. He was fighting against despair and the overwhelming desire to give up, to let gravity win. A voice in his head told him that his efforts were pointless. His chest and shoulders ached.

A cramp in his right bicep made Max wince. He tried to stretch his arm, but the cramp would not release. He clenched his teeth and kept cutting. His hands were shaking, but he kept going. He kept cutting. He methodically destroyed a whole section of hull, slicing it into jagged chunks. He could see the piping for the maneuvering thrusters. He started cutting those up too. He lost track of time. He was cutting and cutting, throwing anything loose over his shoulder and looking for more.

"I'm almost out of loose junk in here," Li said. She floated out the airlock door, kicking a broken computer screen toward the sun.

Max did not respond. He cut an instrument cluster from the lander's hull. He let it float into the black as he cut another piece.

Pain suddenly erupted from his left hand. He had cut through his glove with the laser. He could hear air whistle through the hole. He stared as pink blood bubbled from his hand.

Li appeared at his side. She wrapped gray tape around his hand and the whistling of air stopped.

"Give me that," she said, taking the laser welder from him. She produced a safety line and clipped Max to the hull. Max felt dazed.

"How much time do we have?" Max asked.

"Don't worry about that," Li said.

"How much?" Max asked.

"Less than an hour," Li said quietly.

Max said nothing. He gazed at the moon. It was so close now.

"You need to take a rest. I'll take over for a while," Li said.

"Thank you," Max murmured.

"Take a rest, Max. It is going to be okay," Li said.

"Okay," he said.

The pain faded away, but unconscious terror rose in his tired brain. He grayed out. He felt himself falling, falling toward certain doom. He tried to grab something. His arms were pinioned, spread-eagled. He was in the grip of forces he could not comprehend. He could not fight. He was helpless. Time lost all meaning. He drifted in a hostile cosmos that would consume him.

Then Max heard the voices. He saw the familiar light. There was something so different about manmade light compared to the harsh, unfiltered light of the sun. One was manmade, imperfect, and comforting. The other was implacable, uncaring, infinite.

"We've got you, Max," Miranda's voice said. Her helmet lights were shining into his eyes.

There was a gentle tugging at Max's waist. He was being pulled.

His eyes were open. They felt dry and he blinked hard, vision clearing.

The Orion spacecraft floated in front of him. Miranda was holding him with a space suited arm. A taut space line led back to the open hatch. Li was already waiting at the hatch, smiling.

"You found us," Max croaked.

"We found you," Miranda agreed.

Max let himself be pulled to safety. They entered the Orion capsule and closed the hatch. Max was guided to his seat and the vehicle was repressurized. He sighed when his tight pressure suit deflated, internal pressure equalizing with the spacecraft's atmosphere. Miranda helped Li out of her bulky EVA suit while Albert strapped Max in.

Eighteen minutes later the empty lunar lander smashed into the side of a mountain and exploded. Max watched it on his screen while Albert piloted the Orion spacecraft back to orbit. He was glad the lander had exploded. It would have been a letdown had it just hit the mountain and crumpled, disappearing quietly into the impenetrable shadow of a lunar cliff side.

"What made it explode?" Li asked.

"There were tanks of high-pressure oxygen onboard. Maybe

they combusted with residual hydrazine in the fuel system," Max guessed.

"I'm sure that the next lander will be better built," Li said.

The engine cut off and they coasted toward trans-Earth injection. Max felt his mental facilities return. He was filled with exhausted relief.

They were going home.

EPILOGUE

"This is going to be the next lunar lander?" Max asked.

"Moon lander, Mars lander, asteroid lander. It will be capable of flying nearly anywhere in the solar system. It will be able to land on and take off from anything Mars-sized or smaller," Victoria answered.

The big rocket sat on the launch pad. A white cloud generated by venting liquid oxygen drifted ten stories over Max's head. The gentle breeze wafted the cloud, disappearing as it diffused in the Florida heat.

"This is the biggest rocket we have ever made, and soon it will be the cheapest. We have the construction process automated: raw materials come in, finished rocket goes out. We can make as many as we want. It flies itself. It lands itself. It will be able refuel in orbit and it's fully reusable," Victoria added.

"This is going to be the future of space travel," Georgy said with approval. The collar of his loose Hawaiian shirt fluttered in the warm sea breeze.

It had only been one year since Max, Li, Albert, and Miranda returned to Earth, but already three more crews, two American and one Chinese, had landed on the moon. Construction of humanity's first lunar base was progressing rapidly. Li was up there now, supervising the paving of a proper launch pad. Multiple return flights had flown without incident.

It was finally happening. Humans would colonize the solar system. They would leave their earthly cradle and spread out into the cosmos. The future of humanity had never looked so bright.

"So, what do you think?" Georgy asked.

"Is it safe?" Max asked.

Georgy laughed. He slapped Max on the back. "It will be," he said. "When you're done with it."

Max grinned. "Let's go to space," he said.

9 798803 879299